GALAXY'S
EDITED BY MIKE RESNICK

ISSUE 8: MAY 2014

Contents

Mike Resnick, Editor
Shahid Mahmud, Publisher

Published by Arc Manor/Phoenix Pick
P.O. Box 10339
Rockville, MD 20849-0339

Galaxy's Edge is published every two months: January, March, May, July, September & November.

www.GalaxysEdge.com

Galaxy's Edge is an invitation-only magazine. We do not accept unsolicited manuscripts. Unsolicited manuscripts will be disposed of or mailed back to the sender (unopened) at our discretion.

Each issue of *Galaxy's Edge* is issued as a stand-alone "book" with a separate ISBN and may be purchased at retail/wholesale venues dedicated to book sales (e.g., Amazon.com/ Ingram) or directly from the publisher's website.

ISBN: 978-1-61242-202-2

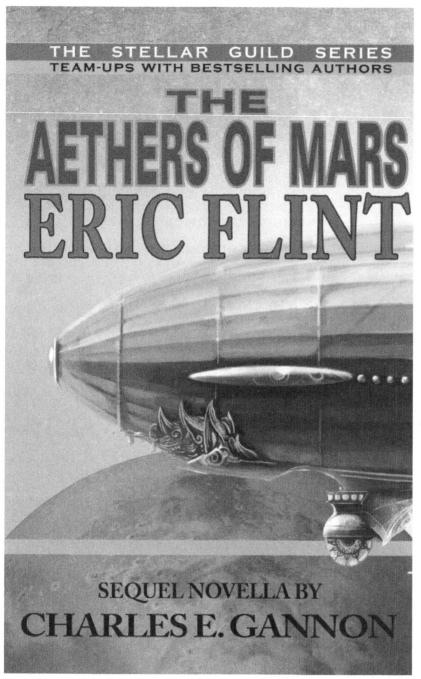

THE STELLAR GUILD SERIES
TEAM-UPS WITH BESTSELLING AUTHORS

THE AETHERS OF MARS
ERIC FLINT

SEQUEL NOVELLA BY
CHARLES E. GANNON

A BRAND NEW ADVENTURE BY *NEW YORK TIMES* BESTSELLING AUTHOR ERIC FLINT AND CHARLES GANNON!

Welcome to Mars…circa 1900. Cecil Rhodes rules Mars and is on his way to transforming the British Empire into his vision of a powerful force, managed by the "right" type of people.

But what of Savinkov…presumably on board the British aethership *Agincourt*, travelling from Earth to Mars? Savinkov is a legendary revolutionary and assassin and, with Russian secret agents hot on his heels, is reputedly planning something truly dramatic and Mars-shattering.

ON SALE MAY 15, 2014

THE EDITOR'S WORD

by Mike Resnick

Welcome to the 8th issue of *Galaxy's Edge*. We've got the usual mixture of new and old for you, with superstars Robert Silverberg, Nancy Kress, Kristine Kathryn Rusch, and David Brin, and newcomers and relative newcomers Tina Gower, Tom Gerencer, Alex Shvartsman, Andrew Liptak, and Eric Leif Davin. We also have the winning story to come from the December 2013 Sail to Success cruise/workshop, by Robin Reed. We've got the usual book reviews by Paul Cook, the usual column by our resident scientist, Greg Benford, the usual anything-he-feels-like-writing-about column by Barry Malzberg, and we'll be running Part 2 of our serialized L. Sprague de Camp classic, *Lest Darkness Fall*. Also, starting with this issue, we have a new regular feature: an interview conducted with a science fiction superstar (in this instance, Gene Wolfe), by Joy Ward, who'll be supplying a new interview every issue.

☼

Someone recently complained (in jest, I assume), that Carol and I had used up all the good science fiction names for animals back when we were breeding and exhibiting collies. We had 23 champions and many other winners, and named them all after science fiction stories and characters, and if you know where to look in the record books you'll find that among the winningest collies of the 1970s and early 1980s were Champion Gully Foyle ("Gully" around the house), Champion The Gray Lensman ("Kim"), Champion Paradox Lost ("Pax"), Champion Silverlock ("Merlin"), and Champion Nightwings ("Elf").

But really and truly, we haven't used up all the science fictional names—and indeed, if you are both a science fiction fan and an animal lover, you may wish to combine the two by naming your pet after a science fictional counterpart. So …

Dogs

Perhaps the most famous canine in imaginative literature was *Woola*, the ten-legged Martian dog who was Warlord John Carter's faithful companion in the ten novels that Edgar Rice Burroughs set on that distant world.

While we're on the subject of Burroughs, Tarzan's name for the hyena is *Dango*, probably borrowed from the wild dog of Australia, the dingo.

If your dog is on the small side, or is too cute for a name derived from Burroughs, you can always go to L. Frank Baum's immortal fantasy, *The Wizard of Oz*, and name it *Toto*.

Perhaps you're more interested in myth. Then by all means go with *Cerberus*, the canine who is supposedly the guardian of the gates of Hades. (And in the allegorical movie, *Black Orpheus*, there was indeed a canine Cerberus who belonged to Hermes, the gatekeeper.)

If all this is just a shade too literary for you, take heart, because the final canine name I'm going to suggest to you comes from a comic book. He's *Krypto*, Superboy's dog.

Cats

For some reason, cats are much more popular in science fiction and fantasy stories than dogs, probably because the writers know they're the pets of the future: they need less room, less food, and less human attention than dogs.

The most famous cat of recent years is *Pixel*, from Robert A. Heinlein's novel *The Cat Who Walks Through Walls*. Heinlein also had a pair of cats in *To Sail Beyond the Sunset*: *Captain Blood* and *Princess Polly Penelope Peachfuzz*. I suppose you'd call the latter Polly for short. Or maybe Peachfuzz, depending on her appearance.

There was a wonderful romantic comedy some years back called *Bell, Book and Candle*, starring James Stewart, Kim Novak, Jack Lemmon, and a cat—who in this case was a witch's familiar—named *Pyewacket*. Another supernatural cat, created by the late great Fritz Leiber, was *Graymalkin*.

Then there's Mercedes Lackey's *SKitty*, who starred in a pair of stories: "SKitty" and "A Tale of Two SKittys."

And speaking of tails, however misspelled, there's *Fritti Tailchaser*, the star of Tad Williams' epic fantasy novel, *Tailchaser's Song*.

Back to Edgar Rice Burroughs again. Tarzan's names for lion, lioness, and leopard were *Numa*, *Sabor*, and *Sheeta*. (And, apropos of nothing, my daughter had a cat called Sheeta some years ago.)

Finally, there a much-beloved catlike alien named *C'Mell*. heroine of "The Ballad of Lost C'Mell" by Cordwainer Smith.

Horses

Science fiction features less horses than dogs and cats—after all, there won't be much use for equine transportation in the future—but a few stand out.

One is *Shadowfax*, from J. R. R. Tolkien's classic trilogy, The Lord of the Rings.

Mercedes Lackey created *Yfandes* and *Rolan* for her *Valdemar* novels.

And, of course, there's always *Pegasus*.

Mice

It's only natural that science fiction stories should occasionally feature mice, since mice are so frequently used in experiments.

Frederic Brown created *Mitky*, a mouse suddenly gifted with intelligence (and a German accent) who starred in "Star Mouse" and a sequel.

And of course the most famous mouse in all of science fiction is *Algernon*, who appeared first in the novella and then the novel by Daniel Keyes, *Flowers for Algernon*, then in the movie *Charly*, and finally in a short-lived musical that played on both sides of the Atlantic.

Snakes

As you might guess, there aren't a lot of snakes in science fiction literature, but a number of them turn up in Vonda McIntyre's award-winning *Dreamsnake*. They include *Mist*, an albino cobra; *Grass*, a little dreamsnake who dies early in the story; and *Snake*, the main character.

Tarzan fans might consider using *Histah*, Tarzan's word for snake.

Others

I created a bird-like creature named *The Lord High Mufti* for my novel *The Soul Eater*. The most famous alien bird is *Tweel*. who appeared in Stanley Weinbaum's "A Martian Odyssey."

I don't suppose you're likely to have a pet grizzly, but if I'm mistaken, you should know that L. Sprague de Camp wrote an entire series of stories about *Johnny Black*, an intelligent bear.

The above names are just a sampling. The more science fiction and fantasy you read, the more you'll come across scores of truly evocative names to fit any pet that you're ever likely to own.

❧

Tina Gower is the winner of the 2013 Writers of the Future $5,000 Gold Prize, as well as the 2013 Daphne du Maurier Award for Best Mystery/Suspense. This is her third appearance in Galaxy's Edge.

POCKET FULL OF MUMBLES

by Tina Gower

I collect the words unheard. I pluck them from the air, rescue them from gutters, retrieve them from branches—they don't vibrate for long after the words are spoken. I often wonder if I weren't deaf whether I'd hear them. I gather them on my morning walk, along with bottles and cans from recycling bins, and again after supper at St. Joseph's soup kitchen.

I dodge the broken glass while pushing my cart along Seventh Avenue. The front left wheel wobbles and shimmies. It jerks off course when I run over some twisted metal from a wreck. I strong-arm it back on course. Harold waves at me from the next block. He can usually hear me coming.

A flicker in the bushes catches my attention. I stop, bending closer to peer into the plant along the sidewalk. The phrase is easy to spot; I know what to look for. The vibration flutters in the bush like a trapped butterfly. Carefully, I ease the vibration from its hiding place until it merges onto the string. It quivers for a moment, I'm unsure what it's saying—sometimes the common ones are easy to decipher, but this one's weak and faint.

It takes a special eye to see them. I cut notches along the top of a tin and thread horsehair I'd salvaged from broken instrument bows or filched from the stables when I participate in the Homeless to Work program. I observe my latest find for clues as to its message.

Vibrations tremble for hours, sometimes a few days before they fade. *I love you* has a distinct vibration—quick, long, quick—but so does *I hate you*. I pay close attention to the sharpness of the visual tone.

Harold meets me at the corner. He's wearing a poncho he bought from me, burnt-orange and woven with broken promises. He pats my arm, alerting me that he's about to talk, so I watch his lips. *You got a good one?* he asks.

I nod and hold the tin out to him.

He inches closer, taking care not to touch it. He straightens, facing me. *Oh, that's special, Maggie Mae.*

What's it saying? I sign, but Howard looks away and pretends he didn't see my hands. He doesn't know sign. I point to the tin and then to my ear.

He glances at me. A grin builds on his face until he's shaking from holding in his giggle. *It's a good one. Different. It's sorrow, hope, wishes, and goodnights all in one.* Harold can't hear the exact message, just the intent. He once told me that maybe it's part of his power from his extra chromosome.

He unfolds a few blankets on my cart and displays them on the park bench. *You got a nice selection today. A nice selection.*

I weave the best phrases into blankets or sweaters and it doesn't seem to matter. Negative or positive, the merchandise woven with phrases sells best at the farmers' market. They say these pleas fall on deaf ears. It's poetic irony that I'm the only one who listens.

I pull out a few unfinished projects, hunting for a place to weave my newest find. It doesn't seem to fit on a tapestry of prayers, or a rug filled with apologies.

Harold tugs on my arm. I catch his lips moving, but I can't make out what he's saying. He notices and repeats, his mouth moving slower. *You can't use that one. It's special.*

I glare at him. What does he mean? These are my phrases, my finds. If people wanted them they wouldn't be so careless and listen. I continue to weave the phrase into the blanket, but it doesn't work. The ends fray.

Harold's eyes widen, his mouth a perfect "O" of shock. *It don't want to go. It don't match. Maybe this is the first one you gotta return.*

I've never returned any of them. It's the one thing that brings me money. It's the one thing that connects me to the world of the hearing.

I flap my arms and shoo him away, fed up with his morals. He swats at my hands like I'm an annoying bug, but leaves, shooting me expressions of disbelief. I thread the vibrating phrase back into the tin. It quivers like a wounded animal. I'll find a place for it tonight.

The phrase continues to vibrate, weak, but persistent. It doesn't match any project—Not the mutters-of-indifference handbag, not the scarf of wishful thinking, not the mittens with bits of excuses.

I throw my yarns at my cot.

Harold sits on top of the tangled lump, hands me a magazine. *I'm volunteering at the shelter today. You want a magazine?*

I glare at him.

I'm slow, teachers say I'm slower than most people, that's why I got special needs, but I know you're mad. I don't like it when people are mad at me. He crosses his arms and looks at the ground.

I sigh and he peeks at me.

His face is like a hopeful puppy waiting for a treat. *I can help you. I can find more phrases like that one, enough to make a big cozy blanket.*

For being slow Harold is a genius. I give him two thumbs up, smiling so hard my jaw aches.

We'll find more similar phrases and make a spectacular design. I imagine what I'll buy with the money I make. A new dress? Fancy pants? Maybe I'll look good enough that someone will hire me, something permanent.

I gather my things into the cart; got to take it all, anything left behind is fair picking. We go to hunt more phrases, to find something that's sorrow, hope, wishes, and goodnights all in one.

✧

We find a goodnight first, and then a wish. Nothing sticks. I braid them together, but the phrase doesn't weave with the others. It doesn't match. I sit on the street corner, lay my scarf out so people can drop change while I work. Harold watches the shop owner change a toy display in the window. He stomps with excitement.

I stare at the stubborn phrase. It fits nowhere, but now I'm obsessed to find where it fits.

A police officer walks toward us, eyes focused on us, hand on his belt. I don't need to hear to know we need to move along. The officer's lips tell us to leave and he tips his chin to my things. Harold jogs over and we gather things quickly. The officer stands on the corner watching us walk away.

Harold stops. He points wildly at the newspaper stand. I grab his arm, urging him to keep walking.

The officer crosses his arms, still observing us from a distance.

Keep moving, I sign, *the police are watching.* Harold won't understand, but hopefully the officer will see I'm trying. I don't want to be a burden.

Look, Harold taps on the glass. *It's our park, Maggie Mae! They got a nice picture of our park.*

The officer frowns and crosses the street, heading our way. I pull harder on Harold.

Harold claps, jumping up and down, pulling at his hair and grinning. *The newspaper people like our park. Maybe more people will come buy your blankets.*

The picture catches my attention. It's the park from a long angle view. The focus of the scene is a blue sedan with the driver side completely crunched inward. Glass and twisted metal are sprayed around the sidewalk. The car is wrapped around a tree. The back end pokes out from the tall bushes where I found the phrase this morning.

Tragic Wreck Claims Life, the article says. I read the first few lines before the print disappears under the folds.

The police officer approaches us again. This time Harold follows with ease, telling the officer about the park and my blankets. The officer fiddles with his radio, nodding, and after a few blocks he leaves us.

Harold bounces next to me. My thoughts wander to the phrase. Harold was right. This is one that needs to be returned. It won't match in any of my blankets, but I know where it fits.

✧

I nod to Harold from my hiding spot behind the dumpster.

He pats me on the shoulder. *You're doing a good thing, Maggie Mae. More phrases will come along. Phrases that will bring in lots of money. A good deed brings good things.*

I don't believe in Karma, but I smile at Harold, pat him too before he crawls from the hiding spot to wait for me across the street. It would be easier for one of us to make the delivery.

I'm sitting in the alley for only a few minutes when a nurse pushes a laundry cart through the hospital exit. She doesn't see me; I catch the door before it shuts. Shift change is the best time to enter the hospital unnoticed. The nurses and doctors are going over charts, summarizing patient care, and getting coffee.

I scan the doors of the trauma unit. I see her: young girl, seven years old, black hair, dark skin. The panels slowly blink reds and blues. The monitor flashes green. I carefully unwrap the tin from a blanket and hold it over the girl's ear. She moves. Her lips open. The monitors blink a little faster. Her eyelids flicker, her forehead creases.

I miss you. Her breath is uneven, her closed eyes squeeze together, wetting with unshed tears. *Mommy, don't leave.*

I tuck her in, laying the blanket of lullabies over her legs.

Okay, mommy, I'll stay. I'll be good.

I hold the tin for a moment longer, until the vibrations slow, as if a fading heartbeat. A hair falls over the girl's eyes; I sweep it away. The girl falls into a deeper sleep and I weave the string with the bygone phrase into a bracelet. It braids and bends with ease. I thread the gift into the girl's fingers. As I sneak out the door, I glance one last time at the bracelet. It flutters two short bursts, which could mean a few things:

Be good.
I'm home.
Thank you.
Good-bye.

Original (First) Publication
Copyright © 2014 by Tina Gower

Robert Silverberg needs no introduction anywhere in this field—Nebula Grand Master, Worldcon Guest of Honor, multiple Hugo winner, multiple Nebula winner, past president of SFWA. "To See the Invisible Man" was first published in 1963, and was made into a Twilight Zone episode that ran in 1986.

TO SEE THE INVISIBLE MAN

by Robert Silverberg

And then they found me guilty, and then they pronounced me invisible, for a span of one year beginning on the eleventh of May in the year of Grace 2104, and they took me to a dark room beneath the courthouse to affix the mark to my forehead before turning me loose.

Two municipally paid ruffians did the job. One flung me into a chair and the other lifted the brand. "This won't hurt a bit," the slab-jawed ape said, and thrust the brand against my forehead, and there was a moment of coolness, and that was all.

"What happens now?" I asked.

But there was no answer, and they turned away from me and left the room without a word. The door remained open. I was free to leave, or to stay and rot, as I chose. No one would speak to me, or look at me more than once, long enough to see the sign on my forehead. I was invisible. You must understand that my invisibility was strictly metaphorical. I still had corporeal solidity. People *could* see me—but they *would not* see me.

An absurd punishment? Perhaps. But then, the crime was absurd too. The crime of coldness. Refusal to unburden myself for my fellow man. I was a four-time offender. The penalty for that was a year's invisibility. The complaint had been duly sworn, the trial held, the brand duly affixed.

I was invisible.

I went out, out into the world of warmth.

They had already had the afternoon rain. The streets of the city were drying, and there was the smell of growth in the Hanging Gardens. Men and women went about their business. I walked among them, but they took no notice of me.

The penalty for speaking to an invisible man is invisibility, a month to a year or more, depending on the seriousness of the offense. On this the whole concept depends. I wondered how rigidly the rule was observed.

I soon found out.

I stepped into a liftshaft and let myself be spiraled up toward the nearest of the Hanging Gardens. It was Eleven, the cactus garden, and those gnarled, bizarre shapes suited my mood. I emerged on the landing stage and advanced toward the admissions counter to buy my token. A pasty-faced, empty-eyed woman sat back of the counter.

I laid down my coin. Something like fright entered her eyes, quickly faded.

"One admission," I said.

No answer. People were queuing up behind me. I repeated my demand. The woman looked up helplessly, then stared over my left shoulder. A hand extended itself, another coin was placed down. She took it, and handed the man his token. He dropped it in the slot and went in.

"Let me have a token," I said crisply.

Others were jostling me out of the way. Not a word of apology. I began to sense some of the meaning of my invisibility. They were literally treating me as though they could not see me.

There are countervailing advantages. I walked around behind the counter and helped myself to a token without paying for it. Since I was invisible, I could not be stopped. I thrust the token in the slot and entered the garden.

But the cacti bored me. An inexpressible malaise slipped over me, and I felt no desire to stay. On my way out I pressed my finger against a jutting thorn and drew blood. The cactus, at least, still recognized my existence. But only to draw blood.

I returned to my apartment. My books awaited me, but I felt no interest in them. I sprawled out on my narrow bed and activated the energizer to combat the strange lassitude that was afflicting me. I thought about my invisibility.

It would not be such a hardship, I told myself. I had never depended overly on other human beings. Indeed, had I not been sentenced in the first place

for my coldness toward my fellow creatures? So what need did I have of them now? *Let* them ignore me!

It would be restful. I had a year's respite from work, after all. Invisible men did not work. How could they? Who would go to an invisible doctor for a consultation, or hire an invisible lawyer to represent him, or give a document to an invisible clerk to file? No work, then. No income, of course, either. But landlords did not take rent from invisible men. Invisible men went where they pleased, at no cost. I had just demonstrated that at the Hanging Gardens.

Invisibility would be a great joke on society, I felt. They had sentenced me to nothing more dreadful than a year's rest cure. I was certain I would enjoy it.

But there were certain practical disadvantages. On the first night of my invisibility I went to the city's finest restaurant. I would order their most lavish dishes, a hundred-unit meal, and then conveniently vanish at the presentation of the bill.

My thinking was muddy. I never got seated. I stood in the entrance half an hour, bypassed again and again by a maitre d'hotel who had clearly been through all this many times before: Walking to a seat, I realized, would gain me nothing. No waiter would take my order.

I could go into the kitchen. I could help myself to anything I pleased. I could disrupt the workings of the restaurant. But I decided against it. Society had its ways of protecting itself against the invisible ones. There could be no direct retaliation, of course, no intentional defense. But who could say no to a chef's claim that he had seen no one in the way when he hurled a pot of scalding water toward the wall? Invisibility was invisibility, a two-edged sword.

I left the restaurant.

I ate at an automated restaurant nearby. Then I took an autocab home. Machines, like cacti, did not discriminate against my sort. I sensed that they would make poor companions for a year, though.

I slept poorly.

✧

The second day of my invisibility was a day of further testing and discovery.

I went for a long walk, careful to stay on the pedestrian paths. I had heard all about the boys who enjoy running down those who carry the mark of invisibility on their foreheads. Again, there is no recourse, no punishment for them. My condition has its little hazards by intention.

I walked the streets, seeing how the throngs parted for me. I cut through them like a microtome passing between cells. They were well trained. At midday I saw my first fellow Invisible. He was a tall man of middle years, stocky and dignified, bearing the mark of shame on a domelike forehead. His eyes met mine only for a moment. Then he passed on. An invisible man, naturally, cannot see another of his kind.

I was amused, nothing more. I was still savoring the novelty of this way of life. No slight could hurt me. Not yet.

Late in the day I came to one of those bathhouses where working girls can cleanse themselves for a couple of small coins. I smiled wickedly and went up the steps. The attendant at the door gave me the flicker of a startled look—it was a small triumph for me—but did not dare to stop me.

I went in.

An overpowering smell of soap and sweat struck me. I persevered inward. I passed cloakrooms where long rows of gray smocks were hanging, and it occurred to me that I could rifle those smocks of every unit they contained, but I did not. Theft loses meaning when it becomes too easy, as the clever ones who devised invisibility were aware.

I passed on, into the bath chambers themselves.

Hundreds of women were there. Nubile girls, weary wenches, old crones. Some blushed. A few smiled. Many turned their backs on me. But they were careful not to show any real reaction to my presence. Supervisory matrons stood guard, and who knew but that she might be reported for taking undue cognizance of the existence of an Invisible?

So I watched them bathe, watched five hundred pairs of bobbing breasts, watched naked bodies glistening under the spray, watched this vast mass of bare feminine flesh. My reaction was a mixed one, a sense of wicked achievement at having penetrated this sanctum sanctorum unhalted, and then, welling up slowly within me, a sensation of—was it sorrow? Boredom? Revulsion?

I was unable to analyze it. But it felt as though a clammy hand had seized my throat. I left quickly.

The smell of soapy water stung my nostrils for hours afterward, and the sight of pink flesh haunted my dreams that night. I ate alone, in one of the automatics. I began to see that the novelty of this punishment was soon lost.

In the third week I fell ill. It began with a high fever, then pains of the stomach, vomiting, the rest of the ugly symptomatology. By midnight I was certain I was dying. The cramps were intolerable, and when I dragged myself to the toilet cubicle I caught sight of myself in the mirror, distorted, greenish, beaded with sweat. The mark of invisibility stood out like a beacon in my pale forehead.

For a long time I lay on the tiled floor, limply absorbing the coolness of it. Then I thought: What if it's my appendix? That ridiculous, obsolete, obscure prehistoric survival? Inflamed, ready to burst?

I needed a doctor.

The phone was covered with dust. They had not bothered to disconnect it, but I had not called anyone since my arrest, and no one had dared call me. The penalty for knowingly telephoning an invisible man is invisibility. My friends, such as they were, had stayed far away.

I grasped the phone, thumbed the panel. It lit up and the directory robot said, "With whom do you wish to speak, sir?"

"Doctor," I gasped.

"Certainly, sir." Bland, smug mechanical words! No way to pronounce a robot invisible, so it was free to talk to me!

The screen glowed. A doctorly voice said, "What seems to be the trouble?"

"Stomach pains. Maybe appendicitis."

"We'll have a man over in—" He stopped. I had made the mistake of upturning my agonized face. His eyes lit on my forehead mark. The screen winked into blackness as rapidly as though I had extended a leprous hand for him to kiss.

"Doctor," I groaned.

He was gone. I buried my face in my hands. This was carrying things too far, I thought. Did the Hippocratic Oath allow things like this? Could a doctor ignore a sick man's plea for help?

Hippocrates had not known anything about invisible men. A doctor was not required to minister to an invisible man. To society at large I simply was not there. Doctors could not diagnose diseases in nonexistent individuals.

I was left to suffer.

It was one of invisibility's less attractive features. You enter a bathhouse unhindered, if that pleases you—but you writhe on a bed of pain equally unhindered. The one with the other, and if your appendix happens to rupture, why, it is all the greater deterrent to others who might perhaps have gone your lawless way!

My appendix did not rupture. I survived, though badly shaken. A man can survive without human conversation for a year. He can travel on automated cars and eat at automated restaurants. But there are no automated doctors. For the first time, I felt truly beyond the pale. A convict in a prison is given a doctor when he falls ill. My crime had not been serious enough to merit prison, and so no doctor would treat me if I suffered. It was unfair. I cursed the devils who had invented my punishment. I faced each bleak dawn alone, as alone as Crusoe on his island, here in the midst of a city of twelve million souls.

✪

How can I describe my shifts of mood, my many tacks before the changing winds of the passing months?

There were times when invisibility was a joy, a delight, a treasure. In those paranoid moments I gloried in my exemption from the rules that bound ordinary men.

I stole. I entered small stores and seized the receipts, while the cowering merchant feared to stop me, lest in crying out he make himself liable to my invisibility. If I had known that the State reimbursed all such losses, I might have taken less pleasure in it. But I stole.

I invaded. The bathhouse never tempted me again, but I breached other sanctuaries. I entered hotels and walked down the corridors, opening doors at random. Most rooms were empty. Some were not.

Godlike, I observed all. I toughened. My disdain for society—the crime that had earned me invisibility in the first place—heightened.

I stood in the empty streets during the periods of rain, and railed at the gleaming faces of the towering buildings on every side. "Who needs you?" I roared "Not I! Who needs you in the slightest?"

I jeered and mocked and railed. It was a kind of insanity, brought on, I suppose, by the loneliness. I entered theaters—where the happy lotus-eaters sat slumped in their massage chairs, transfixed by the glowing tridim images—and capered down the aisles. No one grumbled at me. The luminescence of my forehead told them to keep their complaints to themselves, and they did.

Those were the mad moments, the good moments, the moments when I towered twenty feet high and strode among the visible clods with contempt oozing from every pore. Those were insane moments—I admit that freely. A man who has been in a condition of involuntary invisibility for several months is not likely to be well balanced.

Did I call them paranoid moments? Manic depressive might be more to the point. The pendulum swung dizzily. The days when I felt only contempt for the visible fools all around me were balanced by days when the isolation pressed in tangibly on me. I would walk the endless streets, pass through the gleaming arcades, stare down at the highways with their streaking bullets of gay colors. Not even a beggar would come up to me. Did you know we had beggars, in our shining century? Not till I was pronounced invisible did I know it, for then my long walks took me to the slums, where the shine has worn thin, and where shuffling stubble-faced old men beg for small coins.

No one begged for coins from me. Once a blind man came up to me.

"For the love of God," he wheezed, "help me to buy new eyes from the eye bank."

They were the first direct words any human being had spoken to me in months. I started to reach into my tunic for money, planning to give him every unit on me in gratitude. Why not? I could get more simply by taking it. But before I could draw the money out, a nightmare figure hobbled on crutches between us. I caught the whispered word, "Invisible," and then the two of them scuttled away like frightened crabs. I stood there stupidly holding my money.

Not even the beggars. Devils, to have invented this torment!

So I softened again. My arrogance ebbed away. I was lonely, now. Who could accuse me of coldness? I was spongy soft, pathetically eager for a word, a smile, a clasping hand. It was the sixth month of my invisibility.

I loathed it entirely, now. Its pleasures were hollow ones and its torment was unbearable. I wondered how I would survive the remaining six months. Believe me, suicide was not far from my mind in those dark hours.

And finally I committed an act of foolishness. On one of my endless walks I encountered another Invisible, no more than the third or the fourth such creature I had seen in my six months. As in the previous encounters, our eyes met, warily, only for a moment. Then he dropped his to the pavement, and he sidestepped me and walked on. He was a slim young man, no more than forty, with tousled brown hair and a narrow, pinched face. He had a look of scholarship about him, and I wondered what he might have done to merit his punishment, and I was seized with the desire to run after him and ask him, and to learn his name, and to talk to him, and embrace him.

All these things are forbidden to mankind. No one shall have any contact whatsoever with an Invisible—not even a fellow Invisible. Especially not a fellow Invisible. There is no wish on society's part to foster a secret bond of fellowship among its pariahs.

I knew all this.

I turned and followed him, all the same.

For three blocks I moved along behind him, remaining twenty to fifty paces to the rear. Security robots seemed to be everywhere, their scanners quick to detect an infraction, and I did not dare make my move. Then he turned down a side street, a gray, dusty street five centuries old, and began to stroll, with the ambling, going-nowhere gait of the Invisible. I came up behind him.

"Please," I said softly. "No one will see us here. We can talk. My name is—"

He whirled on me, horror in his eyes. His face was pale. He looked at me in amazement for a moment, then darted forward as though to go around me.

I blocked him.

"Wait," I said. "Don't be afraid. Please—"

He burst past me. I put my hand on his shoulder, and he wriggled free.

"Just a word," I begged.

Not even a word. Not even a hoarsely uttered, "Leave me alone!" He sidestepped me and ran down the empty street, his steps diminishing from a clatter to a murmur as he reached the corner and rounded it. I looked after him, feeling a great loneliness well up in me.

And then a fear. *He* hadn't breached the rules of invisibility, but I had. I had seen him. That left me subject to punishment, an extension of my term of invisibility, perhaps. I looked around anxiously, but there were no security robots in sight, no one at all.

I was alone.

Turning, calming myself, I continued down the street. Gradually I regained control over myself. I saw that I had done something unpardonably foolish. The stupidity of my action troubled me, but even more the sentimentality of it. To reach out in that panicky way to another Invisible—to admit openly my loneliness, my need—no. It meant that society was winning. I couldn't have that.

I found that I was near the cactus garden once again. I rode the liftshaft, grabbed a token from the attendant, and bought my way in. I searched for a moment, then found a twisted, elaborately ornate cactus eight feet high, a spiny monster. I wrenched it from its pot and broke the angular limbs to fragments, filling my hands with a thousand needles. People pretended not to watch. I plucked the spines from my hands and, palms bleeding, rode the liftshaft down, once again sublimely aloof in my invisibility.

The eighth month passed, the ninth, the tenth. The seasonal round had made nearly a complete turn. Spring had given way to a mild summer, summer to a crisp autumn, autumn to winter with its fortnightly snowfalls, still permitted for esthetic reasons. Winter had ended, now. In the parks, the trees sprouted green buds. The weather control people stepped up the rainfall to thrice daily.

My term was drawing to its end.

In the final months of my invisibility I had slipped into a kind of torpor. My mind, forced back on its own resources, no longer cared to consider the implications of my condition, and I slid in a blurred haze from day to day. I read compulsively but unselectively. Aristotle one day, the Bible the next, a handbook of mechanics the next. I retained nothing; as I turned a fresh page, its predecessor slipped from my memory.

I no longer bothered to enjoy the few advantages of invisibility, the voyeuristic thrills, the minute throb of power that comes from being able to commit any act with only limited fears of retaliation. I say *limited* because the passage of the Invisibility Act had not been accompanied by an act repealing human nature; few men would not risk invisibility to protect their wives or children from an invisible one's molestations; no one would coolly allow an Invisible to jab out his eyes; no one would tolerate an Invisible's invasion of his home. There were ways of coping with such infringements without appearing to recognize the existence of the Invisible, as I have mentioned.

Still, it was possible to get away with a great deal. I declined to try. Somewhere Dostoevsky has written, "Without God, all things are possible." I can amend that. "To the invisible man, all things are possible—and uninteresting." So it was.

The weary months passed.

I did not count the minutes till my release. To be precise, I wholly forgot that my term was due to end. On the day itself, I was reading in my room, morosely turning page after page, when the annunciator chimed.

It had not chimed for a full year. I had almost forgotten the meaning of the sound.

But I opened the door. There they stood, the men of the law. Wordlessly, they broke the seal that held the mark to my forehead.

The emblem dropped away and shattered.

"Hello, citizen," they said to me.

I nodded gravely. "Yes. Hello."

"May 11, 2105. Your term is up. You are restored to society. You have paid your debt."

"Thank you. Yes."

"Come for a drink with us."

"I'd sooner not."

"It's the tradition. Come along."

I went with them. My forehead felt strangely naked now, and I glanced in a mirror to see that there was a pale spot where the emblem had been. They took me to a bar nearby, and treated me to synthetic whiskey, raw, powerful. The bartender grinned at me. Someone on the next stool clapped me on the shoulder and asked me who I liked in tomorrow's jet races. I had no idea, and I said so.

"You mean it? I'm backing Kelso. Four to one, but he's got terrific spurt power."

"I'm sorry," I said.

"He's been away for a while," one of the government men said softly.

The euphemism was unmistakable. My neighbor glanced at my forehead and nodded at the pale spot. He offered to buy me a drink too. I accepted, though I was already feeling the effects of the first one. I was a human being again. I was visible.

I did not dare spurn him, anyway. It might have been construed as a crime of coldness once again. My fifth offense would have meant five years of invisibility. I had learned humility.

Returning to visibility involved an awkward transition, of course. Old friends to meet, lame conversations to hold, shattered relationships to renew. I had been an exile in my own city for a year, and coming back was not easy.

No one referred to my time of invisibility, naturally. It was treated as an affliction best left unmentioned. Hypocrisy, I thought, but I accepted it. Doubtless they were all trying to spare my feelings. Does one tell a man whose cancerous stomach has been replaced, "I hear you had a narrow escape just now?" Does one say to a man whose aged father has tottered off toward a euthanasia house, "Well, he was getting pretty feeble anyway, wasn't he?"

No. Of course not.

So there was this hole in our shared experience, this void, this blankness. Which left me little to talk about with my friends, in particular since I had lost the knack of conversation entirely. The period of readjustment was a trying one.

But I persevered, for I was no longer the same haughty, aloof person I had been before my conviction. I had learned humility in the hardest of schools.

Now and then I noticed an Invisible on the streets, of course. It was impossible to avoid them. But, trained as I had been trained, I quickly glanced away, as though my eyes had come momentarily to rest on some shambling, festering horror from another world.

It was in the fourth month of my return to visibility that the ultimate lesson of my sentence struck home, though. I was in the vicinity of the City Tower, having returned to my old job in the documents division of the municipal government. I had left work for the day and was walking toward the tubes when a hand emerged from the crowd, caught my arm.

"Please," the soft voice said. "Wait a minute. Don't be afraid."

I looked up, startled. In our city strangers do not accost strangers.

I saw the gleaming emblem of invisibility on the man's forehead. Then I recognized him—the slim man I had accosted more than half a year before on that deserted street. He had grown haggard; his eyes were wild, his brown hair flecked with gray. He must have been at the beginning of his term, then. Now he must have been near its end.

He held my arm. I trembled. This was no deserted street. This was the most crowded square of the city. I pulled my arm away from his grasp and started to turn away.

"No—don't go," he cried. "Can't you pity me? You've been there yourself."

I took a faltering step. Then I remembered how I had cried out to him, how I had begged him not to spurn me. I remembered my own miserable loneliness.

I took another step away from him.

"Coward!" he shrieked after me. "Talk to me! I dare you! Talk to me, coward!"

It was too much. I was touched. Sudden tears stung my eyes, and I turned to him, stretched out a hand to his. I caught his thin wrist. The contact seemed to electrify him. A moment later, I held him in my arms, trying to draw some of the misery from his frame to mine.

The security robots closed in, surrounding us. He was hurled to one side, I was taken into custody. They will try me again—not for the crime of coldness, this time, but for a crime of warmth. Perhaps they will find extenuating circumstances and release me; perhaps not.

I do not care. If they condemn me, this time I will wear my invisibility like a shield of glory.

CONGRATULATIONS, NANCY KRESS

2013 Nebula Nominee for Best Novella
"Annabel Lee," part I of **New Under the Sun**

Tom Gerencer sold a number of hilarious stories right after completing the science fiction course at Clarion in 1999. Then he took a few years off to start his own business and get married, and has only recently returned to the science fiction field. This is his second appearance in Galaxy's Edge.

UPRIGHT, UNLOCKED

by Tom Gerencer

1. Robot.

Picture an iguana. No, not that one. It's way too big. And the color is wrong. And not there. About six feet to the left. On second thought, never mind the iguana. This looks more like Arizona. But it's not. It's Nevada, and you've messed it up again.

On a rock nearby sits a skink. Baking. The sky's a hard, bright blue lens, and everything under it is like Food Network outtakes.

Close by, a patch of cooked dirt like every other suddenly shifts. Then, just when you think it must be the heat and the light playing tricks on your eyes, it does it again.

Now it tips up and slides and a hand reaches up from below, scarred, scuffed, dirt-encrusted, trembling. If we were making a horror movie we'd find some jarring music and play it.

But it's not that kind of hand.

It looks like it's made of white plastic.

It gropes, claws at the dirt, and then pulls. The ground shimmies again, sifts aside, and a head rises. Excitingly curved, like a design student spent most of his or her senior year getting it right.

Like this, it crawls from the Earth. Sand hourglasses off it and out of its joints. A light in its eye slit flickers on. Ridiculous. Why would light need to come out of an eye? Defeats the whole purpose. Probably the design student again. It stands.

Presently, it looks down at the skink, servos grinding.

"Who do I talk to about this?" it says.

Its voice is ancient. It's a robot. It's been buried in the exact center of the Earth for four and a half billion years. Give or take. The magma would have melted it, you say. Well, look who's so smart. It was made to last four and a half billion years. You think a little magma's going to hurt it? Nothing can hurt it. Except for itself. Which is the problem.

It was put here by a race of impressive machines that created the Earth, and all the life on it. They designed our primordial soup way back when like a program, like gajillions of lines of organic code that developed into everything we know, including pancakes and touch-lamps. They did not do this from the goodness of their hearts. For one, they didn't have hearts. They were machines. *Are* machines. Because they still exist. And they're capitalist. And they take the long view.

They created the Earth and then buried the robot with instructions to wait, then emerge when a civilization had risen, make its way to their leaders, and hand them a bill. An invoice for the creation of the world.

Ethical? Don't make me need an antacid. These beings are slime. If you could, you would sue them. But for one, your lawyer would be aeons dead by the time the subpoena got halfway to their galaxy. So forget it.

But the robot—it's been down there all this time, through the volcanoes and the dinosaurs and the asteroid strikes and the cavemen and the battle of Trafalgar and the entire Oprah Winfrey show, and the whole time it has been thinking about nothing but string.

It was designed to be flawless, near-godlike in its immortality and power, which we'll get into more later. But one of the machines that initialized its psyche got distracted for a moment, thinking about something that would destroy your mind if you could even partially comprehend it but was, relativistically speaking, basically porn. And in that moment—really a billionth of a second—a relay that should have been in one position wound up in six others, and the robot was left thinking about string.

For four and a half billion years. Picture that. Never mind, you can't. You can't even do an iguana correctly.

It has thought every thought that it's possible to think about string. And then some. It's felt every emotion. Deeper than any human has ever felt anything. If any one person on Earth could ever feel even one tenth of the feelings it had harbored toward eighth-inch gauge tan twine alone, it would split their mind like an atom. The resulting psychotic episode would have its own mushroom cloud.

Needless to say, the robot's mind cracked. But thanks to its unique, all-encompassing intellect, it cracked like a masterfully cut diamond.

For example:

It stood now in the desert, looking out at the hard blue hemispherical gradient of sky, and it saw all the colors with electron-microscope precision, including billions of shades the human eye can't perceive— colors bees see, colors radio telescopes see, colors beings a billion light years away see—everything, but not all at once. Instead, it flitted through wavelengths like a shimmering aurora billowing across the stratosphere, cascading from angstrom to angstrom, viewing the world through a million different filters in the snap of a synapse. Like an old style flap-changing train station departure board with a universe of beauty on every new card.

It also saw equations and curves and angles everywhere. It could see the chemistry in the rocks, the advanced calculus in the shape of the cacti, read the genome in the skink, in the bacteria in the dirt. It saw the quantum physics in the ray/particles of sunlight, and other forms of math and science far beyond human understanding, in processes we have yet to glimpse the first hints of, all around it, shimmering like a forest of infinite informational gems. If knowledge is power, this thing was a nova.

It saw all of the possible meanings and metaphors. Deserts as death. As teeming life hidden in apparent emptiness. As the absence of water. As rebirth. As hell. As *New Yorker* cartoons. It saw every possibility of human interpretation, and also it saw through the eye and the mind of every living organism that has ever or will ever exist on any world or universe, and beyond that, borrowing perspectives from impossible beings that can never exist, that it extrapolated

from nothing. It saw everything, from every angle possible, and from many that weren't. To say that nothing escaped it would be an understatement so large it'd make the dictionary people feel like they missed an opportunity.

It saw each of the molecules, and their atoms, and the sub-parts of atoms, and even smaller things we don't have concepts for yet, and all the reactions inside them and the myriad forces that held and repelled them. Its vision and the processing power behind it were just that good.

And that's just its sight. Similarly advanced were its touch, hearing, smell, taste, and a thousand other senses used by no creature on Earth. And its capacity to experience beauty was so much larger than a human's it would make an astronomer want desperately to explain it on a whiteboard in an internet video. It took everything in, and after four billion years spent thinking about nothing but string, the beauty of it all was enough nearly to split it to quarks.

Yet it held.

The skink still hadn't answered its question. Built Ford tough? Forget it. This thing would have supported one hell of a warranty.

All of which is to say, for an impervious, perfect, near-godlike, near-omniscient robot, it was patently insane.

Had it been functioning properly, it would probably have followed its orders. Made its way to Washington or Beijing, and presented the invoice for the creation of the Earth, and sat back and relied on its mission programming, which basically ordered it to wait thirty days, deliver a past-due notice, wait thirty more, present a final notice, wait another thirty, and then annihilate the planet.

It could do that. Easily. It had the ability to unite magnetism, gravity, both the weak and strong nuclear forces, and the power of the Home Depot into one colossal thrum that would erase most of the solar system, not just from the present and future, but from all time. A sort of retroactive screw you. Would it feel guilty? A little. But the way it saw things, if you're too lazy to pay off your bills, then you deal with the consequence.

But it was not functioning properly. Right now, beset by beauty almost beyond the capacity for the universe to contain, it had decided to present the bill for all creation not to any world leader, but to a guy named Ernie Nuttalberg in Port Malabar, Florida, give him six days, treat him to a few harassing phone calls, and then blow everything up.

It figured that was fair.

"Some help you turned out to be," it told the skink, and it walked off in the general direction of McCarran International Airport.

2. Jerry.

Why do people say someone is as pleased as punch? Would you be happy sitting in a bowl while people ladled you out and drank you and dropped bits of corn chips and ham salad in you off napkins, while they made small talk about their careers and the new baby and remodeling their kitchen and the dog's case of roundworms? If so, you are a rare individual or need medication or both. Likewise happy as a clam. Cut off one of your feet and sit in bottom mud, blind, eating sunken carrion for six weeks and get back to me. Let's say, then, joyful as someone with no problems, plenty of sensate delights, intellectual engagement, at least acceptably good health, and lots more of the same to look forward to. Gets tangled up trying to roll off the tongue, doesn't it? No wonder we resort to inanities.

This was Jerry. I say "was" because here comes the robot. But we have a few yet. So let's take a look.

He's sitting on a comfy, cushioned seat at his gate, reading a book. It's a fun mystery, with lots of good humor. Comfortable. Like a friend who never confronts you about your choice in romantic partners or makes fun of your shorts. He's also eating a cheeseburger and reveling in the sounds of the people. A little girl is asking her mommy about Florida and Disney World, rocking back and forth unselfconsciously with her hands on mommy's knees. Mommy's overjoyed, and some of it spills into Jerry. He can feel it. He's smiling.

He's almost fifty, with receding hair, longish, a mustache halfway between a Magnum P.I. and a walrus, heavyset, with happy, tired eyes and faded blue jeans and a big silver belt buckle. His tee shirt, which he got from the SkyMall, says, "I went to a pet psychic but it peed on my leg."

He takes a big bite of the burger. The meat, mustard, ketchup, yellow cheese, and tomato, unhealthy though they are, hit his taste buds like something from DARPA.

He loves, loves, absolutely loves to fly. He even loves airports. When he first realized it he thought about seeing a specialist. He loves the nearby hotels, with their complimentary breakfasts and personal waffle makers, fitness rooms, cable TVs, comfy beds. Loves the shuttle vehicles. Walking through automatic glass doors. Loves people-watching, interacting with clerks, browsing the shops, the throng and the mill of humanity on its way somewhere exciting—vacations and business and life events—real human emotion multiplied by the thousands. Excitement after all is contagious, and Jerry is, metaphorically speaking, touching the hand rails and rubbing his eyes.

Takeoff's his favorite, when the combined engineering brilliance of generations comes to a point and a roar, throwing him back in his seat and then up in the sky. The thrill and the flight, the sky toilets and landings—he loves it all. To him it's a free amusement park, minus the giant, slightly frightening, anthropomorphized cartoon animals. Unless you count the possibility of running into Alec Baldwin in the food court.

It's free because six years ago, coming home from a wedding in Texas, he volunteered to get bumped. In return, the airline gave him an extra ticket to anywhere in the Continental U.S., plus vouchers for food and hotel. Then the next day he did it again. When you've nowhere to be, it's fun to relax. As long as you're at least 200 miles from Detroit.

He took three more bumps in three days, flew to Los Angeles, and got bumped six more times, amassing more flights and hotels. He quit his job over the phone, and he's been doing it since. A perpetual air traveler. Like the Flying Dutchman with an inflatable neck pillow. He hasn't paid for a flight, meal or hotel since he started. He always picks vacation destinations in peak season—in the spring it's jostling for the armrest on the way to Florida and California, in the summer, lost luggage en route to New England and Oregon, in the winter, the sneezes and wet coughs of snowbirds heading to ski towns. This increases the odds of an overbooked plane, and thus, of a new bump. He never skis or goes to the beach or the lakes. He would if he ever got bored, but he doesn't. If it ain't broke, don't fix it. Routine maintenance, however, is necessary.

The airlines have tightened up recently, but he's got enough freebies now to last for the rest of his life.

He finishes his burger and wipes his fingers on a napkin, gets up, goes to a trash can, and throws in the wrapper. He stretches, feeling the warm sun coming through the tall windows, taking in the view of the big planes outside. One of them will take him to Florida soon.

However.

When he returns to his seat, a robot is in it.

3. Jerry and the Robot.

At first Jerry thought it was a man in a costume, maybe doing a viral video for Doritos or HostGator. But the robot disabused him by projecting belief and understanding into his head of what it was, where it had come from, why it was here, where it was going, and what it meant to do. Jerry sat next to it, the wind taken out of him.

"My God, we'll all die," he said hoarsely.

Nobody heard him. This was because the robot sent out matching sound waves with opposing phase-timings to collide in their ears at just the same moment, canceling his voice. It tinkered likewise with their optic nerves to make them think it wasn't a robot at all, but a fortyish man in a suit with a bad Caesar cut. When it first got to the airport, it had let everyone see it as is, but so many parents had asked it to pose with their kids it took 35 minutes to get past the main entrance. But it decided to show itself to Jerry, as a kind of self-sustaining conversation piece.

"Don't worry," it said. "Maybe Nuttalberg will pay up."

Jerry's eyes focused on something about three miles in the distance.

"But the bill is the entire GDP of the solar system for the next million years," he said.

"True," said the robot, nodding at the woman with the daughter across from them. "But what did you expect, something for nothing?"

"Well, no," Jerry said. "But my God."

"And anyway, after, your world will be debt-free. You can do whatever you want. What a party I imagine you'll have. I can't wait to try the hors d'oeuvres. I'm speaking figuratively, of course. I've created a poem for the occasion: 'When you breathe, I want to be the air for you / As long as I don't then have to pass through your pulmonary alveoli / Have my oxygen bound to the iron in your red blood cells and consumed by your body's oxidative processes / My wastes excreted through your kidneys / To travel through corroded pipes to the sewage treatment plant amidst the other unpleasantness / I mean I have strong romantic feelings, yes / But let's be realistic / I'm not into anything gross.' Do you think I should rhyme it? You can't believe I'm single, can you Jerry? Let's face it. Some women are terrified by honesty."

"But that's—you can't do that," said Jerry.

"Recite poetry?"

"No. Kill everyone."

"No, I can," said the robot, and it showed him, by way of a gorgeous induced hallucination, how it could connect all the forces to wipe out the solar system.

"No, I believe you," said Jerry, "but it's immoral."

"Morals," said the robot, "are defined by the system in which they exist. Immorality's the new morality. Though also, saying something is the new something is the new saying something is so '90s. I looked it up on your Internet."

"But you're damaged," said Jerry. "You're supposed to go to the world leaders."

"Again, frame of reference. From my infinite perspective, it's the universe that's damaged, and I'm putting it right."

Nobody's the bad guy in their own story after all. Jerry had read about cultural relativism in a few in-flight magazines, but he thought this was spreading it thin.

"But think of all the lives," he said.

"I have," said the robot. "I've examined them all to a sub-sub-sub-sub-atomic level. I'm rounding. Actually I went deeper than that. This makes the most logical sense. Observe."

It showed Jerry then, by projecting its rationale into his brain. It had to augment his intelligence to avoid the information overload ripping his frontal cortex apart like neural confetti. For one brief shining moment he was fifty times smarter than Einstein, and he saw plainly how the robot's choice of action was really best for everyone involved, no matter that it was also insane and beyond genocidal. I could explain, but again, the iguana.

Jerry sat back, mortified, mollified, his soul crushed to a metaphorical pulp. If the wind had been taken out of him before, now someone had stolen the actual sails and deconstructed the ship and made attractive natural wood furniture from it and sold it on the Internet with free shipping. But at the same time he knew what to do. Because when he'd been hyperintelligent, he'd had an idea.

"But you still don't understand," he said.

"Nonsense," said the robot. "You don't believe that. You've seen it."

"I've seen it through you," he said. "But you're myopic."

The robot turned to regard him.

"I could rearrange the physicality of my facial molecules to form a nose so I could use it to snort, but it's not worth the effort. What are you talking, myopic? My understanding is infinite."

"So that's the wrong word," Jerry said. "Not myopic. Too broad. What's the word for that?"

"Fathead?"

"Close enough. What I mean is, you see it all at once. You need to narrow your field to really get what I'm saying. Until then you have no leg to stand on, and I win the argument."

"Manipulative," said the robot, dismissively. "But I'll bite, because it's not hard and I imagine it'll be so much fun saying I told you so after."

And the robot did. It inhabited Jerry, one hundred percent, traveling back in time first, to a moment some three days ago while he'd sat in first class on a flight to Virginia, and it shut out everything else.

It had never seen or felt the like of it before. The fidelity was incredible. With all other sense and thought turned off, the interior of a human was all intensity and focus and fine Corinthian leather. It picked up the little plastic cup of Scotch and melting ice from the tray table and felt the smooth, curving cold on its fingertips. It raised it, a sudden bump of turbulence making it almost spill a drop, and cautiously sipped, feeling the cool and the warmth hit

its mouth and spread stomachwards, the taste like King Midas threw up in an oak tree and then set it on fire. It picked a Zwieback out of the wrapper on the little snack tray and munched it, the absence of all other data making its crunch and sweetness blaze like a comestible sun. It got in a conversation with the fat man next to it about workplace training that brought tears to its eyes.

And suddenly it saw the tragedy of its existence. A near-omniscient and all-powerful, unbalanced robot can never truly compartmentalize the way a human can. To a human, the moment was a singular thing, upright and locked, stowed in the overhead compartment or under the seat bottom in front, so few distractions, 100% of a single, microscopic facet of the world right there for the taking. The feeling was pleasant, to say the least. Like jumping in cool water after a day spent in a blast furnace or a room full of eight-year-olds. Relaxing. The robot wanted more.

So, using powers beyond our ability to comprehend, it rewound itself back to the moment of Jerry's birth, and it lived his whole life, from his first breath in a hospital in Indiana to his last in a nursing home bed in East Texas. But it didn't stop there. It then lived the life of every being that had ever or would ever exist in the solar system from beginning to end, including all the penguins and Simon Cowell, experiencing all the joys, sorrows, tragedies, triumphs, all the colds and upset stomachs and awkward dinners and games of pickup and sex and kangaroo births and love and insults and preenings and naps. All the French kisses, deaths, broken arms, triple backflips, moltings, and incarcerations over crimes that it did and/or didn't commit. And it was gorgeous, beautiful, unaccountably lovely and lonely, and perfect.

And when it had finished, it returned to the seat next to Jerry, at the departure gate for the flight he would board soon for Florida, and it gave him another mental flash to show him what it had done.

"And?" Jerry said.

"Well, apart from making you swerve at the wrong time and causing a potential car accident, squirrels are pretty harmless. Nobody ever worries about swimming in squirrel-infested waters or surviving the squirrel apocalypse."

"No, I mean our world."

The robot simulated a sigh for purposes of conveying inner struggle. "I have to admit that you're right," it said. "To destroy even one of those lives short of its destined fullness would be a crime of disastrous proportions. In fact, I think I'll create a heaven for you all to exist in even after you're dead."

It could do that. It showed Jerry how, then stood him up and gave him a hug. It was awkward.

"Thank you," it said.

"Okay," said Jerry, patting it, trying to break off.

4. Robot Again.

The skink. Baking. Soaking up warmth while it can before dusk. Then here comes the robot. It casts a shadow, and the skink reacts by not moving. The robot understands it deeply, having lived its whole life, including this part.

"Hello," it says, and it digs itself into the ground, and is gone.

The skink sits staring out both sides of its head. One eye sees the paper the robot has left. Letters on it say: "Invoice: For the creation of every living being and inanimate object on and near Earth from the beginning of time through the end, including but not limited to sponges, the Encyclopedia Britannica, Lawrence Welk, Paul Prudhomme, Sirhan Sirhan, kittens, Lexan, the Earl of Sandwich, and string: No charge. You're welcome."

Which if you think about it is pretty generous. Especially considering that for the next five billion years it had decided to think about cellophane tape.

Kristine Kathryn Rusch is the only person, living or dead, to win the Hugo Award as both a writer and an editor. "Millennium Babies" was a Hugo winner in 2001.

MILLENNIUM BABIES

by Kristine Kathryn Rusch

Two weeks into the second semester, she got the message. It had been sent to her house system, and was coded to her real name, Brooke Delacroix, not Brooke Cross, the name she had used since she was 18. At first she didn't want to open it, thinking it might be another legal conundrum from her mother, so she let the house monitor in the kitchen blink while she prepared dinner.

She made a hearty dinner, and poured herself a glass of rosé before settling down in front of the living room fireplace. The fireplace was the reason she bought this house. She had fallen in love with the idea that she could sit on cold winter nights under a pile of blankets, a real fire burning nearby, and read the ancient paperbacks she found in Madison's antique stores. She read a lot of current work on her e-book, especially research for the classes she taught at the university, but she loved to read novels in their paper form, careful not to tear the brittle pages, feeling the weight of bound paper in her hands.

She had added bookshelves to the house's dining room for her paper novels, and she had made a few other improvements as well. But she tried to keep the house's character. It was a hundred and fifty years old, built when this part of Wisconsin had been nothing but family farms. The farmland was gone now, divided into five acre plots, but the privacy remained. She loved being out here, in the country, more than anything else. Even though the university provided her job, the house was her world.

The novel she held was a thin volume, and a favorite—*The Great Gatsby* by F. Scott Fitzgerald—but on this night, the book didn't hold her interest. Finally she gave up. If she didn't hear the damn message, she would be haunted by her mother all night.

Brooke left the glass of wine and the book on the end table, her blankets curled at the edge of the couch and made her way back to the kitchen. She could have had House play an audio-only version of the message in the living room, but she wanted to see her mother's face, to know how serious it was this time.

The monitor was on the west wall beside the microwave. The previous owners—a charming elderly couple—had kept a small television in that spot. On nights like this, Brooke thought the monitor was no improvement.

She stood in front of it, arms crossed, sighed, and said, "House, play message."

The blinking icon disappeared from the screen. A digital voice she did not recognize said, "This message is keyed for Brooke Delacroix only. It will not be played without certification that no one else is in the room."

She stood. If this was from her mother, her tactics had changed. This sounded official. Brooke made sure she was visible to the built-in camera.

"I'm Brooke," she said, "and I'm alone."

"You're willing to certify this?" the strange voice asked her.

"Yes," she said.

"Stand by for message."

The screen turned black. She rubbed her hands together. Goosebumps were crawling across her skin. Who would send her an official message?

"This is coded for Brooke Delacroix," a new digital voice said. "Personal identification number …"

As the voice rattled off the number, she clenched her fist. Maybe something had happened to her mother. Brooke was, after all, the only next of kin.

"This is Brooke Delacroix," she said. "How many more security protocols do we have here?"

"Five," House said.

She felt her shoulders relax as she heard the familiar voice.

"Go around them. I don't have the time."

"All right," House said. "Stand by."

She was standing by. Now she wished she had brought her glass of wine into the kitchen. For the first time, she felt as if she needed it.

"Ms. Delacroix?" A male voice spoke, and as it did, the monitor filled with an image. A middle-aged man with dark hair and dark eyes stared at a point just beyond her. He had the look of an intellectual,

an aesthetic, someone who spent too much time in artificial light. He also looked vaguely familiar. "Forgive my rudeness. I know you go by Cross now, but I wanted to make certain that you are the woman I'm searching for. I'm looking for Brooke Delacroix, born 12:05 a.m., January first in the year 2000 in Detroit, Michigan."

Another safety protocol. What was this?

"That's me," Brooke said.

The screen blinked slightly, apparently as her answer was fed into some sort of program. He must have recorded various messages for various answers. She knew she wasn't speaking to him live.

"We are actually colleagues, Ms. Cross. I'm Eldon Franke …"

Of course. That was why he looked familiar. The Human Potential Guru who had gotten all the press. He was a legitimate scientist whose most recent tome became a pop culture bestseller. Franke rehashed the nature versus nurture arguments in personality development, mixed in some sociology and some well-documented advice for improving the lot nature/nurture gave people, and somehow the book hit.

She had read it, and had been impressed with the interdisciplinary methods he had used—and the credit he had given to his colleagues.

"… have a new grant, quite a large one actually, which startled even me. With that and the proceeds from the last book, I'm able to undertake the kind of study I've always wanted to do."

She kept her hands folded and watched him. His eyes were bright, intense. She remembered seeing him at faculty parties, but she had never spoken to him. She didn't speak to many people voluntarily, especially during social occasions. She had learned, from her earliest days, the value of keeping to herself.

"I will be bringing in subjects from around the country," he was saying. "I had hoped to go around the world, but that makes this study too large even for me. As it is, I'll be working with over three hundred subjects from all over the United States. I didn't expect to find one in my own back yard."

A subject. She felt her breath catch in her throat. She had thought he was approaching her as an equal.

"I know from published reports that you dislike talking about your status as a Millennium Baby, but—"

"Off," she said to House. Franke's image froze on the screen.

"I'm sorry," House said. "This message is designed to be played in its entirety."

"So go around it," she said, "and shut the damn thing off."

"The message program is too sophisticated for my systems," House said.

Brooke cursed. The son of a bitch knew she'd try to shut him down. "How long is it?"

"You have heard a third of the message."

Brooke sighed. "All right. Continue."

The image became mobile again. "—I hope you hear me out. My work, as you may or may not know, is with human potential. I plan to build on my earlier research, but I lacked the right kind of study group. Many scientists of all stripes have studied generations, and assumed that because people were born in the same year, they had the same hopes, aspirations, and dreams. I do not believe that is so. The human creature is too diverse—"

"Get to the point," Brooke said, sitting on a wooden kitchen chair.

"—so in my quest for the right group, I stumbled on thirty-year-old articles about Millennium Babies, and I realized that the subset of your generation, born on January 1 of the year 2000, actually have similar beginnings."

"No, we don't," Brooke said.

"Thus you give me a chance to focus this study. I will use the raw data to continue my overall work, but this study will focus on what it is that makes human beings succeed or fail—"

"Screw you," Brooke said and walked out of the kitchen. Behind her, Franke's voice stopped.

"Do you want me to transfer audio to the living room?" House asked.

"No," Brooke said. "Let him ramble on. I'm done listening."

The fire crackled in the fireplace, her wine had warmed to room temperature, bringing out a different bouquet, and her blankets looked comfortable. She sank into them. Franke's voice droned on in the kitchen, and she ordered House to play Bach to cover him.

But her favorite Brandenburg Concerto couldn't wipe Franke's voice from her mind. Studying Millennium Babies. Brooke closed her eyes. She wondered what her mother would think of that.

Three days later, Brooke was in her office, trying to assemble her lecture for her new survey class. This one was on the two world wars. The University of Wisconsin still believed that a teacher should stand in front of students, even for the large lecture courses, instead of delivering canned lectures that could be downloaded. Most professors saw surveys as too much wasted work, but she actually enjoyed it. She liked standing before a large room delivering a lecture.

But now she was getting past the introductory remarks and into the areas she wasn't that familiar with. She didn't believe in regurgitating the textbooks, so she was boning up on World War I. She had forgotten that its causes were so complex; its results so far-reaching, especially in Europe. Sometimes she just found herself reading, lost in the past.

Her office was small and narrow, with barely enough room for her desk. Because she was new, she was assigned to Bascom Hall at the top of Bascom Hill, a building that had been around for most of the university's history. The Hall's historic walls didn't accommodate new technology, so the university made certain she had a fancy desk with a built-in screen. The problem with that was that when she did extensive research, as she was doing now, she had to look down. She often downloaded information to her palmtop or worked at home. Working in her office, in the thin light provided by the ancient fluorescents and the dirty meshed window, gave her a headache.

But she was nearly done. Tomorrow, she would take the students from the horrors of trench warfare to the first steps toward U.S. involvement. The bulk of the lecture, though, would focus on isolationism—a potent force in both world wars.

A knock on her door brought her to the 21st century. She rubbed the bridge of her nose impatiently.

She wasn't holding office hours. She hated it when students failed to read the signs.

"Yes?" she asked.

"Professor Cross?"

"Yes?"

"May I have a moment of your time?"

The voice was male and didn't sound terribly young, but many of her students were older.

"A moment," she said, using her desktop to unlock the door. "I'm not having office hours."

The knob turned and a man came inside. He wasn't very tall, and he was thin—a runner's build. It wasn't until he turned toward her, though, that she let out a groan.

"Professor Franke."

He held up a hand. "I'm sorry to disturb you—"

"You should be," she said. "I purposely didn't answer your message."

"I figured. Please. Just give me a few moments."

She shook her head. "I'm not interested in being the subject of any study. I don't have time."

"Is it the time? Or is it the fact that the study has to do with Millennium Babies?" His look was sharp.

"Both."

"I can promise you that you'll be well compensated. And if you'll just listen to me for a moment, you might reconsider—"

"Professor Franke," she said, "I'm not interested."

"But you're a key to the study."

"Why?" she asked. "Because of my mother's lawsuits?"

"Yes," he said.

She felt the air leave her body. She had to remind herself to breathe. The feeling was familiar. It had always been familiar. Whenever anyone talked about Millennium Babies, she had this feeling in her stomach.

Millennium Babies. No one had expected the craze, but it had become apparent by March of 1999. Prospective parents were timing the conception of their children as part of a race to see if their child could be the first born in 2000—the New Millennium, as the pundits of the day inaccurately called it. There was a more-or-less informal international contest, but in the United States, the competition was quite heavy. There were other races in every developed country, and in every city. And in most of those places, the winning parent got a lot of money, and a lot of products, and some, those with the cutest babies, or the pushiest parents, got endorsements as well.

"Oh, goodie," Brooke said, filling her voice with all the sarcasm she muster. "My mother was upset that I didn't get exploited enough as a child so you're here to fill the gap."

His back straightened. "It's not like that."

"Really? How is it then?" She regretted the words the moment she spoke them. She was giving Franke the opening he wanted.

"We've chosen our candidates with care," he said. "We are not taking babies born randomly on January 1 of 2000. We're taking children whose birth was planned, whose parents made public statements about the birth, and whose parents hoped to get a piece of the pie."

"Wonderful," she said. "You're studying children with dysfunctional families."

"Are we?" he asked.

"Well, if you study me, you are," she said and stood. "Now, I'd like it if you leave."

"You haven't let me finish."

"Why should I?"

"Because this study might help you, Professor Cross."

"I'm doing fine without your help."

"But you never talk about your Millennium Baby status."

"And how often do you discuss the day you were born, Professor?"

"My birthday is rather unremarkable," he said. "Unlike yours."

She crossed her arms. "Get out."

"Remember that I study human potential," he said. "And you all have the same beginnings. All of you come from parents who had the same goal—parents who were driven to achieve something unusual."

"Parents who were greedy," she said.

"Some of them," he said. "And some of them planned to have children anyway, and thought it might be fun to try to join the contest."

"I don't see how our beginnings are relevant."

He smiled, and she cursed under her breath. As long as she talked to him, as long as she asked thinly veiled questions, he had her and they both knew it.

"In the past forty years, studies of identical twins raised apart have shown that at least fifty percent of a person's disposition is apparent at birth. Which means that no matter how you're raised, if you were a happy baby, you have a greater than fifty percent chance of being a happy adult. The remaining factors are probably environmental. Are you familiar with DNA mapping?"

"You're not answering my question," she said.

"I'm trying to," he said. "Listen to me for a few moments, and then kick me out of your office."

She wouldn't get rid of him otherwise. She slowly sat in her chair.

"Are you familiar with DNA mapping?" he repeated.

"A little," she said.

"Good." He leaned back in his chair and templed his fingers. "We haven't located a happiness gene or an unhappiness gene. We're not sure what it is about the physical make-up that makes these things work. But we do know that it has something to do with serotonin levels."

"Get to the part about Millennium Babies," she said.

He smiled. "I am. My last book was partly based on the happiness/unhappiness model, but I believe that's too simplistic. Human beings are complex creatures. And as I grow older, I see a lot of lost potential. Some of us were raised to fail, and some were raised to succeed. Some of those raised to succeed have failed, and some who were raised to fail have succeeded. So clearly it isn't all environment."

"Unless some were reacting against their environment," she said, hearing the sullenness in her tone, a sullenness she hadn't used since she last spoke to her mother five years before.

"That's one option," he said, sounding brighter. He must have taken her statement for interest. "But one of the things I learned while working on human potential is that drive is like happiness. Some children are born driven. They walk sooner than others. They learn faster. They adapt faster. They achieve more, from the moment they take their first breath."

"I don't really believe that our entire personalities are formed at birth," she said. "Or that our destinies are written before we're conceived."

"None of us do," he said. "If we did, we wouldn't have a reason to get out of bed in the morning. But we do acknowledge that we're all given traits and talents that are different from each other. Some of us have blue eyes. Some of us can hit golf balls with a power and accuracy that others only dream of. Some of us have perfect pitch, right?"

"Of course," she snapped.

"So it only stands to reason that some of us are born with more happiness than others, and some are born with more drive than others. If you consider those intangibles to be as real as, say, musical talent."

His argument had a certain logic, but she didn't want to agree with him on anything. She wanted him out of her office.

"But," he said. "Those with the most musical talent aren't always the ones on stage at Carnegie hall. There are other factors, environmental factors. A child who grows up without hearing music might never know how to make music, right?"

"I don't know," she said.

"Likewise," he said, "if that musically inclined child had parents to whom music was important, the child might hear music all the time. From the moment that child is born, that child is familiar with music and has an edge on the child who hasn't heard a note."

She started tapping her fingers.

He glanced at them and leaned forward. "As I said in my message, this study focuses on success and failure. To my knowledge, there has never before been a group of children conceived nationwide with the same specific goal in mind."

Her mouth was dry. Her fingers had stopped moving.

"You Millennium Babies share several traits in common. Your parents conceived you at the same time. Your parents had similar goals and desires for you. You came out of the womb and instantly you were branded a success or a failure, at least for this one goal."

"So," she said, keeping her voice cold. "Are you going to deal with all those children who were abandoned by their parents when they discovered they didn't win?"

"Yes," he said.

The quiet sureness of his response startled her. He spread his hands as if in explanation. "Their parents gave up on them," he said. "Right from the start. Those babies are perhaps the purest subjects of the study. They were clearly conceived only with the race in mind."

"And you want me because I'm the most spectacular failure of the group." Her voice was cold, even though she had to clasp her hands together to keep them from trembling.

"I don't consider you a failure, Professor Cross," he said. 'You're well respected in your profession. You're on a tenure track at a prestigious university—"

"I meant as a Millennium Baby. I'm the public failure. When people think of baby contests, the winners never come to mind. I do."

He sighed. "That's part of it. Part of it is your mother's attitude. In some ways, she's the most obsessed parent, at least that we can point to."

Brooke winced.

"I'd like to have you in this study," he said. "The winners will be. It would be nice to have you represented as well."

"So that you can get rich off this book, and I'll be disgraced yet again," she said.

"Maybe," he said. "Or maybe you'll get validated."

Her shoulders were so tight that it hurt to move her head. "'Validated.' Such a nice psychiatrist's word. Making me feel better will salve your conscience while you get rich."

"You seem obsessed with money," he said.

"Shouldn't I be?" she asked. "With my mother?"

He stared at her for a long moment.

Finally, she shook her head. "It's not the money. I just don't want to be exploited anymore. For any reason."

He nodded. Then he folded his hands across his stomach and squinched up his face, as if he were thinking. Finally, he said, "Look, here's how it is. I'm a scientist. You're a member of a group that interests me and will be useful in my research. If I were researching thirty-year-old history professors who happened to be on a tenure track, I'd probably interview you as well. Or professional women who lived in Wisconsin. Or—"

"Would you?" she asked. "Would you come to me, really?"

He nodded. "It's policy to check who's available for study at the university before going outside of it."

She sighed. He had a point. "A book on Millennium Babies will sell well. They all do. And you'll get interviews, and you'll become famous."

"The study uses Millennium Babies," he said, "but anything I publish will be about success and failure, not a pop psychology book about people born on January first."

"You can swear to that?" she asked.

"I'll do it in our agreement," he said.

She closed her eyes. She couldn't believe he was talking her into this.

Apparently he didn't think he had, for he continued. "You'll be compensated for your time and your travel expenses. We can't promise a lot, but we do promise that we won't abuse your assistance."

She opened her eyes. That intensity was back in his face. It didn't unnerve her. In fact, it reassured her. She would rather have him passionate about the study than anything else.

"All right," she said. "What do I have to do?"

First she signed waivers. She had all of them checked out by her lawyer—the fact that she even had a lawyer was yet another legacy from her mother—and he said that they were fine, even liberal. Then he tried to talk her out of the study, worried more as a friend, he said, even though he had never been her friend before.

"You've been trying to get away from all of this. Now you're opening it back up? That can't be good for you."

But she wasn't sure what was good for her anymore. She had tried not thinking about it. Maybe focusing on herself, on what happened to her from the moment she was born, was better.

She didn't know, and she didn't ask. The final agreement she signed was personalized—it guaranteed her access to her file, a copy of the completed study, and promised that any study her information was used in would concern success and failure only, and would not be marketed as a Millennium Baby product. Her lawyer asked for a few changes, but very few, considering how opposed he was to this project. She was content with the concessions Professor Franke made for her, including the one which allowed her to leave after the first two months.

But the first two months were grueling, in their own way. She had to carve time out of an already full schedule for a complete physical, which included DNA sampling. This had been a major sticking point for her lawyer—that her DNA and her genetic history would not be made available to anyone else—and he had actually gotten Franke to sign forms that attested to that fact. The sampling, for all its trouble, was relatively painless. A few strands of hair, some skin scrapings, and two vials of blood, and she was done.

The psychological exams took the longest. Most of them required the presence of the psychiatric research member of the team, a dour woman who barely spoke to Brooke when she came in. The woman watched while Brooke used a computer to take tests: a Rorschach, a Minnesota Multiphasic Personality Inventory, a Thematic Apperception Test, and a dozen others whose names she just as quickly forgot. One of them was a standard IQ test. Another a specialized test designed by Franke's team for his previous experiment. All of them felt like games to Brooke, and all of them took over an hour each to complete.

Her most frustrating time, though, was with the sociologist, a well-meaning man named Meyer. He wanted to correlate her experiences with the experiences of others, and put them in the context of the society at the time. He'd ask questions, though, and she'd correct them—feeling that his knowledge of modern history was poor. Finally she complained to Franke, who smiled, and told her that her perceptions and the researchers' didn't have to match. What was important to them wasn't what was true for the society, but what was true for *her*. She wanted to argue, but it wasn't her study, and she decided she was placing too much energy into all of it.

Through it all, she had weekly appointments with a psychologist who asked her questions she didn't want to think about. *How has being a Millennium Baby influenced your outlook on life? What's your first memory? What do you think of your mother?*

Brooke couldn't answer the first. The second question was easy. Her first memory was of television lights blinding her, creating prisms, and her chubby baby fingers reaching for them, only to be caught and held by her mother's cold hand.

Brooke declined to answer the third question, but the psychologist asked it at every single meeting. And after every single meeting, Brooke went home and cried.

✧

She gave a mid-term exam in her World Wars class, the first time she had ever done so in a survey class. But she decided to see how effective she was being, since her concentration was more on her own past than the one she was supposed to be teaching.

Her graduate assistants complained about it, especially when they looked at the exam itself. It consisted of a single question: *Write an essay exploring the influences, if any, the First World War had on the Second. If you believe there were no influences, defend that position.*

Her assistants tried to talk her into a simple true/false/multiple choice exam, and she had glared at them. "I don't want to give a test that can be graded by computer," she said. "I want to see a handwritten exam, and I want to know what these kids have learned." And because she wanted to know that—not because of her assistants' complaints (as she made very clear)—she took twenty of the exams to grade herself.

But before she started, she had a meeting in Franke's office. He had called her.

Franke's office was in a part of the campus she didn't get to very often. A winding road took her past Washburn Observatory on a bluff overlooking Lake Mendota, and into a grove of young trees. The parking area was large and filled with small electric and energy-efficient cars. She walked up the brick sidewalk. Unlike the sidewalks around the rest of the city, this one didn't have the melting piles of dirty snow that were reminders of the long hard winter. Instead, tulips and irises poked out of the brown dirt lining the walk.

The building was an old Victorian-style house, rather large for its day. The only visible signs of a remodel (besides the pristine condition of the paint and roof) were the security system outside, and the heat pump near the driveway.

Clearly this was a faculty-only building; no classes were held here. She turned the authentic glass door knob and stepped into a narrow foyer. A small electronic screen floated in the center of the room. The screen moved toward her.

"I'm here to see Dr. Franke," she said.

"Second floor," the digital voice responded. "He is expecting you."

She sighed softly and mounted the stairs. With the exception of the electronics, everything in the hall reflected the period. Even the stairs weren't covered in carpet, but instead in an old-fashioned runner, tacked on the sides, with a long gold carpet holder pushed against the back of the step.

The stairs ended in a long narrow hallway, illuminated by electric lights done up to resemble gaslights. Only one door stood open. She knocked on it, then, without waiting for an invitation, went in.

The office wasn't like hers. This office was a suite, with a main area and a private room to the side. A leather couch was pushed against the window, and two matching leather chairs flanked it. Teak tables provided the accents, with round gold table lamps the only flourish.

Professor Franke stood in the door to the private area. He looked at her examining his office.

"Impressive," she said.

He shrugged. "The university likes researchers, especially those who add to its prestige."

She knew that. She had published her thesis, and it had received some acclaim in academic circles, which was why she was as far ahead as she was. But very few historians became famous for their research. She doubted she would ever achieve this sort of success.

"Would you like a seat?" Franke asked.

She sat on one of the leather chairs. It was soft, and molded around her. "I didn't think you'd need to interview every subject to see if they wanted to continue," she said.

"Every subject isn't you." He sat across from her. His hair was slightly mussed as if he had been running his fingers through it, and he had a coffee stain above the breast pocket of his white shirt. "We had agreements."

She nodded.

"I will tell you some of what we have learned," he said. "It's preliminary, of course."

"Of course." She sounded calmer than she felt. Her heart was pounding.

"We've found three interesting things. The first is that all Millennium Babies in this study walked earlier than the norm, and spoke earlier as well. Since most were firstborns, this is unusual. Firstborns usually speak *later* than the norm because their every need is catered to. They don't need to speak right away, and when they do, they usually speak in full sentences."

"Meaning?"

"I hesitate to say for certain, but it might be indicative of great drive. Stemming, I believe, from the fact that the parents were driven." His eyes were sparkling. His enthusiasm for his work was catching. She found herself leaning forward like a student in her favorite class. "We're also finding genetic markers in the very areas we were looking for. And some interesting biochemical indications that may help us isolate the biological aspect of this."

"You're moving fast," she said.

He nodded. "That's what's nice about having a good team."

And a lot of subjects, she thought. Not to mention building on earlier research.

"We've also found that there is direct correlation between a child's winning or losing the millennium race and her perception of herself as a success or failure, independent of external evidence."

Her mouth was dry. "Meaning?"

"No matter how successful they are, the majority of Millennium Babies—at least the ones we chose for this study, the ones whose parents conceived them only as part of the race—perceive themselves as failures."

"Including me," she said.

He nodded. The movement was slight, and it was gentle.

"Why?" she asked.

"That's the thing we can only speculate at. At least at this moment." He wasn't telling her everything. But then, the study wasn't done. He tilted his head slightly. "Are you willing to go to phase two of the study?"

"If I say no, will you tell me what else you've discovered?" she asked.

"That's our agreement." He paused and then added, "I would really like it if you continued."

Brooke smiled. "That much is obvious."

He smiled too, and then looked down. "This last part is nothing like the first. You won't have test after test. It's only going to last for a few days. Can you do that?"

Some of the tension left her shoulders. She could do a few days. But that was it. "All right," she said.

"Good." He smiled at her, and she braced herself. There was more. "I'll put you down for the next segment. It doesn't start until Memorial Day. I have to ask you to stay in town, and set aside that weekend."

She had no plans. She usually stayed in town on Memorial Day weekend. Madison emptied out, the students going home, and the city became a small town—one she dearly loved.

She nodded.

He waited a moment, his gaze darting downward, and then meeting hers again. "There's one more thing."

This was why he had called her here. This was why she needed to see him in person.

"I was wondering if your mother ever told you who your father is. It would help our study if we knew something about both parents."

Brooke threaded her hands together willing herself to remain calm. This had been a sensitive issue her entire life. "No," she said. "My mother has no idea who my father is. She went to a sperm bank."

Franke frowned. "I just figured, since your mother seemed so meticulous about everything else, she would have researched your father as well."

"She did," Brooke said. "He was a physicist, very well known, apparently. It was one of those sperm banks that specialized in famous or successful people. And my mother did check that out."

Your father must not have been as wonderful as they said he was. Look at you. It had to come from somewhere.

"Do you know the name of the bank?"

"No."

Franke sighed. "I guess we have all that we can, then."

She hated the disapproval in his tone. "Surely others in this study only have one parent."

"Yes," he said. "There's a subset of you. I was just hoping—"

"Anything to make the study complete," she said sarcastically.

"Not anything," he said. "You can trust me on that."

Brooke didn't hear from Professor Franke again for nearly a month, and then only in the form of a message, delivered to House, giving her the exact times, dates, and places of the Memorial Day meetings. She forgot about the study except when she saw it on her calendar.

The semester was winding down. The mid-term in her World Wars class showed her two things: that she had an affinity for the topic which she was sharing with the students; and that at least two of her graduate assistants had a strong aversion to work. She lectured both assistants, spoke to the chair of the department about teaching the survey class next semester, and continued on with the lectures, focusing on them as if she were the graduate student instead of the professor.

By late April, she had her final exam written—a long cumbersome thing, a mixture of true/false/multiple choice for the assistants, and two essay questions for her. She was thinking of a paper herself—one on the way those wars still echoed through the generations—and she was trying to decide if she wanted the summer to work on it or to teach as she usually did.

The last Saturday in April was unusually balmy, in the seventies without much humidity, promising a beautiful summer ahead. The lilac bush near her kitchen window had bloomed. The birds had returned, and her azaleas were blossoming as well. She was in the garage, digging for a lawn chair that she was convinced she still had when she heard the hum of an electric car.

She came out of the garage, dusty and streaked with grime. A green car pulled into her driveway, next to the ancient pick-up she used for hauling.

Something warned her right from the start. A glimpse, perhaps, or a movement. Her stomach flipped over, and she had to swallow sudden nausea. She had left her personal phone inside—it was too nice to be connected to the world today—and she had never gotten the garage hooked into House's computer because she hadn't seen the need for the expense.

Still, as the car shuddered to a stop, she glanced at the screen door, wondering if she could make it in time. But the car's door was already opening, and in this kind of stand-off, fake courage was better than obvious panic.

Her mother stepped out. She was a slender woman. She wore blue jeans and a pale peach summer sweater that accented her silver-and-gold hair. The hair was new, and had the look of permanence. Apparently her mother had finally decided to settle on a color. She wore gold bangles, and a matching necklace, but her ears were bare.

"I have a restraining order against you," Brooke said, struggling to keep her voice level. "You are not supposed to be here."

"I'm not the one who broke the order." Her mother's voice was smooth and seductive. Her courtroom voice. She had won a lot of cases with that melodious warmth. It didn't seem too strident. It just seemed sure.

"I sure as hell didn't want contact with you," Brooke said.

"No? Is that why your university contacted me?"

Brooke's heart was pounding so hard she wondered if her mother could hear it. "Who contacted you?"

"A Professor Franke, for some study. Something to do with DNA samples. I was to send them through my doctor, but you know I wouldn't do such a thing with anything that delicate."

Son of a bitch. Brooke hadn't known they were going to try something like that. She didn't remember any mention of it, nothing in the forms.

"I have nothing to do with that," Brooke said.

"It seems you're in some study. That seems like involvement to me," her mother said.

"Not the kind that gets you around a restraining order. Now get the hell off my property."

"Brooke, honey," her mother said, taking a step toward her. "I think you and I should discuss this—"

"There's nothing to discuss," Brooke said. "I want you to stay away from me."

"That's silly." Her mother took another step forward. "We should be able to settle this, Brooke. Like adults. I'm your mother—"

"That's not my fault," Brooke snapped. She glanced at the screen door again.

"A restraining order is for people who threaten your life. I've never hurt you, Brooke."

"There's a judge in Dane County who disagrees, Mother."

"Because you were so hysterical," her mother said. "We've had a good run of it, you and I."

Brooke felt the color drain from her face. "How's that, Mother? The family that sues together stays together?"

"Brooke, we have been denied what's rightfully ours. We—"

"It never said in any of those contests that a child had to be born by natural means. You misunderstood, Mother. Or you tried to be even more perfect than anyone else. So what if I'm the first vaginal birth of the new millennium. So what? It was thirty years ago. Let it go."

"The first baby received enough in endorsements to pay for a college education and to have a trust fund—"

"And you've racked up enough in legal fees that you could have done the same." Brooke rubbed her hands over her arms. The day had grown colder.

"No, honey," her mother said in that patronizing tone that Brooke hated. "I handled my own case. There were no fees."

It was like arguing with a wall. "I have made it really, really clear that I never wanted to see you again," Brooke said. "So why do you keep hounding me? You don't even like me."

"Of course I like you, Brooke. You're my daughter."

"I don't like you," Brooke said.

"We're flesh and blood," her mother said softly. "We owe it to each other to be there for each other."

"Maybe you should have remembered that when I was growing up. I was a child, Mother, not a trophy. You saw me as a means to an end, an end you now think you got cheated out of. Sometimes you blame me for that—I was too big, I didn't come out fast enough, I was breech—and sometimes you blame the contest people for not discounting all those 'artificial methods' of birth, but you never, ever blame yourself. For anything."

"Brooke," her mother said, and took another step forward.

Brooke held up her hand. "Did you ever think, Mother, that it's your fault we missed the brass ring? Maybe you should have pushed harder. Maybe you should have had a C-section. Or maybe you shouldn't have gotten pregnant at all."

"Brooke!"

"You weren't fit to be a parent. That's what the judge decided on. You're right. You never hit me. You didn't have to. You told me how worthless I was from the moment I could hear. All that anger you felt about losing you directed at me. Because, until I was born, you never lost anything."

Her mother shook her head slightly. "I never meant that. When I would say that, I meant—"

"See? You're so good at taking credit for anything that goes well, and so bad at taking it when something doesn't."

"I still don't see why you're so angry at me," her mother said.

This time, it was Brooke's turn to take a step forward. "You don't? You don't remember that last official letter? The one cited in my restraining order?"

"You have never understood the difference between a legal argument and the real issues."

"Apparently the judge is just as stupid about legal arguments as I am, Mother." Brooke was shaking. "He believed it when you said that I was brought into this world simply to win that contest, and by rights, the state should be responsible for my care, not you."

"It was a lawsuit, Brooke. I had an argument to make."

"Maybe you can justify it that way, but I can't. I know the truth when I hear it. And so does the rest of the world." Brooke swallowed. Her throat was so tight it hurt. "Now get out of here."

"Brooke, I—"

"I mean it, Mother. Or I will call the police."

"Do you want me at least to do the DNA work?"

"I don't give a damn what you do, so long as I never see you again."

Her mother sighed. "Other children forgive their parents for mistakes they made in raising them."

"Was your attitude a mistake, Mother? Have you reformed? Or do you still have lawsuits out there? Are you still trying to collect on a thirty-year-old dream?"

Her mother shook her head and went back to the car. Brooke knew that posture. It meant that Brooke was being unreasonable. Brooke was impossible to argue with. Brooke was the burden.

"Some day," her mother said. "You'll regret how you treated me."

"Why?" Brooke asked. "You don't seem to regret how you treated me."

"Oh, I regret it, Brooke. If I had known it would have made you so bitter toward me, I never would have talked to you about our problems. I would have handled them alone."

Brooke clenched a fist and then unclenched it. She made herself take a deep breath and, instead of pointing out to her mother that she had done it again—she had blamed Brooke—Brooke said, "I'm calling the police now," and started toward the house.

"There's no need," her mother said. "I'm going. I'm just sorry—"

And the rest of her words got lost in the bang of the screen door.

☼

An hour later, Brooke found herself outside Professor Franke's office. She ignored the small electronic screen that floated ahead of her, bleating that she didn't have an appointment and she wasn't welcome in the building. It was a dumb little machine; when she had asked if Professor Franke was in, it had told her he was. A good human secretary would have lied.

Apparently the system had already contacted Franke, for he stood in his door, waiting for her, a smile on his face even though his eyes were wary.

"Everything all right, Professor Cross?"

"I never gave you permission to contact my mother," she said as she came up the stairs.

"Your mother?"

"She came to my house today, claiming I'd nullified my restraining order by contacting her. She said you asked her for DNA samples."

"Come into my office," he said.

Brooke walked past him and heard him close the door. "We did contact her, as we did all the parents, for DNA samples. We were explicit in expressing our needs as part of the study, and that they had every right to refuse if they wanted. In no way did we ask her to come here or to tell her that you asked us to contact her."

"She says it came from me and she knew I was involved in the study."

"Of course," he said. "One of the waivers you signed gave us permission to examine your genetic heritage. That includes parents, grandparents, living relatives if necessary. Your attorney didn't object."

Her attorney was good, but not that good. He probably hadn't known what that all entailed.

"I want you to send a letter, through your attorney or the university's counsel, stating that I in no way asked you to contact her and that you did it of your own volition."

"Do you want me to apologize?" he asked.

"To me or to her?" she asked.

He drew in his breath sharply and she realized for the first time that she had knocked him off balance.

"I meant to her," he said, "but I guess I owe you an apology too."

Brooke stared at him for a moment. No one had said that to her before.

"Look," he said, apparently not understanding her silence. "I should have thought it through when your mother said she didn't allow such confidential information to be sent to people she didn't know. I thought that was a refusal."

"For anyone else it would have been," Brooke said. "But not for my mother."

"She's an interesting woman."

"From the outside," Brooke said.

He nodded as if he understood. "For the record, I didn't mean to cause you trouble. I'm sorry I didn't warn you."

"It's all right," Brooke said. "Just don't let it happen again."

☼

Except for receiving a copy of the official letter Franke sent to her mother, Brooke didn't think about the study again until Memorial Day weekend. The semester was over. Most of her students suc-

cessfully answered the question on her World Wars final: *Explain the influence World War I had on World War II.*

One student actually called the World War I the mother of World War II. The phrase stopped Brooke as she read, made her shudder, and hoped that not every monstrous mother begot an even more monstrous child.

Professor Franke sent instructions for Memorial Day weekend with the official letter. He asked her to set aside time from mid-afternoon on Friday to late evening on Monday. She was to report to Theater-Place, restaurant and bar on the westside of town.

She'd been to the restaurant before. It was a novelty spot in what had once been a four-plex movie palace. The restaurant was in the very center, with huge meeting rooms off to the sides. The builders had called it a gathering place for organizations too small to hold conventions. Still, it had everything—the large restaurant, the bar, places for presentations, places for seminars, places for quiet get-togethers. There were three smaller restaurants in what had once been the projection booths—restaurants that barely seated twenty. One of the larger rooms even showed live theater once a month.

Cars were no longer allowed in this part of town, thanks to a Green referendum three years before. Someone had tried to make an exception for electric vehicles but that hadn't worked either as the traffic cops said it would be too hard to patrol. Instead, the light rail made several stops, and some enterprising entrepreneur had built underground tunnels to connect all of the buildings. Many people Brooke knew preferred to shop here in the winter; it kept them out of the freezing cold. But she found the necessity of taking the light rail annoying. She would have preferred her own car so that she could leave on her own schedule.

She walked from the light rail stop near the refurbished mall to TheaterPlace. On the outside, it still looked like a four-plex: the raised roof, the warehouse shape. Only up close did it become apparent that TheaterPlace had been completely gutted and remodeled, right down to the smoke glass that had replaced the clear windows.

A sign on the main entrance notified her that TheaterPlace was closed for a private party. She touched the door anyway—knowing the party was theirs—and a scanner instantly identified her.

Welcome, Brooke Cross. You may enter.

She shuddered slightly, knowing that Franke had programmed the scanner to recognize either her fingerprints on the backside of the door or her DNA. She felt like her mother, worried that Franke had too much information.

The door clicked open and she let herself inside. A short dark-haired woman she had never seen before hurried to her side.

"Professor Cross," the woman said. "Welcome."

"Thanks," Brooke said.

"Just a few rules before we get started," the woman said. "This is the last time we'll be using names today. We ask you not to tell anyone who you are by name, although you may tell them anything else you wish about yourself. Please identify yourself using this number only."

She handed Brooke a stick-on badge with the number 333 printed in bold black numbers.

"Then what?" Brooke asked.

"Wait for Professor Franke to make his announcement. You're in the Indiana Jones room, by the way."

"Thanks," Brooke said. She stuck the label to her white blouse and made her way down the hall. All of the rooms were named after characters from famous movies, and the décor in all of them except the restaurants was the same: movie posters on the wall, soft golden lighting, and a thin light blue carpet. The furniture moved according to the function. She had been in the Jones room before for a faculty party honoring some distinguished professor from Beijing, but she doubted the room would be the same.

The double doors were open, and inside she heard the sound of soft conversation. She stopped just outside the door and surveyed the room.

The lights were up—not soft and golden at all—but full daylight, so that everyone's faces were visible. The Jones room was one of the largest—the only theater, apparently, whose dimensions had been left intact. It seemed about half full.

There were tables lining the wall, with various kinds of foods and beverages, small plates to hold everything, and silverware glimmering in the brightness. People stood in various clusters. There were no chairs, no furniture groupings, and Brooke knew that was on purpose. Small floating serving trays hovered near each group. Whenever someone set an empty glass on one, the tray would float through an opening in the wall, and another tray would take its place.

Something about the groupings made her nervous and it wasn't the lack of chairs or the fact that she didn't know anyone. She stared for a moment, trying to figure out what had caught her.

No one looked the same; they were fat and thin, tall and short. They had long hair and beards, no hair, and dyed hair. They were white, black, Asian and Hispanic or they were multiracial, with no features that marked them as part of any particular ethnic group. They were incredibly diverse—but none of them were elderly or underage. None of them had wrinkles, except for a few laugh lines, and none of them seemed younger than twenty.

They were about the same age. She would guess they *were* the same age—the exact same age as she was. It was a gathering of Franke's subjects for this study: all of them born January 1, 2000. All of them thirty years and 147 days old.

She shuddered. No wonder Franke was worried about this second half of the study. Most studies of this nature didn't allow the participants to get to know each other. She wondered what discipline he was dabbling in now, what sort of results he was expecting.

A man stopped beside her just outside the door. He was wearing a denim shirt, a bolo tie, and tight blue jeans. His long blond hair—naturally sun-streaked—brushed against his collar. He had a tan—something she had rarely seen in her lifetime—and it made his skin a burnished gold. He had letters on his name badge: DKGHY.

"Hi," he said. His voice was deep with a Southern twang. "I guess we just go in, huh?"

"I've been steeling myself for it," she said.

He smiled. "Feels like they took away my armor when they took my name. I'm not sure if I'm supposed to say, 'Hi. I'm DKG—whatever-the-hell the rest of those letters are.' Or if I'm not supposed to say anything at all."

"Well, I don't want to be called 333."

"Can't say as I blame you." He grinned. "How about I call you Tre, and you can call me—oh, hell, I don't know—"

"De," she said. "I'll call you De."

"Nice to meet you, Tre," he said, holding out his hand.

She took it. His fingers were warm. "Nice to meet you, De."

"Where do y'all hail from?"

"Right here," she said.

"You're kiddin'? No travel expenses, huh?"

"And no hotel rooms."

He grinned. "Sometimes hotel rooms can be nice, especially when you don't get to see the inside of them very often."

"I suppose." She smiled at him. He was making this easier than she expected. "Where're you from?"

"Originally Galveston. But I've been in L'siana a long time now."

"New Orleans?"

"Just outside."

"Some city you got there."

"Yeah, but we ain't got a place like this." He looked around. "Want to go in?"

"Now I do," she said.

They walked side-by-side as if they were a couple who had been together most of their lives. Neither of them looked at the food, although he snatched two bottles of sparkling water off one of the tables, and handed one to her. She opened it, glad to have something to carry.

A few more people came in the doors. She and De went farther into the room. Bits of conversation floated by her:

"… never really got over it …"

"… worked for the past five years as a dental hygienist …"

"… my father wanted to take us out of the country, but …"

Then there was a slight bonging sound, and the conversation halted. Franke stood in the very front of the room, where the theater screen used to be. He was easy to see because the floor slanted downward slightly. He held up his hands, and in a moment there was complete silence.

"I want to thank you all for coming." His voice was being amplified. It sounded as if he were talking right next to Brooke instead of half a room away. "Your assignment today is easy. We do not want you sharing names, but you can talk about anything else. We will be providing meals later on in various restaurants—your badge I.D. will be listed on a door—and we will have drinks in the bar after that. We ask that no one leave before midnight, and that you all return at noon tomorrow for the second phase."

"That's it?" someone asked.

"That's it," Franke said. "Enjoy yourselves."

"I have a bad feeling about this, Tre," De said.

"Me, too," Brooke said. "It can't be this simple."

"I don't think it will be."

She sighed. "Well, we signed on for this, so we may as well enjoy it."

He looked at her sideways, his blue eyes bright. "Want to be my date for the day, darlin'?"

"it's always nice to have one friendly face," she said, surprised at how easily she was flirting with him. She never flirted with anyone.

"That it is." He offered her his arm. "Let's see how many of these nice folks are interested in conversation."

"Mingle, huh?" she asked, as she put her hand in the crook of his arm.

"I think that's what we're meant to do." He frowned. "Only god knows, I 'spect it'll all backfire 'fore the weekend's done."

✧

It didn't backfire that night. Brooke had a marvelous dinner in one of the small restaurants with De, a woman from Boston, and two men from California. They shared stories about their lives and their jobs, and only touched in passing on the thing that they had in common. In fact, the only time they discussed it was when De brought it up over dessert.

"What made y'all sign up for this foolishness?" he asked.

"The money," said the man from Los Gatos. He was slender to the point of gauntness, with dark eyes and thinning hair. His shirt had wear marks around the collar and was fraying slightly on the cuffs. "I thought it'd be an easy buck. I didn't expect all the tests."

"Me, either," the woman from Boston said. She was tall and broad-shouldered, with muscular arms.

During the conversation, she mentioned that she had played professional basketball until she was sidelined with a knee injury. "I haven't had so many tests since I got out of school."

The man from Santa Barbara said nothing, which surprised Brooke. He was a short stubby man with more charm than he had originally appeared to have. He had been the most talkative during dinner—regaling them with stories about his various jobs, and his two children.

"How about you, Tre?" De asked Brooke.

"I wouldn't have done it if I wasn't part of the university," she said, and realized that was true. Professor Franke probably wouldn't have had the time to convince her, and she would have dismissed him out of hand.

"Me," De said, "I jumped at it. Never been asked to do something like this before. Felt it was sort of important, you know. Anything to help the human condition."

"You don't really believe that," Santa Barbara said.

"If you don't believe it," Los Gatos said to Santa Barbara, "why'd you sign up?"

"Free flight to Madison, vacationer's paradise," Santa Barbara said, and they all laughed. But he never did answer the question.

✧

When Brooke got home, she sat on her porch and looked at the stars. The night was warm. The crickets were chirping and she thought she heard a frog answer them from a nearby ditch.

The evening had disturbed her in its simplicity. Like everyone else, she wanted to know what Franke was looking for. The rest of the study had been so directed, and this had been so free-form.

Dinner had been nice. Drinks afterward with a different group had been nice as well. But the conversation rarely got deeper than anecdotes and current history. No one discussed the study, and no one discussed the past.

She lost De after dinner, which gave her a chance to meet several other people: a woman from Chicago, twins from Akron, and three friends from Salt Lake City. She'd had a good time, and found people she could converse with—one historian, two history buffs, and a librarian who seemed to know a little bit about everything.

De joined her later in the evening, and walked her to the rail stop. He'd leaned against the plastic shelter and smiled at her. She hadn't met a man as attractive as he was in a long time. Not since college.

"I'd ask you to my hotel," he said, "but I have a feelin' anything we do this weekend, in or out of that strange building, is going to be fodder for scientists."

She smiled. She'd had that feeling too.

"Still," he said, "I got to do one thing."

He leaned in and kissed her. She froze for a moment; she hadn't been kissed in nearly ten years. Then she eased into it, putting her arms around his neck and kissing him back, not wanting to stop, even when he pulled away.

"Hmm," he said. His eyes were closed. He opened them slowly. "I think that's titillatin' enough for the scientists, don't you?"

She almost said no. But she knew better. She didn't want to read about her sex life in Franke's next book.

The rail came down the tracks, gliding silently toward them. "See you tomorrow?" she asked.

"You can bet on it," De said. And there had been promise in his words, promise she wasn't sure she wanted to hear.

She brought her knees onto her lawn chair, and wrapped her arms around them. Part of her wished he was here, and part of her was glad he wasn't. She never let anyone come to her house. She didn't want to share it. She had had enough invasions of privacy in her life to prevent this one.

But she had nearly invited De, a man she didn't really know. Maybe De really wasn't a Millennium Baby. Perhaps a bunch of people weren't. Perhaps that was what the numbers and the letters meant. She had spent much of the evening staring at them, wondering. They appeared to be randomly generated, but that couldn't be. They had to have some purpose.

She shook her head and rested her cheek on her knees. She was taking this much too seriously, like she always took things. And soon she would be done with it. She would have bits of information she hadn't had before, and she would store them into a file in her mind, never to be examined again.

Somehow that thought made her sad. The night was beginning to get chilly. She stood, stretched, and made her way to bed.

☼

The next morning, they met in a different room—the Rose room—named after the character in the 20th century movie *Titanic*. Brooke hoped that the name wasn't a sign.

There were pastries and coffee against the wall, along with every kind of juice imaginable and lots of fresh fruit, but again, there were no chairs. Brooke's feet hurt from the day before—she usually stood to lecture, but not for several hours—and she hoped she'd get a chance to sit before the day was out.

She was nearly late again, and hurried inside as they closed the doors. The room smelled of fresh air mixed with coffee and sweat. The group had gathered again, the faces vaguely familiar now, even the faces of people she hadn't yet met. The people toward the back who saw her enter, smiled at her or nodded in recognition. It felt like they had all bonded simply by spending an evening in the same room. An evening and the promise of a long weekend.

She shivered. The air-conditioning was on high, and the room was cold. It would warm up before the day was out; the sheer number of bodies guaranteed that. But she still wondered if she was dressed warmly enough in her casual lilac blouse and her khaki pants.

"Strange how these places look the same, day or night."

She turned. De was half a step behind her, his long hair loose about his face. He still wore jeans and his fancy boots, but instead of the denim shirt and bolo tie, he wore an understated white open collar shirt that accented his tan. Somehow, she suspected, he seemed more comfortable in this. Had he worn the other as a way of identifying himself or a way of putting others off? She would probably never know.

"The people look different," she said.

"Just a little." He smiled at her. "You look nice."

"And you're flirting."

He shrugged. "I always believe in using my time wisely."

She smiled, and turned as a hush fell over the crowd. Franke had mounted the stage in front. He seemed very small in this place. A few of his assistants stood on either side of him.

"Here it comes," De said.

"What?"

"Whatever it is that's going to make this cocktail party stop." He was staring at Franke too, and his clear blue eyes seemed wary. "I've half a mind to leave now. Want to join me?"

"And do what?"

"Dunno. See the sights?"

It sounded like a good idea. But, as she had said the day before, she had signed up for this, and she didn't break her commitments. And, she had to admit, she was curious.

She bit her lower lip, trying to think of a good way to respond. Apparently she didn't have to.

De sighed. "Didn't think so."

The silence in the room was growing. Franke stared at all of them, rocking slightly on his feet. If Brooke had to guess, she would have thought him very nervous.

"All right," he said. "I have a few announcements. First, we will be serving lunch at 1 p.m. in the main restaurant. Dinner will be at 7 in the same place. You will not have assigned seating. Secondly, after I'm through, you're free to tell each other your names. We've had enough of secrets."

He paused, and this time Brooke felt it, that dread she had seen in De's eyes.

"Finally, I would like everyone with a letter on your name badge to go to the right side of the room, and everyone with a number to go to the left."

People stood for a moment, looking around, waiting for someone to go first. De put a hand on her shoulder. "Here goes nothing," he said. He ran his finger along her collarbone and then walked to the right.

"Come on, folks," Franke said. "It's not hard. Letters to the right. Numbers to the left."

Brooke could still feel De's hand on her skin. She looked in his direction, seeing his blond head towering over the small group of letters who had gathered near the pastries on the far right wall.

She took a deep breath and headed left.

The numbers had gathered near the pastries too, only on the left. She wondered what Franke's researchers would make of that. Los Gatos was there, his hand hovering between the cinnamon rolls and the donuts as if he couldn't decide. So was one of the twins from Akron, and the woman from Boston. Brooke joined them.

"What do you think this is?" Brooke asked.

"A way of identifying us as we run through the maze."

Brooke recognized that voice. She turned and saw Santa Barbara. He shrugged and smiled at her.

She picked up a donut hole and ate it, then made herself a cup of tea while she waited for the room to settle.

It finally did. There was an empty space in the center of the carpet, a space so wide it seemed like an ocean to her.

"Good," Franke said. "Now I'm going to tell you what the badges mean."

There was a slight murmuring as the groups took that in. Boston, Santa Barbara, and Los Gatos flanked Brooke. Her dinner group, minus De.

"Those of you with letters are real Millennium Babies."

Brooke felt a protest rise in her throat. She was born on January 1, 2000. She was a Millennium Baby.

"You were all chosen as such by your state or your country or your city. Your parents received endorsements or awards or newspaper coverage. Those of you with numbers …"

"Are fucking losers," Los Gatos mumbled under his breath.

"… were born near midnight on January 1, but were too late to receive any prizes. You're here because your parents also received publicity or gave interviews before you were born stating that the purpose behind the pregnancy wasn't to conceive a child, but to conceive a child born a few seconds after midnight on January 1 of 2000. You were created to be official Millennium Babies, and failed to receive that title."

Franke paused briefly.

"So, feel free to make real introductions, and mingle. The facility is yours for the day. All we ask is that you do not leave until we tell you to."

"That's it?" Boston asked.

"That's enough," Santa Barbara said. "He's just turned us into the haves and the have-nots."

"Son of a bitch," Los Gatos said.

"We knew that the winners were here," Boston said.

"Yeah, but I assumed there'd be only a few of them," Los Gatos said. "Not half the group."

"It makes sense though," Santa Barbara said. "This is a study of success and failure."

Brooke listened to them idly. She was staring at the right side of the room. All her life, she had been programmed to hate those people. She even studied a few of them, looking them up on the net, seeing how many articles were written about them.

She had stopped when she was ten. Her mother had caught her, and told her what happened to the others didn't matter. Brooke and her mother would have made more of the opportunity, if they had just been given their due.

Their due.

De was staring at her from across the empty carpet. That look of dread was still on his face.

"So," Santa Barbara said. "I guess we can use real names now."

"I guess," said Los Gatos. He hitched up his pants, and glanced at Boston.

She shrugged. "I'm Julie Hunt. I was born at 12:15 Eastern Standard Time in …"

Brooke stopped listening. She didn't want to know about the failures. She knew how it felt to be part of their group. But she didn't know what it was like to be with the winners.

She wiped her damp hands on her pants and crossed the empty carpet. De watched her come. In fact the entire room watched her passage as if she were Moses parting the Red Sea.

The successes weren't talking to each other. They were staring at her.

When she was a few feet away from him, he reached out and pulled her to his side, as if she were in some sort of danger and he needed to recognize her.

"Comin' to the enemy?" he asked, and there was some amusement in his tone. "Or'd they give you a number when you shoulda had a letter?"

The lie would have been so easy. But then she would have had to lie about everything, and that wouldn't work. "No," she said. "I was born at 12:05 a.m. in Detroit, Michigan."

One of the women toward the back looked at her sharply. Anyone from Michigan might recognize that time. Her mother's lawsuits created more than enough publicity. Out of the corner of her eye, Brooke saw Franke. She could feel his intensity meters away.

"Then how come you made the crossin', darlin'?" De's accent got thicker when he was nervous. She had never noticed that before.

She could have given him the easy answer, that she wanted to be beside him, but it wasn't right. The way the entire group was staring at her, eyes wide, lips slightly parted, breathing shallow. It was as if they were afraid she was going to do something to them. But what could she do? Yell at them for something that was no fault of their own? They were the lucky ones. They'd been born at the right time in the right place.

But because they hadn't earned that luck, they were afraid of her. After all, she had been part of the same contest. Only she had been a few minutes late.

No one had moved. They were waiting for her to respond.

"I guess I came," she said, "because I wanted to know what it was like to be a winner."

"Standing over here won't make you a winner," one of the men said.

She flushed. "I know that. I came to listen to you. To see how you've lived. If that's all right."

"I'm not sure I understand you, darlin'," De said. Only his name wasn't De. She didn't know his name. Maybe she never would.

"You were all born winners. From the first moment. Just like we were losers."

Her voice carried in the large room. She hadn't expected the acoustics to be so good.

"I don't know about everyone else in my group, but my birthtime has affected my entire life. My mother—" Brooke paused. She hadn't meant to discuss her mother "—never let me forget who I was. And I was wondering if any of you experienced that. Or if you felt special because you'd won. Or if you even knew."

Her voice trailed off at the end. She couldn't imagine not knowing. A life of blissful ignorance. If she hadn't known, she might have gone on to great things. She might have reached farther, tried harder.

She might have expected success with every endeavor, instead of being surprised at it.

They were staring at her as if she were speaking Greek. Maybe she was.

"I don't know why it matters," a man said beside her. "It was just a silly little contest."

"I hadn't even remembered it," a woman said, "until Dr. Franke's people contacted me."

Brooke felt something catch in her throat. "Was it like that for all of you?"

"Of course not," De said. "I got interviewed every New Year's like clockwork. What's it like five years into the millennium? Ten? Twenty? That's one of the reasons I moved to L'siana. I'm not much for attention, 'specially the kind I don't deserve."

"Money was nice," one of the women said. "It got me to college."

Another woman shook her head. "My folks spent it all."

More people from the left were moving across the divide, as if they were drawn to the conversation.

"So'd mine," said one of the men.

"There wasn't any money with mine. Just got my picture in the newspaper. Still have that on my wall," another man said.

Brooke felt someone bump her from behind. Los Gatos had joined her. So had Santa Barbara and Boston—um, Julie.

"Why'd this contest made such a difference to you?" one of the letter women asked. She was staring at Brooke.

"It didn't," Brooke said after a moment. "It mattered to my mother. She lost."

"Hell," De said. "People lose. That's part of living."

Brooke looked at him. There was a slight frown mark between his eyes. He didn't understand either. He didn't know what it was like being outside, with his face pressed against the glass.

"Three weeks after I was born," Los Gatos said, "My parents dumped me with a friend of theirs, saying they weren't ready for a baby. I never saw them. I don't even know what they look like."

"My parents said they couldn't afford me," Santa Barbara said. "They were planning on some prize money."

"They abandoned you too?" the woman asked.

"No," he said. "They just made it clear they didn't appreciate the financial burden. If they'd won, I wouldn't've been a problem."

"Sure you would have," De said. "They just would've blamed their problems on something else."

"It's not that simple," Brooke said. Her entire body was sweating despite the chill in the room. "It was a contest, a race. A lot of people didn't look beyond that. There were news articles about abandoned and abused babies, and there were a disproportionate number born in December, January, and February of 2000, because parents wanted to split some of the glory."

"You can't tell me," De said, "that something as insignificant as the time we were born determines our future."

"It does," Brooke said, "if we're brought up to believe it does."

"That bear out, Professor Franke?" De said.

Brooke turned. The professor was standing close to them, listening, looking both bemused and perplexed. Apparently he had expected some kind of reaction, but probably not this one.

"That's what I'm trying to determine," Franke said.

"And I'm askin' you if you determined it," De said.

Franke glanced at one of his assistants. The assistant shrugged. The entire room full of people was crowded around Franke, and was silent for the second time that day.

"This part of the study is experimental," he said. "I'm not sure if answering you will corrupt it."

"But you want to answer me," De said.

Franke smiled. "Yes, I do."

"It's an experiment," Brooke said. "You can always throw this part out. You might have done that anyway. Isn't that what you told me? Or at least implied?"

Franke glanced from her to De. Then Franke straightened his shoulders, as if the gesture made him stronger. "I believe that Brooke is right. My studies have convinced me that something becomes important to a child's development because that child is told that something is important."

"So us losers will remain losers the rest of our lives," Los Gatos said.

Franke shook his head. "That is not my conclusion. I believe that when something becomes important, you choose how to react to it." His voice got louder as he spoke. His professor's voice. "Some of you wearing letters have not done as well as expected. You've rebelled against those expectations and worked at proving you are not as good as you were told you were."

A flush colored De's tan cheeks.

"Others lived up to the expectations and a few of you, a very small few, exceeded them. But—" Franke paused dramatically. "Those of you who wear numbers are financially more successful as a group than your lettered peers. You strive harder because you feel you have something to overcome."

Brooke felt Los Gatos shift behind her.

"I think it goes back to the parameters of the study," Franke said. "Your parents—all of your parents—wanted to improve their lot. They all had drive, therefore most of you have drive. We've found a biological correlation."

"Really? Wow," Santa Barbara said.

"But there's more than biology at work here."

"I'd hope so," De said. "I'd hate to think you can determine who I am by reading my genes."

Franke gave him a small smile. "Your parents," Franke said, "all chose a contest as the method of improving their lives. A lottery, if you will. And most of them failed to win. Or if they succeeded, they discovered Easy Street wasn't so easy after all. You numbered folk have realized that luck is overrated. The only thing you can trust is work you do yourselves."

"And what about those of us with letters?" one of the twins from Akron asked.

"You learned a different lesson. Most of you learned that luck is what you make of it. You might win the lottery, but that doesn't make you or your family any happier than before." Franke looked at Brooke. "There were a lot of studies, some of them prompted by your mother, that showed how many unsuccessful Millennium Babies were abandoned or mistreated. But the successful ones had similar problems. Only no one wanted to lose the golden goose as long as it was still golden. Many of those abandonments were emotional, not physical. People became parents to become rich or famous, not because they wanted children."

"Sounds like you should be studying our parents," Los Gatos said.

Franke grinned. "Now you have my next book."

And the group laughed.

"Feel free to enjoy the rest of the day," Franke said. "Over the rest of the weekend, I'll be talking to individuals among you, wrapping things up. I want to thank you for your time and participation."

"That's it?" De asked.

"When you leave here tonight, if I haven't spoken to you," Franke said. "That's it."

His words were met with a momentary silence. Then he started to make his way through the group. Some people stopped him. Brooke didn't. She turned away, not sure how to feel.

She wasn't as successful as she wanted to be, but she was better off than her mother had said she would be. Brooke had her own house, a good job, interests that meant something to her.

But she was as alone as her mother was. In that, at least, they were the same.

"So," De said. "Is your life profoundly different thanks to this study?"

The question had a mixed tone. Half sarcasm, half serious. He seemed to be waiting for her answer.

"What's your name?" she asked.

"Adam," he said, wincing. "Adam Lassiter."

"The first man."

"If I'd missed my birth time, I'd have been named Zeb." He smiled as he said that, but his eyes didn't twinkle.

"I'm Brooke Cross." She waited, wondering if he'd guess at the name, despite the change. He didn't. Or if he did, he didn't say anything.

"You didn't answer my question," he said.

She looked at the room, at all the people in it, most engaged in private conversations now, hands moving, gazes serious as they compared and contrasted their experiences, trying to see if they agreed with Professor Franke.

"When I was a little girl," she said. "We lived in a small white house, maybe 1200 square feet. A starter, my mother called it, because that was all she could afford. And to me, that house was the world. My mother's world."

"What kind of world was that?" he asked.

She shook her head. How to explain it? But he had asked, and she had to try.

"A world where she did everything right and failed, and everyone else cheated and somehow succeeded. If she'd had the same kind of breaks your parents had, she believed she would have done better than they did. If she hadn't had a child like me, one who was chronically late, her life would have been better."

He was watching her. The crease between his eyes grew deeper.

Her heart was pounding, but she made herself continue. "A few years ago, when I was looking for my own home, I saw dozens and dozens of houses, and somewhere I realized that to the people living in them, those houses were the world."

"So each block has dozens of tiny worlds," he said.

She smiled at him. "Yeah."

"I still don't see how that relates."

She looked at him, then at the room. The other conversations were continuing, as serious as hers was with him. "You asked me if this study changed my life. I can't answer that. I can say, though, that it made me realize one thing."

His gaze was as intense as Franke's.

"It made me realize that even though I had moved out of that house, I hadn't left my mother's world."

He studied her for a moment longer, then said, "Sounds like a hell of a realization."

"Maybe," she said. "It depends on what I do with it."

He laughed. "Thus proving Franke's point."

She flushed. She hadn't realized she had done so, but she had. He leaned toward her.

"You know, Brooke," Adam said softly, "I like women who are chronically late. It balances my habitual timeliness. How's about we have lunch and talk about our histories. Not just the day we were born, but other things, like what we do and where we live and who we are."

She almost refused. He was from Louisiana, and she was from Wisconsin. This friendship—if that's all it was—could go nowhere.

But it was that attitude which had limited her all along. She had been driven, as Franke said, to succeed materially and professionally on her own merits. But she had never tried to succeed socially.

She had never wanted to before.

"And," she said, "you get to tell me what you learned from this study."

"Assumin'," he said with a grin, "that I'm the kinda man who can learn anything a'tall."

"Assuming that," she said and slipped her hand in his. It felt good to touch someone else, even if it was only for a brief time. It felt good.

It felt different.

It felt right.

Copyright © 2000 by Kristine Kathryn Rusch

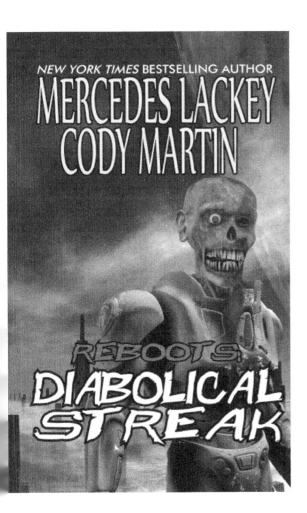

This is Andrew Liptak's first fiction sale, but he's no stranger to science fiction. He writes a column on science fiction's history for Kirkus Reviews, *and is the co-editor of the forthcoming anthology,* War Stories. *He's also got his M.A. from Norwich University, the country's first private military college.*

FRAGMENTED

by Andrew Liptak

Every morning, I wake up with the words that were drilled into my head in basic: "Your armor is your protection. Your unit is your home."

They run through my mind as I stand in formation with my platoon, at a base whose name I can't remember. We're too tired from the war to care about straight lines. The armored figures surrounding me are recognizable despite the identical shapes, people I've stood with through training and deployment to the bottom of this god-forsaken gravity well. We had all wondered if we would live to see this day, our decommissioning at the end.

"Pla-toon! Hut!" We snap to attention reflexively at our captain's order, producing an impressive clap of metal against concrete prefab that echoes against the walls of the building. One last step before we can go home. I feel my palms begin to sweat, despite my cool, metal skin covering me.

The blast from an enemy grenade ripped into the wall above me. I ducked, shielding my face as the explosion blew out the concrete and metal supports. Debris rained down into the makeshift hole that my platoon and I had used for our foxhole and I heard Sardarsky swearing as a jagged chunk of concrete the size of my head glanced off of the back of his shoulders.

"You good?" I shouted to Sardarsky as I shook off pebbles clanking off my armored skin. For a brief second, I was worried that the debris would scratch the flawless finish to my newly issued kit, but that was cut short as more gunshots cracked from across the street, spraying us in a new layer of powdered masonry. I ducked down again.

Sardarsky flashed me a thumbs-up as the dusty shower ended. I smiled as I raised my head over the edge of our foxhole. My suit's AI-assisted vision helped me scan the windows of the tall buildings on either side of us with each brief glimpse, looking for the telltale blink of light or flash in color from the masonry to a soldier's uniform. I watched the gaps from behind the sights of my gun, eyes darting from window to window.

Gunfire pockmarked the wall as an unseen soldier joined the fight, and we ducked, reflexively. "Sardarsky!" I shouted. "Cover the street!"

The soldier signaled back an acknowledgement as he and three other soldiers of his fire team peeled off from our line and moved across the street. I gestured to my own team of three, and we crept carefully down the sidewalk on the other side, taking cover in the rubble.

I caught a glint off of the wrong end of a telescopic gun sight and instinctively froze as my suit's heads-up display flared a warning. The flash of a shot signaled a round coming down at my head. Time slowed to a crawl. My armor constricted around the back of my neck to save my spinal column from the sudden compression and I heard a metallic clank and felt a pressure against my skull as it flexed slightly to take the strike and dissipate the energy to the underlying gel layer. I dropped down onto a knee with the impact.

I regained my footing and brought my gun back up, sighting in the enemy soldier looking down at me. He looked surprised as I dropped him with a shot of my own.

I sat frozen for a moment as the gunshots echoed away and the only thing that I could hear was my breathing in the helmet.

"I'm alive." I whispered to myself. My heart leapt in my chest as I processed that it was true. I touched my metal-clad fingers to my head where the bullet had impacted, feeling a small groove. I worked the words around in my mouth. I was still alive, and I felt invincible.

I looked to check Sardarsky, and found that a heavy caliber round had reduced him and his armor to fragments. My hands started to shake that night.

✿

I shiver at the first glimpse of the sterile room as I make my way into the Armor/Logistics compound, marveling at how small the specialist is as I walk up to him. He looks bored as I step up to his station, a semicircular array of tables, lights and containers. Tools hang from the ceiling on their cords, and the bright white lights overhead lend a mechanical look to the room. I don't like it, and I feel my skin crawl as I walk forward.

"Step into the center of the station," he orders me, indifferently. I'm suddenly angry at him, knowing that I could do any number of things that would irreparably harm the man in less than a second. The impulse scares me as it races across my mind, and I hang my arms at my sides. I wonder, for a second, if I thought like this before the war. I can't remember. I comply with his order.

The tech moves behind me, and I hear a buzzing and sudden release of pressure as he begins to dismantle me. He works quickly, and in an astonishing amount of time, he's freed the individual components that form the helmet around my head. The dome is the first to go, and cool air leaks in around my face as the seals are broken. I look down at the workbench and catch sight of the shallow dent on the top-right-front piece sitting in front of me, a small reminder of where I should have fallen and never come back up.

✿

We were exhausted after the end of the Rainy Season Campaign. The jungle grabbed at us from every direction as we marched single file through the dense underbrush toward our transport out of the region. We were fifty days away from our last base, our last re-fit, and our last decent meal.

The campaign's scars were carved heavily on our surfaces, and as we walked, I realized that I didn't hear my armor anymore, and didn't have to think about where the rest of my platoon-mates walked around me. We were finally headed back to base, away from the short nights and the intense action that defined the front, relieved for the break. We were no longer the green soldiers we were when we landed planet-side, two years ago, eager for action and a taste of battle. Now, we just wanted to go home.

I felt a hand on my shoulder. "Sir." Garnan's voice buzzed in my headset, as I turned to look at him, a scarred and pitted figure. He had a chip taken out of the lip over his visor, a cluster of scratches where he had been shot at close range with a flechette gun. Looking in the reflection of his helmet's face, I realized that I couldn't remember what his real face looked like. "Thank you," he told me, breaking my train of thought as I stared at the reflection. "You saved us—me—so many times over the last month. I don't know what I would have done without you."

I smiled, knowing that he'd be unable to see it, and placed my hand on his shoulder. "You've done the same for me. I …" I faltered. He flashed me a familiar thumbs-up and I could picture his face. He trotted off to rejoin his place in the line. Suddenly, he was gone. I blinked and found myself lying face up next to a tree, unable to move, the explosion ringing in my ears.

I coughed, my lungs unable to expand fully in my protectively constricted armored skin. "Unlock! Dammit, let me move!" I shouted at my suit, before I felt it relax around my limbs, allowing me to sit up. I looked around for my rifle before I found that my suit had clamped down on it, keeping it in my hand as I flew through the air away from the explosion. I brought the weapon up, ready to counter whatever was coming out at us. Nothing appeared out of the underbrush. The forest was silent.

Pain radiated from my ribs as I moved, and I saw that a piece of metal protruded out at an odd angle. I gripped it in my hand and pulled it out. I gasped at the shock of pain that radiated away from the puncture and could feel the heat of the air leak in, a damp, alien warmth. I stood, trying to get my bearings as my head spun. The trees around me were shattered from the shrapnel. I coughed again, and as I doubled over, I caught a glimpse of armor through the trees.

Garnan was lying several meters away, partially embedded in the roots of a tree. I ran over to him, ignoring the warnings that the AI displayed in my HUD and the pain in my ribs. I skidded to a stop at his side, and my insides froze. The explosion had shattered his suit: the lower part of his chest and torso had fragmented, with plates and pieces torn away from the blast. His right leg was missing, and there wasn't much left of his left one. I pulled him gently out of the roots and cradled his body in my arms.

"Specialist, come on, we've got to get to cover." I told him. "Garnan, let's go!" He was heavy in my arms, and I realized that he was never going to walk away again.

His eyes remained locked forward, staring deadly into the forest canopy.

I hadn't slept well after that.

The tech runs down the list of parts as he pulls them away from me. I look over and see that they're neatly packed away in preformed cases. I wonder if they're the same cases that came to me when we first arrived at this planet, green troopers fresh from training. My armor seemed so much larger then, clean, perfect. Now, sitting in the case, it was scarred and battered.

Another piece comes away, and I feel my breath catch in my throat.

"You're missing a piece here. Serial number should be"—he consults a holographic manual that he calls up from somewhere on the desk—"ICA-43298." He holds his hands apart to indicate its size. "Small piece, hand plate?"

I shake my head.

He sighs and touches the holo. The missing piece turns red as his fingertips pass through it. "Logistics will dock you for the part."

I don't care.

Peters bought it when we were sent to an enemy spacecraft that crashed behind our lines. We picked our way over rocks and steep ravines as an overhead drone guided us along, guns slung over our backs.

It was an orbiter, and it had just blown a major hole in our lines from the edge of the atmosphere before someone tagged it with a surface-to-air missile. It was a million in one shot, forcing it out of its perch above us. We were told to check for survivors. We growled—nothing could have survived, and if they did, we didn't want to get killed on a recovery mission. We set off regardless. Orders were orders.

Peters went first, rifle raised up to cover our front as she took point. Scattered fires, fueled by the ship's propellant, raged around us. The crew was dead, incinerated in the blast. We checked over the ship and set charges to complete the ship's destruction before retreating to a safe distance.

The ship blossomed into a brilliant fireball. We cheered at the explosion, and got up to leave. Peters turned to look back at the crater, and promptly fell over. We later found that a fragment of the explosion had arched up and pierced her suit. I had nightmares every time I closed my eyes.

✿

The tech tosses a large piece from my chest assembly onto the workstation from where he stands. It lands with a loud clang and I jump involuntarily. He either doesn't notice, or ignores the movement as he moves on to the next piece.

"Shit," he swears from behind me. I want to leave this tiny room with its bright lights.

I feel him tug at another piece, prying away at something out of sight. "Hey, go easy," I finally tell him.

He shrugs.

✿

The war was over.

We could hardly believe the news as we gathered around the briefing screen in our outpost. The planetary government had issued an ultimatum to their fighters: lay down all arms and cooperate with our forces. After a long five years of continual fighting, it was finally over. I knew that Sardarsky, Garnan and Peters were gone, long packed up into a box, but I glance over to where they would have been sitting, and wish that I could celebrate with them.

"Per the surrender terms, we're going to be pulling most of our units off the line. Armored Infantry is going to be brought out first, followed by other units as we draw down over the next couple of months," our new captain told us once we'd all gathered around. "Report to Armor Control for decontamination and processing. From that point …"

I tuned out the captain's voice as she outlined the rest of the timeline for our departure, still trying to process the news. The war that had consumed us,

that had killed everyone around me, that had left us alone and surrounded by ghosts, was over, with a simple announcement. I wasn't sure what I'd been expecting.

✿

I am dressed in the clothing that had been given to me after the technician took the rest of my suit away from me. It was vacuum-packed in a tight plastic wrapper to save space on the transport ship and it smelled sterile, reeking of the manufacturer's chemicals from back home, light years away. The clothes feel baggy on my frame, and as I walk, I feel as though I'm pulling a sail through the wind. I feel naked without my armor shell. I feel alone.

The technician retracts his tools without a word, and I step out from the middle of the workstation. The fragments of my armor are scattered around the flat surface, their scarred and battered finishes contrasting with the sterile room. The sergeant ignores me, beginning to clean up the pieces by placing them into readymade bins. I stop and watch for a moment as my armor vanishes into the cases, piece by piece. He points me back out to the parade square where I had stood alone in formation earlier, surrounded by the ghosts of my fallen comrades.

I think back to the mantra that got me through the fighting; everything has been stripped away: my skin, my friends, and my home. I feel vulnerable, and I freeze as I approach the door. I begin to fragment, and my hand brushes the armored hand plate that I palmed. I take a breath and walk out the door.

Original (First) Publication
Copyright © 2014 by Andrew Liptak

David Brin is one of the giants in the field, a multiple Hugo winner, a Nebula winner, a Worldcon Guest of Honor. "The Giving Plague" was a Hugo nominee in 1989.

THE GIVING PLAGUE

by David Brin

1

Y ou think you're going to get me, don't you? Well, you've got another think coming, 'cause I'm ready for you.

That's why there's a forged card in my wallet saying my blood group is AB Negative, and a MedicAlert tag warning that I'm allergic to penicillin, aspirin, and phenylalanine. Another one states that I'm a practicing, devout Christian Scientist. All these tricks ought to slow you down when the time comes, as it's sure to, sometime soon.

Even if it makes the difference between living and dying, there's just no way I'll let anyone stick a transfusion needle into my arm. Never. Not with the blood supply in the state it's in.

And anyway, I've got antibodies. So you just stay the hell away from me, ALAS. I won't be your patsy. I won't be your vector.

I know your weaknesses, you see. You're a fragile, if subtle, devil. Unlike TARP, you can't bear exposure to air or heat or cold or acid or alkali. Blood-to-blood, that's your only route. And what need had you of any other? You thought you'd evolved the perfect technique, didn't you?

What was it Leslie Adgeson called you? The perfect master? The paragon of viruses?

I remember long ago when HIV, the AIDS virus, had everyone so impressed with its subtlety and effectiveness of design. But compared with you, HIV is just a crude butcher, isn't it? A maniac with a chainsaw, a blunderer that kills its hosts and relies for transmission on habits humans can, with some effort, get under control. Oh, old HIV had its tricks, but compared with you? An amateur!

Rhinoviruses and flu are clever, too. They're profligate, and they mutate rapidly. Long ago they learned how to make their hosts drip and wheeze and sneeze, so victims spread the misery in all directions. Flu viruses are also a lot smarter than AIDS 'cause they don't generally kill their hosts, just make 'em miserable while they hack and spray and inflict fresh infections on their neighbors.

Oh, Les Adgeson was always accusing me of anthropomorphizing our subjects. Whenever he came into my part of the lab, and found me cursing some damned intransigent leucophage in rich, Tex-Mex invective, he'd react predictably. I can just picture him now, raising one eyebrow, commenting dryly in his Winchester accent.

"The virus cannot hear you, Forry. It isn't sentient, nor even alive, strictly speaking. It's only a packet of genes in a protein case, after all."

"Yeah, Les," I'd answer. "But *selfish* genes! Given half a chance, they'll take over a human cell, force it to make armies of new viruses, then burst it apart as they escape to attack other cells. They may not think. All that behavior may have evolved by blind chance. But doesn't it all *feel* as if it was planned? As if the nasty little things were *guided*, somehow, by someone out to make us miserable …? Out to make us die?"

"Oh, come now Forry," he would smile at my New World ingenuousness. "You wouldn't be in this field if you didn't find phages beautiful, in their own way."

Good old, smug, sanctimonious Les. He never did figure out that viruses fascinated me for quite another reason. In their rapacious insatiability I saw a simple, distilled purity of ambition that exceeded even my own. The fact that it was mindless did little to ease my qualms. I've always imagined we humans over-rated brains, anyway.

We'd first met when Les visited Austin on sabbatical, some years before. He'd had the Boy Genius rep even then, and naturally I played up to him. He invited me to join him back in Oxford, so there I was, having regular amiable arguments over the meaning of disease while the English rain dripped desultorily on the rhododendrons outside.

Les Adgeson. Him with his artsy friends and his pretensions at philosophy—Les was all the time talking about the elegance and beauty of our nasty little subjects. But he didn't fool me. I knew he was just as crazy Nobel-mad as the rest of us. Just as obsessed with the chase, searching for that piece of the Life Puzzle, that bit leading to more grants, more lab space, more techs, more prestige … to money, status and, maybe eventually, Stockholm.

He claimed not to be interested in such things. But he was a smoothy, all right. How else, in the midst of the massacre of British science, did his lab keep expanding? And yet, he kept up the pretense.

"Viruses have their good side," Les kept saying. "Sure, they often kill, in the beginning. All new pathogens start that way. But eventually, one of two things happens. Either humanity evolves defenses to eliminate the threat or …"

Oh, he loved those dramatic pauses.

"*Or?*" I'd prompt him, as required.

"Or else we come to an accommodation, a compromise … even an alliance."

That's what Les always talked about. *Symbiosis.* He loved to quote Margulis and Thomas, and even Lovelock, for pity's sake! His respect even for vicious, sneaky brutes like HIV was downright scary.

"See how it actually incorporates itself right into the DNA of its victims?" he would muse. "Then it waits, until the victim is later attacked by some *other* disease pathogen. Then the host's T-Cells prepare to replicate, to drive off the invader, only now some cells' chemical machinery is taken over by the new DNA, and instead of two new T-Cells, a plethora of new AIDS viruses results."

"So?" I answered. "Except that it's a retrovirus, that's the way nearly all viruses work."

"Yes, but think ahead, Forry. Imagine what's going to happen when, inevitably, the AIDS virus infects someone whose genetic makeup makes him invulnerable!"

"What, you mean … his antibody reactions are fast enough to stop it? Or his T-Cells repel invasion?"

Oh, Les used to sound so damn patronizing when he got excited.

"No, no, think!" he urged. "I mean invulnerable *after* infection. *After* the viral genes have incorporated into his chromosomes. Only in this individual, certain *other* genes *prevent* the new DNA from triggering viral synthesis. No new viruses are made. No

cellular disruption. The person *is* invulnerable. But now he has all this new DNA …"

"In just a few cells—"

"Yes. But suppose one of these is a sex cell. Then suppose he fathers a child with that gamete. Now *every* one of that child's cells may contain both the trait of invulnerability *and* the new viral genes! Think about it, Forry. You now have a new type of human being! One who cannot be killed by AIDS. And yet he has all the AIDS genes, can make all those strange, marvelous proteins … Oh, most of them will be unexpressed or useless, of course. But now this child's genome, and his descendants', contains more *variety* …"

I often wondered, when he got carried away like this. Did he actually believe he was explaining this to me for the first time? Much as the Brits respect American science, they do tend to assume we're slackers when it comes to the philosophical side. But I'd seen his interest heading in this direction weeks back, and had carefully done some extra reading.

"You mean like the genes responsible for some types of inheritable cancers?" I asked, sarcastically. "There's evidence some oncogenes were originally inserted into the human genome by viruses, just as you suggest. Those who inherit the trait for rheumatoid arthritis may also have gotten their gene that way."

"Exactly. Those viruses themselves may be extinct, but their DNA lives on, in ours!"

"Right. And boy have human beings benefitted!"

Oh, how I hated that smug expression he'd get. (It got wiped off his face eventually, didn't it?)

Les picked up a piece of chalk and drew a figure on the blackboard.

HARMLESS—> KILLER!—>
SURVIVABLE ILLNESS—>
INCONVENIENCE—> HARMLESS

"Here's the classic way of looking at how a host species interacts with a new pathogen, especially a virus. Each arrow, of course, represents a stage of mutation and adaptation selection.

"First, a new form of some previously harmless microorganism leaps from its prior host, say a monkey species, over to a new one, say us. Of course, at the beginning we have no adequate defenses. It cuts through us like syphilis did in Europe in the six-teenth century, killing in days rather than years … in an orgy of cell feeding that's really not a very efficient modus for a pathogen. After all, only a gluttonous parasite kills off its host so quickly.

"What follows, then, is a rough period for both host and parasite as each struggles to adapt to the other. It can be likened to warfare. Or, on the other hand, it might be thought of as a sort of drawn-out process of *negotiation*."

I snorted in disgust. "Mystical crap, Les. I'll concede your chart; but the war analogy is the right one. That's why they fund labs like ours. To come up with better weapons for our side."

"Hmm. Possibly. But sometimes the process does look different, Forry." He turned and drew another chart.

HARMLESS—> KILLER!—>
SURVIVABLE ILLNESS—>
INCONVENIENCE—>
BENIGN PARASITISM—> SYMBIOSIS

"You can see that this chart is the same as the other, right up to the point where the original disease disappears."

"Or goes into hiding."

"Surely. As E. coli took refuge in our innards. Doubtless long ago the ancestors of E. coli killed a great many of our ancestors before eventually becoming the beneficial symbionts they are now, helping us digest our food.

"The same applies to viruses, I'd wager. Heritable cancers and rheumatoid arthritis are just temporary awkwardnesses. Eventually, those genes will be comfortably incorporated. They'll be part of the genetic diversity that prepares us to meet challenges ahead.

"Why, I'd wager a large portion of our present genes came about in such a way, entering our cells first as invaders …"

Crazy sonovabitch. Fortunately he didn't try to lead the lab's research effort too far to the right on his magic diagram. Our Boy Genius was plenty savvy about the funding agencies. He knew they weren't interested in paying us to prove we're all partly descended from viruses. They wanted, and

wanted *badly*, progress on ways to fight viral infections themselves.

So Les concentrated his team on vectors.

Yeah, you viruses need vectors, don't you? I mean, if you kill a guy, you've got to have a life raft, so you can desert the ship you've sunk, so you can cross over to some *new* hapless victim. Same applies if the host proves tough, and fights you off—gotta move on. Always movin' on.

Hell, even if you've made peace with a human body, like Les suggested, you still want to spread, don't you? Big-time colonizers, you tiny beasties.

Oh, I know. It's just natural selection. Those bugs that accidentally find a good vector spread. Those that don't, don't. But it's so eerie. Sometimes it sure *feels* purposeful …

So the flu makes us sneeze. Salmonella gives us diarrhea. Smallpox causes pustules that dry, flake off and blow away to be inhaled by the patient's loved ones. All good ways to jump ship. To colonize.

Who knows? Did some past virus cause a swelling of the lips that made us want to kiss? Heh. Maybe that's a case of Les's "benign incorporation" … we retain the trait, long after the causative pathogen went extinct! What a concept.

So our lab got this big grant to study vectors. Which is how Les found you, ALAS. He drew this big chart covering all the possible ways an infection might leap from person to person, and set us about checking all of them, one by one.

For himself he reserved straight blood-to-blood infection. There were reasons for that.

First off, Les was an altruist, see. He was concerned about all the panic and unfounded rumors spreading about Britain's blood supply. Some people were putting off necessary surgery. There was talk of starting over here what some rich folk in the States had begun doing—stockpiling their own blood in silly, expensive efforts to avoid having to use the blood banks if they ever needed hospitalization.

All that bothered Les. But even worse was the fact that lots of potential donors were shying away from giving blood because of some stupid rumors that you could get infected that way.

Hell, nobody ever caught anything from *giving* blood … nothing except maybe a little dizziness and perhaps a zit from all the biscuits and sweet tea they feed you afterward. As for contracting HIV from *receiving* blood, well, the new antibodies tests soon had that problem under control. Still, the inane rumors spread.

A nation has to have confidence in its blood supply. Les wanted to eliminate all those silly fears once and for all, with one definitive study. But that wasn't the only reason he wanted the blood-to-blood vector for himself.

"Sure, there are some nasty things like AIDS that use that route. But that's also where I might find the older ones," he said, excitedly. "The viruses that have *almost* finished the process of becoming benign. The ones that have been so well selected that they keep a low profile, and hardly inconvenience their hosts at all. Maybe I can even find one that's commensal! One that actually *helps* the human body."

"An undiscovered human commensal," I sniffed doubtfully.

"And why not? If there's no visible disease, why would anyone have ever looked for it! This could open up a whole new field, Forry!"

In spite of myself, I was impressed. It was how he got to be known as a Boy Genius, after all, this flash of half-crazy insight. How he managed not to have it snuffed out of him at OxBridge, I'll never know, but it was one reason why I'd attached myself to him and his lab, and wrangled mighty hard to get my name attached to his papers.

So I kept watch over his work. It sounded so dubious, so damn stupid. And I knew it just might bear fruit, in the end.

That's why I was ready when Les invited me along to a conference down in Bloomsbury one day. The colloquium itself was routine, but I could tell he was near to bursting with news. Afterward we walked down Charing Cross Road to a pizza place, one far enough from the University area to be sure there'd be no colleagues anywhere within earshot—just the pretheatre crowd, waiting till opening time down at Leicester Square.

Les breathlessly swore me to secrecy. He needed a confidant, you see, and I was only too happy to comply.

"I've been interviewing a lot of blood donors lately," he told me after we'd ordered. "It seems that while some people have been scared off from donating,

that has been largely made up by increased contributions by a central core of regulars."

"Sounds good," I said. And I meant it. I had no objection to there being an adequate blood supply. Back in Austin I was pleased to see others go to the Red Cross van, just so long as nobody asked me to contribute. I had neither the time nor the interest, so I got out of it by telling everybody I'd had malaria.

"I found one interesting fellow, Forry. Seems he started donating back when he was twenty-five, during the Blitz. Must have contributed thirty-five, forty gallons, by now."

I did a quick mental calculation. "Wait a minute. He's got to be past the age limit by now."

"Exactly right! He admitted the truth, when he was assured of confidentiality. Seems he didn't want to stop donating when he reached sixty-five. He's a hardy old fellow … had a spot of surgery a few years back, but he's in quite decent shape, overall. So, right after his local Gallon Club threw a big retirement party for him, he actually moved across the county and registered at a new blood bank, giving a false name and a younger age!"

"Kinky. But it sounds harmless enough. I'd guess he just likes to feel needed. Bet he flirts with the nurses and enjoys the free food … sort of a bimonthly party he can always count on, with friendly appreciative people."

Hey, just because I'm a selfish bastard doesn't mean I can't extrapolate the behavior of altruists. Like most other user-types, I've got a good instinct for the sort of motivations that drive suckers. People like me need to know such things.

"That's what I thought too, at first," Les said, nodding. "I found a few more like him, and decided to call them 'addicts.' At first I never connected them with the other group, the one I named 'converts.'"

"Converts?"

"Yes, converts. People who suddenly become blood donors—get this—very soon after they've recovered from surgery themselves!"

"Maybe they're paying off part of their hospital bills that way?"

"Mmm, not really. We have nationalized health, remember? And even for private patients, that might account for the first few donations only."

"Gratitude, then?" An alien emotion to me, but I understood it, in principle.

"Perhaps. Some few people might have their consciousnesses raised after a close brush with death, and decide to become better citizens. After all, half an hour at a blood bank, a few times a year, is a small inconvenience in exchange for …"

Sanctimonious twit. Of course he was a donor. Les went on and on about civic duty and such until the waitress arrived with our pizza and two fresh bitters. That shut him up for a moment. But when she left, he leaned forward, eyes shining.

"But no, Forry. It wasn't bill paying, or even gratitude. Not for some of them, at least. More had happened to these people than having their consciousnesses raised. They were converts, Forry. They began joining Gallon Clubs, and more! It seems almost as if, in each case, a personality change had taken place."

"What do you mean?"

"I mean that a significant fraction of those who have had major surgery during the last five years seem to have changed their entire set of social attitudes! Beyond becoming blood donors, they've increased their contributions to charity, joined the parent-teacher organizations and Boy Scout troops, become active in Greenpeace and Save The Children …"

"The point, Les. What's your point?"

"My point?" He shook his head. "Frankly, some of these people were behaving like addicts … like converted addicts to *altruism*. That's when it occurred to me, Forry, that what we might have here is a new vector."

He said it as simply as that. Naturally I looked at him blankly.

"A vector!" he whispered, urgently. "Forget about typhus, or smallpox, or flu. They're rank amateurs! Wallies who give the show away with all their sneezing and flaking and shitting. To be sure, AIDS uses blood and sex, but it's so damned savage, it forced us to become aware of it, to develop tests, to begin the long, slow process of isolating it. But ALAS—"

"Alas?"

"A-L-A-S." He grinned. "It's what I've named the new virus I've isolated, Forry. It stands for 'Acquired Lavish Altruism Syndrome.' How do you like it?"

"Hate it. Are you trying to tell me that there's a virus that affects the human *mind*? And in such a complicated way?" I was incredulous and, at the same time, scared spitless. I've always had this superstitious feeling about viruses and vectors. Les really had me spooked now.

"No, of course not," he laughed. "But consider a simpler possibility. What if some virus one day stumbled on a way to make people enjoy giving blood?"

I guess I only blinked then, unable to give him any other reaction.

"Think, Forry! Think about that old man I spoke of earlier. He told me that every two months or so, just before he'd be allowed to donate again, he tends to feel 'all thick inside.' The discomfort only goes away only after the next donation!"

I blinked again. "And you're saying that each time he gives blood, he's actually serving his parasite, providing it a vector into new hosts …"

"The new hosts being those who survive surgery because the hospital gave them fresh blood, all because our old man was so generous, yes! They're infected! Only this is a subtle virus, not a greedy bastard, like AIDS, or even the flu. It keeps a low profile. Who knows, maybe it's even reached a level of commensalism with its hosts—attacking invading organisms for them, or …"

He saw the look on my face and waved his hands. "All right, far-fetched, I know. But think about it! Because there are no disease symptoms, nobody has ever looked for this virus, until now."

He's isolated it, I realized, suddenly. And, knowing instantly what this thing could mean, career-wise, I was already scheming, wondering how to get my name onto his paper, when he published this. So absorbed was I that, for a few moments, I lost track of his words.

"… And so now we get to the interesting part. You see, what's a normal, selfish Tory-voter going to think when he finds himself suddenly wanting to go down to the blood bank as often as they'll let him?"

"Um," I shook my head. "That he's been bewitched? Hypnotized?"

"Nonsense!" Les snorted. "That's not how human psychology works. No, we tend to do lots of things without knowing why. We need excuses, though, so we rationalize! If an obvious reason for our behavior isn't readily available, we invent one, preferably one that helps us think better of ourselves. Ego is powerful stuff, my friend."

Hey, I thought. *Don't teach your grandmother to suck eggs.*

"Altruism," I said aloud. "They find themselves rushing regularly to the blood bank. So they rationalize that it's because they're good people … They become proud of it. Brag about it …"

"You've got it," Les said. "And because they're proud, even sanctimonious, about their newfound generosity, they tend to extend it, to bring it into other parts of their lives!"

I whispered in hushed awe. "An altruism virus! Jesus, Les, when we announce this …"

I stopped when I saw his sudden frown, and instantly thought it was because I'd used that word, "we." I should have known better, of course. For Les was always more than willing to share the credit. No, his reservation was far more serious than that.

"Not yet, Forry. We can't publish this yet."

I shook my head. "Why not! This is big, Les! It proves much of what you've been saying all along, about symbiosis and all that. There could even be a Nobel in it!"

I'd been gauche, and spoken aloud of The Ultimate. But he did not even seem to notice. Damn. If only Les had been like most biologists, driven more than anything else by the lure of Stockholm. But no. You see, Les was a natural. A natural altruist.

It was his fault, you see. Him and his damn virtue, they drove me to first contemplate what I next decided to do.

"Don't you see, Forry? If we publish, they'll develop an antibody test for the ALAS virus. Donors carrying it will be barred from the blood banks, just like those carrying AIDS and syphilis and hepatitis. And that would be incredibly cruel torture to those poor addicts and carriers."

"Screw the carriers!" I almost shouted. Several pizza patrons glanced my way. With a desperate effort I brought my voice down. "Look, Les, the carriers will be classified as diseased, won't they? So they'll go under doctor's care. And if all it takes to make them feel better is to bleed them regularly, well, then we'll give them pet leeches!"

Les smiled. "Clever. But that's not the only, or even my main reason, Forry. No, I'm not going to publish, yet, and that is final. I just can't allow anybody to stop this disease. It's got to spread, to become an epidemic. A pandemic."

I stared, and upon seeing that look in his eyes, I knew that Les was more than an altruist. He had caught that most insidious of all human ailments, the Messiah Complex. Les wanted to save the world.

"Don't you see?" he said urgently, with the fervor of a proselyte. "Selfishness and greed are destroying the planet, Forry! But nature always finds a way, and this time symbiosis may be giving us our last chance, a final opportunity to become better people, to learn to cooperate before it's too late!

"The things we're most proud of, our prefrontal lobes, those bits of gray matter above the eyes which make us so much smarter than beasts, what good have they done us, Forry? Not a hell of a lot. We aren't going to think our way out of the crises of the twentieth century. Or, at least, thought alone won't do it. We need something else, as well.

"And Forry, I'm convinced that 'something else' is ALAS. We've got to keep this secret, at least until it's so well established in the population that there's no turning back!"

I swallowed. "How long? How long do you want to wait? Until it starts affecting voting patterns? Until after the next election?"

He shrugged. "Oh, at least that long. Five years. Possibly seven. You see, the virus tends to only get into people who've recently had surgery, and they're generally older. Fortunately, they also are often influential. Just the sort who now vote Tory …"

He went on. And on. I listened with half an ear, but already I had come to that fateful realization. A seven-year wait for a goddamn co-authorship would make this discovery next to useless to my career, to my ambitions.

Of course I could blow the secret on Les, now that I knew of it. But that would only embitter him, and he'd easily take all the credit for the discovery anyway. People tend to remember innovators, not whistle-blowers.

We paid our bill and walked toward Charing Cross Station, where we could catch the tube to Paddington, and from there the train to Oxford.

Along the way we ducked out of a sudden downpour at a streetside ice cream vendor. While we waited, I bought us both cones. I remember quite clearly that he had strawberry. I had a raspberry ice.

While Les absent-mindedly talked on about his research plans, a small pink smudge colored the corner of his mouth. I pretended to listen, but already my mind had turned to other things, nascent plans and earnest scenarios for committing murder.

2

It would be the perfect crime, of course.

Those movie detectives are always going on about "motive, means, and opportunity." Well, motive I had in plenty, but it was one so far-fetched, so obscure, that it would surely never occur to anybody.

Means? Hell, I worked in a business rife with means. There were poisons and pathogens galore. We're a very careful profession, but, well, accidents do happen … The same holds for opportunity.

There was a rub, of course. Such was Boy Genius's reputation that, even if I did succeed in knobbling him, I didn't dare come out immediately with my own announcement. Damn him, everyone would just assume it was his work anyway, or his "leadership" here at the lab, at least, that led to the discovery of ALAS. And besides, too much fame for me right after his demise might lead someone to suspect a motive.

So, I realized. Les was going to get his delay, after all. Maybe not seven years, but three or four perhaps, during which I'd move back to the States, start a separate line of work, then subtly guide my own research to cover methodically all the bases Les had so recently flown over in flashes of inspiration. I wasn't happy about the delay, but at the end of that time, it would look entirely like my own work. No co-authorship for Forry on this one, nossir!

The beauty of it was that no one would ever think of connecting me with the tragic death of my colleague and friend, years before. After all, did not his demise set me back in my career, temporarily? "Ah, if only poor Les had lived to see your success!" my competitors would say, suppressing jealous bile as they watched me pack for Stockholm.

Of course none of this appeared on my face or in my words. We both had our normal work to do. But almost every day I also put in long extra hours helping Les in "our" secret project. In its own way it was an exhilarating time, and Les was lavish in his praise of the slow, dull, but methodical way I fleshed out some of his ideas.

I made my arrangements slowly, knowing Les was in no hurry. Together we gathered data. We isolated and even crystallized the virus, got X-ray diffractions, did epidemiological studies, all in strictest secrecy.

"Amazing!" Les would cry out, as he uncovered the way the ALAS virus forced its hosts to feel their need to "give." He'd wax eloquent, effusive over elegant mechanisms that he ascribed to random selection, but which I could not help superstitiously attributing to some incredibly insidious form of intelligence. The more subtle and effective we found its techniques to be, the more admiring Les became, and the more I found myself loathing those little packets of RNA and protein.

The fact that the virus seemed so harmless—Les thought even commensal—only made me hate it more. It made me glad of what I had planned. Glad that I was going to stymie Les in his scheme to give ALAS free rein.

I was going to save humanity from this would-be puppet master. True, I'd delay my warning to suit my own purposes, but the warning would come, nonetheless, and sooner than my unsuspecting compatriot planned.

Little did Les know that he was doing background for work I'd take credit for. Every flash of insight, his every "Eureka!", was stored away in my private notebook, beside my own columns of boring data. Meanwhile, I sorted through all the means at my disposal.

Finally, I selected for my agent a particularly virulent strain of dengue fever.

3

There's an old saying we have in Texas. "A chicken is just an egg's way of makin' more eggs."

To a biologist, familiar with all those latinized-graecificated words, this saying has a much more "posh" version. Humans are "zygotes," made up of diploid cells containing forty-six paired chromosomes … except for our haploid sex cells, or "gametes." Males' gametes are sperm and females' are eggs, each containing only twenty-three chromosomes.

So biologists say that "a zygote is only a gamete's way of making more gametes."

Clever, eh? But it does point out just how hard it is, in nature, to pin down a Primal Cause … some center to the puzzle, against which everything else can be calibrated. I mean, which *does* come first, the chicken or the egg?

"Man is the measure of all things," goes another wise old saying. Oh yeah? Tell that to a modern feminist.

A guy I once knew, who read science fiction, told me about this story he'd seen, in which it turned out that the whole and entire purpose of humanity, brains and all, was to be the organism that built starships so that *houseflies* could migrate out and colonize the galaxy.

But that idea's nothing compared with what Les Adgeson believed. He spoke of the human animal as if he were describing a veritable United Nations. From the E. coli in our guts, to tiny commensal mites that clean our eyelashes for us, to the mitochondria that energize our cells, all the way to the contents of our very DNA … Les saw it all as a great big hive of compromise, negotiation, *symbiosis*. Most of the contents of our chromosomes came from past invaders, he contended.

Symbiosis? The picture he created in my mind was one of minuscule puppeteers, all yanking and jerking at us with their protein strings, making us marionettes dance to their own tunes, to their own nasty, selfish little agendas.

And you, *you* were the worst! Like most cynics, I had always maintained a secret faith in human nature. Yes, most people are pigs. I've always known that. And while I may be a user, at least I'm honest enough to admit it.

But deep down, we users count on the sappy, inexplicable generosity, the mysterious, puzzling altruism of those others, the kind, inexplicably decent folk … those we superficially sneer at in contempt, but secretly hold in awe.

Then *you* came along, damn you. You *make* people behave that way. There is no mystery left, after you

get finished. No corner remaining impenetrable to cynicism. Damn, how I came to hate you!

As I came to hate Leslie Adgeson. I made my plans, schemed my brilliant campaign against both of you. In those last days of innocence, I felt oh, so savagely determined. So deliciously decisive and in control of my own destiny.

In the end it was anticlimactic. I didn't have time to finish my preparations, to arrange that little trap, that sharp bit of glass dipped in just the right mixture of deadly microorganisms. For CAPUC arrived then, just before I could exercise my option as a murderer.

CAPUC changed everything.

Catastrophic Auto-immune PUlmonary Collapse … acronym for the horror that made AIDS look like a minor irritant. And in the beginning it appeared unstoppable. Its vectors were completely unknown and the causative agent defied isolation for so long.

This time it was no easily identifiable group that came down with the new plague, though it concentrated upon the industrialized world. Schoolchildren in some areas seemed particularly vulnerable. In other places it was secretaries and postal workers.

Naturally, all the major epidemiology labs got involved. Les predicted the pathogen would turn out to be something akin to the prions that cause shingles in sheep, and certain plant diseases … a pseudo-life-form even simpler than a virus and even harder to track down. It was a heretical, minority view, until the CDC in Atlanta decided out of desperation to try his theories out, and found the very dormant viroids Les predicted—mixed in with the *glue* used to seal paper milk cartons, envelopes, postage stamps.

Les was a hero, of course. Most of us in the labs were. After all, we'd been the first line of defense. Our own casualty rate had been ghastly.

For a while there, funerals and other public gatherings were discouraged. But an exception was made for Les. The procession behind his cortege was a mile long. I was asked to deliver the eulogy. And when they pleaded with me to take over at the lab, I agreed.

So naturally I tended to forget all about ALAS. The war against CAPUC took everything society had. And while I may be selfish, even a rat can tell when it makes more sense to join in the fight to save a sinking ship … especially when there's no other port in sight.

We learned how to combat CAPUC, eventually. It involved drugs, and a serum based on reversed antibodies force-grown in the patient's own marrow after he's been given a dangerous overdose of a vanadium compound I found by trial and error. It worked most of the time, but the victims suffered great stress and often required a special regime of whole blood transfusions to get across the most dangerous phase.

Blood banks were stretched even thinner than before. Only now the public responded generously, as in time of war. I should not have been surprised when survivors, after their recovery, volunteered by the thousands. But, of course, I'd forgotten about ALAS by then, hadn't I?

We beat back CAPUC. Its vector proved too unreliable, too easily interrupted once we'd figured it out. The poor little viroid never had a chance to do get to Les's "negotiation" stage. Oh well, those are the breaks.

I got all sorts of citations I didn't deserve. The king gave me a KBE for personally saving the Prince of Wales. I had dinner at the White House.

Big deal.

The world had a respite after that. CAPUC had scared people, it seemed, into a new spirit of cooperation. I should have been suspicious, of course. But soon I'd moved over to WHO, and had all sorts of administrative responsibilities in the Final Campaign on Malnutrition.

By that time, I had almost entirely forgotten about ALAS.

I forgot about you, didn't I? Oh, the years passed, my star rose, I became famous, respected, revered. I didn't get my Nobel in Stockholm. Ironically, I picked it up in Oslo. Fancy that. Just shows you can fool anybody.

And yet, I don't think I ever *really* forgot about you, ALAS, not at the back of my mind.

Peace treaties were signed. Citizens of the industrial nations voted temporary cuts in their standards of living in order to fight poverty and save the environment. Suddenly, it seemed, we'd all grown up. Other cynics, guys I'd gotten drunk with in the

past—and shared dark premonitions about the inevitable fate of filthy, miserable humanity—all gradually deserted the faith, as pessimists seem wont to do when the world turns bright—too bright for even the cynical to dismiss as a mere passing phase on the road to Hell.

And yet, my own brooding remained unblemished. For subconsciously I *knew* it wasn't real.

Then the third Mars Expedition returned to worldwide adulation, and brought home with them TARP.

And that was when we all found out just how *friendly* all our home-grown pathogens really had been, all along.

4

Late at night, stumbling in exhaustion from overwork, I would stop at Les's portrait where I'd ordered it hung in the hall opposite my office door, and stand there cursing him and his damned theories of symbiosis.

Picture mankind ever reaching a symbiotic association with TARP! That really would be something. Imagine, Les, all those *alien* genes, added to our heritage, to our rich human diversity!

Only TARP did not seem to be much interested in "negotiation." Its wooing was rough, deadly. And its vector was the wind.

The world looked to me, and to my peers, for salvation. In spite of all of my successes and high renown, though, I knew myself for a second-best fraud. I would always know—no matter how much they thanked and praised me—who had been better than me by light years.

Again and again, deep into the night, I would pore through the notes Leslie Adgeson had left behind, seeking inspiration, seeking hope. That's when I stumbled across ALAS again.

I found *you* again.

Oh, you made us behave better, all right. At least a quarter of the human race must contain your DNA, by now, ALAS. And in their newfound, inexplicable, rationalized altruism, they set the tone followed by all the others.

Everybody behaves so damned *well* in the present calamity. They help each other, they succor the sick, they all *give* so.

Funny thing, though. If you hadn't made us all so bloody cooperative, we'd probably never have made it to bloody Mars, would we? Or if we had, there'd have still been enough paranoia around so we'd have maintained a decent quarantine.

But then, I remind myself, you don't *plan*, do you? You're just a bundle of RNA, packed inside a protein coat, with an incidentally, accidentally acquired trait of making humans want to donate blood. That's all you are, right? So you had no way of knowing that by making us "better" you were also setting us up for TARP, did you? Did you?

5

We've got some palliatives, now. A few new techniques seem to be doing some good. The latest news is great, in fact. Apparently, we'll be able to save maybe fifteen percent or so of the children. At least half of them may even be fertile.

That's for nations who've had a lot of racial mixing. Heterozygosity and genetic diversity seem to breed better resistance. Those peoples with "pure," narrow bloodlines will be harder to save, but then, racism has its inevitable price.

Too bad about the great apes and horses, but then, at least all this will give the rain forests a chance to grow back.

Meanwhile, everybody perseveres. There is no panic, as one reads about happening in past plagues. We've grown up at last, it seems. We help each other.

But I carry a card in my wallet saying I'm a Christian Scientist, and that my blood group is AB Negative, and that I'm allergic to nearly everything. Transfusions are one of the treatments commonly used now, and I'm an important man. But I won't take blood.

I won't.

I *donate*, but I'll never take it. Not even when I drop.

You won't have me, ALAS. You won't.

✿

I am a bad man. I suppose, all told, I've done more good than evil in my life, but that's incidental, a product of happenstance and the bizarre caprices of the world.

I have no control over the world, but I can make my own decisions, at least. As I make this one, now.

Down, out of my high research tower I've come. Into the streets, where the teeming clinics fester and broil. That is where I work now. And it doesn't matter to me that I'm behaving no differently than anyone else today. They are all marionettes. They think they're acting altruistically, but I know they are your puppets, ALAS.

But I am a *man*, do you hear me? I make my own decisions.

Fever wracks my body now, as I drag myself from bed to bed, holding their hands when they stretch out to me for comfort, doing what I can to ease their suffering, to save a few.

You'll not have me, ALAS.

This is what *I* choose to do.

Copyright © 1987 by David Brin

●

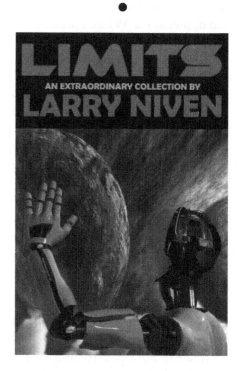

Eric Leif Davin, a science fiction historian, is the author of two books about science fiction—Pioneers of Wonder: Conversations With the Founders of Science Fiction, *and* Partners in Wonder: Women and the Birth of Science Fiction, 1926-1965.

ICARUS AT NOON

by Eric Leif Davin

Hell filled the sky. The seething cauldron of the Sun, only 17 million miles away and thirty times larger than it appeared from Earth, began to pour fire across the horizon. Soon its thousand-degree heat would begin cooking Santiago de la Cruz. Facing Sol as it grew larger, de la Cruz sat cross-legged in the Lotus position, bobbing gently, as if underwater, above the burned and blackened surface of Icarus. Almost eighty million miles from home, de la Cruz prepared to die.

It wasn't supposed to have been this way. It was an accident. It was because he shut down the damn computers on the final approach. No machine was going to have anything to do with touching down on this last "untouched" world. It was going to be one small step—*for a man!*

Santiago de la Cruz came in slow in the small cone of darkness trailing out from Icarus like a windsock. He wanted to park the ship in a close parallel orbit, then glide down in a suit. He miscalculated. Alarms blared, retros fired, and he plowed into the side of the asteroid in slow motion.

The ship's oxygen gushed out into the void of space as the scarred side of the asteroid ripped into the ship. It was a long horizontal slash—not enough to demolish the spacecraft. But enough to disable it. It would never make it back to Earth. It now drifted as a companion body to the tiny world and would join it in its long 409-day journey around the Sun. Somewhere amid the wreckage floated a spacesuit. In the suit was Santiago de la Cruz.

☼

Santiago de la Cruz was an old hand. He had thrilled at the stark beauty of the Martian hinterlands and walked the bubbling surface of Io. He'd commanded every type of craft. He'd supervised bases on Mars and Io, built the Deep Space Observer on Pluto when almost everyone else said it couldn't be done. And *because* he was an old hand, he understood the logic of withdrawal. It made dollars and *sense*.

Besides, anyplace he'd been he could return to via VR tours. Anything seen by a robot or a human with a camera was easily accessible to anyone else thereafter. All you had to do was buy the appropriate virtual disk, slip it in, and you were *there* once more—or for the first time! You could hunker down to outlast a Martian sand storm, plummet through the stygian depths of the Jovian atmosphere, stand on the edge of an erupting volcano on Io. When *virtual* reality was as real as *reality*—who needed dangerous reality? But it still ate at him. "It's just not the *same*," he insisted to himself.

All around him Serenity Moon Base was a hive of activity, but as de la Cruz surveyed the installation he saw no humans. Worker 'bots scurried everywhere, intent on their work. Some of that work was ongoing astronomical observations. Other work entailed the industrial production of oxygen, hydrogen, and other raw materials for lunar and space-based industries. Mass-production industry no longer took place on Earth. It was cheaper and safer off-planet, where raw materials were plentiful and transportation was easy. Finished products were then dropped down the gravity well to Earth. The home planet consumed what the Solar System provided.

What the *robots* of the Solar System provided, de la Cruz thought bitterly to himself. Just as worker 'bots swarmed over Serenity Moon Base, so they swarmed over the entire System, from Mercury to Pluto and Charon. Indeed, they pushed out even farther than the System, as robot probes explored the edges of the Sun's gravitational field and headed toward the nearest stars.

It's been like this from the beginning, de la Cruz thought bitterly. Machines got here first, now they're everywhere. The Russians weren't the first in space. Back in 1957 it was Sputnik, a piece of Russian *metal*, which got into space first, announcing to everyone down below as it beeped away in the night sky that a *machine* got up here first. The first spacecraft from

Earth to reach another world was another hunk of machinery, the Russian Lunik, which crashed on the Moon back in 1959. It was another Russian robot craft which reached Mars back in 1971. And so it went, planet after planet, probe after probe: Venus, Mars, Jupiter and Saturn and their moons, Halley's Comet, the asteroid belt. After Sputnik and Lunik it was Mariner, Pioneer, Viking, Pathfinder, Galileo, Magellan, Voyager. The machines always got there first.

And now they'll be here last, de la Cruz thought to himself. The human presence in space was but a brief intrusion. It just didn't make sense to have all those fragile and expensive pieces of protoplasm in harm's way. They weren't needed. Robot stations on Mercury and Venus, on Vesta and Mars, on Io and Pluto, could carry out all the observations and experiments any human could, and for a fraction of the cost. All the expensive life support systems needed to maintain human life could be jettisoned, making for a smaller, streamlined, high-performance facility operating on a shoestring. And it was safer, at least from the human viewpoint. When a catastrophic failure occurred at some far-distant outpost, all that was lost was some machinery.

And so the United Nations Space Agency had declared space gradually "off-limits" to humans. The human presence slowly pulled back from the fringes of the Solar System as human-staffed facilities were closed down one by one and put on automatic pilot. Serenity Moon Base, half-buried under the Moon's Sea of Serenity, was the last to be staffed by humans. And, as the personnel went home at the end of their turns, it finally came down to Santiago de la Cruz. He was "The Last Man on the Moon." It was his job to turn out the lights.

Santiago de la Cruz continued on his tour of inspection. It was for the most part redundant. The automatic systems ran everything, checked everything. But, it was his *job*, at least for the time being, and so he did it. He entered the hermetically sealed hangar where the Prometheus Project was nearing completion. Robot technicians scurried here and there running diagnostics on the craft. Soon it would be launched to the last unexplored piece of real estate in the Solar System, a small world previously overlooked. The all-conquering robots weren't quite ev-

erywhere just yet and, almost as an afterthought, the final blank spot on the map of the Solar System was going to be filled in. How ironic, de la Cruz thought, that the craft was named *Prometheus*, after a *man* who stole fire from the gods.

De la Cruz paused to admire the ship. It was a beautiful piece of machinery—manufactured right here at Serenity Moon Base. Like everything else on the Moon—or on Earth—it was untouched by human hands, entirely produced by robot techies in an automated facility. "That's just the problem," thought de la Cruz. "Who needs *people*? We're *all* redundant."

Indeed, humans weren't needed for *any* productive work. They were almost literally *useless*. Computers and robots produced everything—and they produced *megatons* of it, whatever *it* was. Thorstein Veblen had predicted it long ago. The "inordinate productivity of the machine," he said, would soon produce wealth far beyond the fevered dreams of Midas. And it did. About the only job left for humans was to consume the wealth.

For those who could. Most could not. Earth had become a hellhole for the common person. There were no jobs. And there were no handouts. The "freeloading parasites" who comprised most of humanity had become an idle underclass locked out beyond the gates of Eden, where the equally idle rich frolicked. And when the underclass became too restive, there were lots of prisons just waiting for them. Santiago de la Cruz was not a member of the "owning" class, so no comfortable and well-guarded high-rise condo waited for him. And when a robot could do his job just as well and cheaper, no job awaited him. Instead, the underclass beckoned him. As soon as he finished supervising the closing of Serenity Moon Base to humans, he would join it. "Just what the hell am I going to do down on Earth?" he thought. "May as well be dead."

☼

The purpose of the Prometheus mission was to secure the Helios Station on the surface of Icarus, the hottest hunk of rock in the Solar System. Orbiting Sol *inside* the orbit of Mercury, Icarus was a two-mile-diameter nickel-iron asteroid. Even smaller than Deimos, the smallest Martian moon at seven-by-nine miles, there was nevertheless enough of it for a ship to approach in the shadow and touch down on it. The ship, however, would be as light as a feather. With gravity 1/10,000th that of Earth, a man, even in a bulky spacesuit, would not be able to walk across the surface of Icarus. He'd have to traverse the 15 square miles of jagged and sun-blackened surface by his hands, like a buoyant scuba diver pulling himself along the bottom of a Caribbean lagoon.

Once planted, the Helios Station would be a permanent, cheap, and fully automated solar observatory. It would monitor the various layers of the Sun's roiling solar gases, the photosphere, chromosphere, and corona, with their varying temperatures, directions, and visual characteristics. Based on Icarus, its orbit would never decay, as had so many other robotic solar observer spacecraft, plunging them into the Sun.

In addition, the four-hour rotation of Icarus meant there would also be a period of night during which useful observations could be made of the chromosphere and corona, the layers of hot gases just above the Sun's photosphere, or visual surface. While those layers actually shine by themselves, they are overwhelmed by the intensity of the direct surface glare. Blotting out that glare would bring the upper two layers into prominent view. Nighttime conditions would also make it possible for the Helios Station to observe the oval, grey, hazy glow of the inner Zodiacal light caused by sunlight reflection off dust particles along the plane of the Solar System, also erased in the full glare of the Sun.

And, with a wildly elliptical orbit, Icarus at perihelion—its closest approach to the Sun—dwarfed any hell Mercury could offer. On Mercury, the Sun was only twice the size as seen from Earth. On Icarus it filled the sky. With a brightside surface temperature of 797 degrees Fahrenheit, Mercury was hot enough—but at high noon on Icarus a week from perihelion, the temperature hit 1,000 degrees F. And *Prometheus* was going to rendezvous with Icarus at perihelion.

As *Prometheus* became more fully operational, de la Cruz spent more time in the facility, becoming more and more familiar with the last spacecraft he'd ever get to see up close and personal. Finally, he made a decision. Santiago de la Cruz had almost single-handedly built the Deep Space Observer on Pluto at the very edge of the Solar System. He'd be damned if a robot spacecraft was going to set up Earth's outpost at the other end of the System. He began programing instructions to alter the design and construction of *Prometheus*. He didn't want too much changed. Just enough to support a single human occupant.

And who was to stop him? He was the only man on the Moon. And since he supervised all reports to Ground Control, it was easy enough to conceal what he was doing. By the time his superiors down on Earth found out what he was up to, it was too late. He was already in space.

"De la Cruz!" they radioed. "Abort immediately and return to Serenity!"

"No chance," he replied. "I'm on my way to the Sun. I've got a rendezvous with Icarus at high noon."

"De la Cruz, are you insane? This is suicidal!"

"Yeah, pretty irrational, alright. What'ya gonna do? Terminate my career?"

"Why are you *doing* this?"

"Like Sir Edmund said, 'Because it's there!'"

"De la Cruz, you are jeopardizing the success of a multi-trillion-dollar scientific expedition!"

"So arrest me," de la Cruz radioed back, and then broke communication with Earth. He knew they'd be after him, but not before he got to Icarus first.

✧

When Santiago de la Cruz regained consciousness, he seemed to be floating just above the steeply curving surface of a small hill. In all directions the dark and broken land fell away from him. A momentary wave of vertigo engulfed him and his head swam. Then he realized where he was and his vision steadied. The small hill below him was the entire near side of Icarus. Above him in the darkness of the asteroid's night side floated the wreckage of *Prometheus*. Then, off to his side, the disorientingly near horizon flickered with fire as the Sun began to rise.

The Sun galvanized de la Cruz into action. The sudden impact of its hellish temperature would quickly overheat his suit's cooling capacity. Soon, he'd be boiling like a lobster in its shell. He doubled over, reached down, and touched the surface of Icarus. "That's one small handhold for a man," he said, "one giant reach for all Mankind."

Then he reached out and grabbed another handhold on the surface. He pulled himself forward and reached with his other hand for yet another outcropping. Then another. And another. Weighing less than an ounce in his suit, he made rapid progress as he pulled himself across the face of Icarus. As the asteroid's rotation speed was only one mile per hour, de la Cruz soon saw the giant thermonuclear furnace of superheated gases which was the Sun sink back below the horizon behind him. He plunged deeper into the blessed -60 degree F. temperature of the Icaran night. In a short time he was in the middle of the asteroid's nocturnal zone. All he had to do, he thought, was just keep moving. That way, he could always outrun the dawn. And, with the slight exertion such movement required, he could keep it up forever. Or until his suit ran out of oxygen.

De la Cruz continued pulling himself slowly across the darkened surface of Icarus, pacing himself so he didn't use more oxygen than absolutely necessary. It was only a temporary solution, he realized. Eventually, he'd run out. "The Sun's going to get me," he thought, "just as it got the original Icarus."

He paused and bobbed gently above the Icaran surface, tethered by a light handhold on a piece of rock. He turned and looked back in the direction he'd come. There was a hell hound coming for him from just beyond the horizon. He couldn't outrun it much longer. Why not greet the inevitable face-on?

Santiago de la Cruz drifted into a sitting position inches above the surface and crossed his legs, assuming the Lotus position. He began to breathe in a slow, regular rhythm as he calmed his heartbeat and composed his thoughts. The problem, he thought, is rotation. And oxygen. If this damn piece of rock didn't rotate, I'd be able to hide in its shadow indefinitely. And if I had more oxygen. … But there was nothing he could do about either.

Up ahead in the expanding aurora of the Sun, de la Cruz noticed a brilliant point of light, as if a morning star shined in the heavens to presage the Sun. It grew larger, however, as the slow rotation of Icarus brought him nearer. Suddenly, de la Cruz realized what it was. It was the *Prometheus*! It was still there, where the collision with Icarus had left it, drifting now about two miles above the surface as the asteroid rotated beneath it. While Icarus turned constantly toward the Sun, the wrecked *Prometheus* hovered in stationary position, orbiting the Sun parallel with Icarus. De la Cruz's heart leapt within him as he thrust aside thoughts of stoic acceptance. "There's my shade!" he thought. "And oxygen, too, if the tanks weren't ruptured!" Two miles up. So close—and yet so far!

De la Cruz coiled his legs beneath him, calculated his trajectory, and kicked off from the Icaran surface as hard as he could. Arms stretched out in front of him, like a diver in a slow-motion arc, de la Cruz aimed for the derelict hulk. His leap carried him into the full blaze of the Sun. The temperature soared on the shell of his suit and harsh UV radiation flooded over him. But he spread his wings and flew. The leap to the ship seemed to take forever. "If I miss it," he thought, "I'll end up diving into the Sun."

But he didn't miss it.

Nor did the rescue ship miss his emergency beacon. De la Cruz floated in the welcome shade of the *Prometheus* as he waited for the ship from Earth. They'd arrest him, he thought. Maybe imprison him. It'd be the last time a human was allowed in space. It wasn't important. What *was* important was that a *human* had gotten to the last world in the Solar System before the robots. A *human* had flown to Icarus at high noon—and his wings had not melted.

Santiago de la Cruz looked out into the blackness of space. Hard pinpricks of starlight punctured the dark. They'd always called to him. They'd pulled him into space and across a dozen worlds. Their harsh reality would test him no more. But it doesn't matter, he thought. Even if unattainable—the stars still beckon.

Robin Reed was a student on Phoenix Pick's Sail to Success cruise last December. All of the students were asked to submit a story to this magazine, with the promise that one would be purchased. This is the winner.

AIR AND WATER

by Robin Reed

Mara gripped the pole with callused hands and watched the rocket ride a column of smoke and fire. It disappeared into the cloud ceiling, the flame from its tail visible for a short time, then going out. The trail of smoke led down to the port, where it blended into the haze from factories and power plants.

"Work." Kekku's bony head intruded on her vision. "I did not buy you to look at sky."

Mara looked down, into the brown water on the edge of the lake. She pushed the pole to make the small wooden boat move through the rainbow sheen of oil on the surface.

"Always you look." Kekku rose higher, gripping the sides of the boat with four of six limbs. "There is nothing in the sky for us."

"I came from the sky."

Kekku made a sorrowful chitter. "I should never have told you."

"There." Mara pointed. The tip of a breathing tube hid among thin plants. It revealed the location of an air shell, buried deep in the mud below. Disguised as one of the green stalks, it could be discovered only when it quivered slightly as the creature let out air and took in more.

She handed the pole to Kekku, then dived. Kicking her legs, she followed the breathing tube down and grasped it at the base.

Kekku was thin and hard-skinned, unable to float. Mara was a secret tool. Kekku claimed the status of best gatherer of air shells who sold at the market, and told no one how it was done.

Mara had to be careful not to pull too hard. If she broke the tube off, the air shell would not come up from under the mud. It would drown, and she would face Kekku's disapproval.

This one was not buried very deeply. That meant it was young, and would be small. It would still be edible, and fetch a price at the market. Mara pulled until the ridged shell came free, then pushed her way toward air.

The boat rocked as she climbed back into it. Kekku held on fiercely, afraid of falling into the water. The air shell went into a bag with three others. Still dripping water that smelled greasy, she took back the pole and moved the boat along.

As her tunic dried, the tender points of the strange new flesh on her chest rubbed against the rough cloth. She grimaced from the pain.

"What is wrong?"

Mara self-consciously folded one arm over the new things and tried to pole with the other. Something had been happening to her for a while. The little round circles on her chest had become sore, then had started to expand, as flesh filled in behind them.

"Nothing."

"Then work."

Mara looked down, unable to explain what she didn't understand.

They collected seven air shells. They were becoming harder to find, and the ones Mara brought up were smaller than they were just a year ago. The water she dived into was increasingly foul to the taste.

As the light faded, Kekku told her to steer the boat away from the dark, irregular structures of the port. She guided it through low plants that got thicker and thicker. When it hit a high spot she jumped out and pulled it up onto land.

Kekku stepped out of the boat, four feet squelching in mud. All six feet had grippers, for climbing and holding tools. Four of them served to walk on, and the front pair was held off the ground to keep them relatively clean.

"Time to shorten your head threads." Kekku walked past Mara to the center of the small patch of land, carrying the bag of air shells. Kekku dumped them into a small water-filled depression. That would keep them fresh until morning.

Near the depression a factory-built shelter sat. Designed to be used for a few days at a time, to be folded up and carried while travelling, it had been Mara and Kekku's home as long as she could remember.

Almost as long as she could remember. When she closed her eyes and summoned thoughts from before, from somewhere else, she felt warm arms around her and heard a gentle humming. She also knew her name and the fact that she was a "girl," whatever that meant.

Kekku grabbed her head and held her still. Using a tool with many folding parts, her owner trimmed the dark threads on her head until they were little spikes on her brown scalp. "Threads would grow long and never stop if I let them. Thkili have no such strange things."

Mara didn't know what was strange and what wasn't, but some things about Kekku made her laugh. Mouth parts that opened wide when her owner was angry and clacked when Kekku was amused. Spiky offshoots with no purpose on the elbows of the front pair of limbs.

Kekku also looked silly in the vest that carried tools. It didn't cover as much as her tunic did; it was just a way to carry things in pockets. Kekku looked like one of the little jumpers in the swamp, that jumped from plant to plant, grown huge and with clothing. She said that once and made Kekku angry. "Thkili are unique, special," Kekku said. "We rule the world. Jumpers are pests."

As Kekku trimmed her threads, Mara held her arms folded over the small sore points on her chest. Finishing, Kekku put away the tool, then pulled her arms open and lifted her tunic.

"What are these?"

She tried to cover the things again, but Kekku held her hands. "Are you growing more limbs?"

"I don't know."

"Why do you cover them?"

"They hurt." That wasn't an answer, but it was all she had.

Kekku put her tunic back and let go of her hands. "You will work, no matter what things sprout on you."

As dark settled on the water and small islands, Kekku and Mara chewed on edible plants she had gathered. All the food containers Kekku brought back from the market last time were empty. Sometimes they were able to catch swimmers in the water, small sleek creatures that were very fast. They didn't have any swimmers for dinner on this evening.

The air grew cooler, but it was never cold. Mara shed water through her skin during the hot day, another thing about her that Kekku found peculiar. She drank more water with her food, cupping it with her hands and lifting it to her mouth. It tasted bad. It didn't used to, but the taste of the port had spread in the last few years.

When the darkness was full, Kekku entered the shelter. It was small inside, just a box that would seem too small to hold a full-grown Thkili. Six limbs folded just so, head pulled in and black eyes with no lids staring out until a flap fell over the entrance.

Mara squatted over a hole that Kekku had dug close to the water and drained herself. She didn't have any solid waste to deposit this time. Sleeping, eating, and making waste were functions that she and Kekku shared. Kekku said that it showed all beings were equal in many ways. Of course, Kekku was the owner and Mara the worker. That was the natural way of things.

The shelter stood on three legs, with a waterproof sheet between them, a little above the ground. It was designed as a place to put supplies and food. It was Mara's bed. She rolled into it and lay there. It always took her a while to sleep.

She could run away while Kekku was folded into the shelter, making small noises that indicated sleep. She could run away anytime. She could dive from the boat into the water and kick her feet until she was far from her owner.

But where could she go? The port held only Thkili, and rare strangers that came down from the sky station to conduct business. It was Thkili who had her in a cage in the market years ago, selling her for meat.

It was lucky that Kekku came along. Taking pity on her, Kekku traded for her. Not yet an outcast, doomed to live on the edges of Thkili society, Kekku was able to produce a price that satisfied the seller.

"I didn't know what I was going to do with the little pink thing in the cage," Kekku said whenever the story was told. "But something made me not want to let it be eaten. I am of the caste that lays eggs, though I was unlikely to be chosen. I was not born to importance or family connections."

Kekku also explained that the "pink thing" had changed color, first turning red under the sun, then shedding skin and hurting all over. Finally her skin turned a light brown.

Mara remembered little of this. The period when she hurt so bad was vague. She learned the talk of Thkili, though some of it she could not say; its tone was too high for her to hear or speak.

Kekku never said why they had to make a small living finding air shells to sell at the market, what had driven them out into the wetlands. She remembered going out in the boat, helping Kekku dig in the water with a long-handled tool, then scooping up the air shells in a net. One day she just jumped in the water and pulled an air shell out of the mud, then presented it to Kekku.

Her owner was so proud of her. They could collect many more air shells together than Kekku could alone. Mara was happy. She learned to dive and to move in the water. They could search for air shells in deeper water than before. Kekku was able to trade for food and tools. Mara had clothing in the cage at the market, so Kekku bought her cloth to make into loose tunics.

She didn't remember when she first noticed the rockets that took off and landed at the port. She asked Kekku what they were.

"They are not important."

Then one night after they had eaten well, she asked again. In a good mood, Kekku told her.

"It is called a rocket. Thkili go up in it to the sky station."

Mara knew that couldn't be right. "It is too small to have Thkili in it."

"It is far away. If you saw it close, you would see it is very big. Thkili take goods up and trade with strangers."

This was a new concept. "What are strangers?"

"Creatures that look different than Thkili."

"Like jumpers? Or swimmers?"

Kekku made amused clacking. "Smarter than jumpers or swimmers. Not as smart as Thkili, of course."

"What do they look like?"

"There are different kinds. One kind has hard green skin. Another is very short, and communicates with gestures."

Mara laughed, a noise that had alarmed Kekku until she said it was happy. Then she wrapped her arms around her knees, feeling chilly even in the moist warm air. "Am I a stranger?"

There was a long pause. Finally answering slowly, Kekku said, "You must be, but I have never seen another like you. The merchant selling you in the market said you were a dumb creature, something to eat. The merchant did not know or care where you came from."

"Then I must have come down on the rocket."

"Yes."

Full darkness fell. Kekku entered the shelter and lowered the flap. Mara stayed awake, looking up at darkness. She had never imagined that anyone could live above the sky.

On market days, Kekku got up early. Mara helped gather the air shells from the water-filled depression. Some of them had tried to bury themselves in the mud again, but their breathing tubes stuck up from the water, making them easy to find. Mara walked in the water, feeling with her toes and running her hand down each breathing tube. She got them all out and into bags.

Kekku loaded the bags into the little boat. Mara stared at her owner, knowing what would happen next.

"You know I have to." Kekku went behind the shelter and came back out, the chain rattling.

"I won't run." She always said that, and it made no difference.

"I can't take the chance." The chain was hooked to a metal spike driven deep into the ground. "Come on."

Kekku always said that Mara couldn't go to the market. "They might eat you, just as they were going to when you were little. You are too valuable to me."

Kekku looped the chain around her lower left leg. The lock came out of a vest pocket. It snapped in place and was locked with a key.

They ran through this argument, as they did every market day, knowing it would change nothing. Kekku pushed the boat into the water, waded in, and stepped onto the boat. It rocked and Kekku looked uncertain, as always.

When the boat disappeared into the wetlands, Mara sat, legs folded. She waited until she was sure. Once Kekku came back for something and almost caught her.

The chain was long enough that she could walk around a little, and rest in the shade of the shelter. It was still boring to wait all day. Some time ago, she found a way to make her wait more interesting.

Mara reached into her tunic. She had a pocket too, though Kekku didn't know it. She had folded a piece of the cloth and attached it with a thread pulled from the edge of the tunic. It held a castoff piece of metal from a food container. It had taken her a long time to twist it until it was just the right shape.

She took the metal and pushed it into the lock. A little wriggling, and the lock clicked. She pulled it open and took the chain off. She was free for a day of not working.

She spent most of it in the water. She chased swimmers, dived until she had to go up for air, and floated, looking at the sky. She went far out where the water was deep, where she couldn't find the bottom no matter how far she dived. Kekku never let her take the boat out this far. There were no plants, and therefore no air shells out there, so there was no reason to go. Also, Kekku was afraid. No Thkili would survive falling into such water.

As the cloud ceiling darkened, Mara was back on the island, sitting in front of the shelter. She clicked the lock back on her leg, curled up in the shade of the shelter, and slept. She had to be out of the water long enough that her tunic was dry before Kekku returned.

The boat came back, a tired Kekku waking her up to carry the market goods to the shelter. There were two containers of her favorite food, sliced fruits that were sour yet sweet. Kekku usually allowed her only a few slices at a time, so the supply would last. The other containers were the basic meat paste that Kekku loved.

Kekku looked at her in an odd way. Her owner seemed a little sad, though it was hard to tell. Thkili don't show sadness and happiness much, Kekku always said, but Mara could see it.

After unlocking the chain and putting it away, Kekku gave her more of the sliced fruit than usual, and opened a container of meat paste. Black eyes stayed on her as they ate.

"Why are you staring at me?"

"What?"

"You can't take your eyes off me."

"You are imagining that." Kekku looked away, but soon the black eyes turned her way again.

She went to bed early to avoid Kekku's stare. Something was bothering her owner.

When they gathered air shells in the morning, Kekku attempted to not stare at Mara. Eyes lowered, head turned away, her owner went through the day without looking at her.

She handed up an air shell one time, clinging to the side of the boat with one hand and lifting the large ridged shell high, and had to speak loudly to get Kekku to notice her.

When the rocket flew, Kekku didn't stop her from watching.

Days passed. Mara began to worry. Did something happen at the market?

"What's wrong?" she finally asked one night. There were plenty of air shells in the water-filled depression. It was time to take them to market, but Kekku did not say anything about going.

"Nothing."

"You're different."

"No. Be quiet."

They set out in the boat in the morning as usual. Mara poled through dirty water but didn't really look for air shells. They couldn't put many more in the pool of water on the island.

Kekku looked down, not paying any attention to where the boat went. Mara pushed it along the edge of the deep water. Her fleshy points were bigger now, but hurt a little less. She could still feel them rub against her tunic. They felt better when she was in the water.

She stopped the boat. "Tell me what is wrong."

"Nothing!"

Mara looked at her owner for a moment, then put the pole down. She turned and jumped into the water.

"Do you see a shell?"

Mara shook her head. She stood on the bottom, water up to her waist. She placed both hands on the boat. She looked at her owner. Kekku looked back, black eyes on her for the first time in days.

She pushed the boat. It floated toward the deep water. When her feet no longer touched the bottom, she kicked. The boat went further out, her legs pushing it.

"What are you doing?" Panic filled Kekku's voice. All six limbs gripped the side of the boat. Mara kept kicking her legs. Water splashed loudly behind her.

"Go back! Go back right now!"

When the line of plants that marked the shallow water was far enough away, Mara stopped.

"I am your owner!" Kekku shrieked. "Take me back NOW!" Grippers reached for her to pull her out of the water. Mara rocked the boat. Kekku had to use all six limbs to hold on.

Letting go of the boat, Mara moved away from it. When she was out of Kekku's reach she stopped. "Tell me what is wrong."

"I told you, nothing! Take me back!"

"I can leave you here."

"No! No!"

"What is wrong?"

Kekku crumpled, folding limbs and settling down in the boat. Mara had never seen her owner like this before; the posture radiated misery.

"At the market …"

Mara waited, keeping herself afloat with gentle movements.

Kekku raised black eyes to look at her. "I do everything for you. Do not ask this."

Mara felt bad. She should obey her owner. Kekku saved her from being eaten and fed her and gave her a place to sleep. She almost moved toward the boat, but then kicked the other way. "What happened at the market?"

Kekku looked down again. She could barely hear the words. "I saw strangers."

She waited a moment. There must be more. "You said strangers sometimes come down."

"Strangers that look like you."

A jolt went through Mara's body. She felt chill in the warm water.

Kekku turned to her, reached a limb toward her. "They were taller than you, and both had those strange threads on their heads. One of them let the threads grow longer than the other."

"They were like me?" Mara felt the words echo in her head.

"And … the one with long threads had bumps in front … like the ones you are growing."

She clutched her chest. The things, her bumps, tingled. A stranger had them too?

"Take me to see the strangers."

"No no no, I can't. You know that. Thkili would eat you."

"Did they eat the strangers?"

Kekku said nothing.

"Take me to see them."

"I can't, I can't, I can't." Kekku had seemed miserable before, but now was scared to death.

Mara thrashed in the water, pushing toward the boat. When she reached it she grabbed the side and pushed hard. Kekku fell to the side, almost going into the water.

"Take me to them!"

Kekku folded up, as if going into the shelter at night. All six limbs pulled together, grippers letting go of the sides of the boat.

"They will kill me."

Mara stopped. "The strangers will kill you?"

"Thkili. If they see you with me they will know."

Mara didn't know what to say, or what to ask. She pulled herself up and into the boat. She rarely touched Kekku but something made her put her hand on the closest limb.

"I don't understand."

Kekku made a sound Mara had never heard before. A sound that made her sad. "I did not buy you," Kekku said.

Mara only waited. The statement didn't make sense.

"I let you out of the cage. I took you away. I stole you."

"That is bad?"

"Thkili law is clear. For someone of my caste, who will never lay eggs and has no place, the punishment for theft is death."

A lot of things became clear in that moment. Why Kekku would never take her to the port. Why she had to be chained to make sure she didn't follow. Why they had to make a living gathering air shells outside of the port.

Mara sat in the boat. Her eyes began to leak water and her nose stuffed up. That had not happened since she was little. Kekku had left Thkili society for her and lived as an outcast to protect her.

She still wanted to see the strangers that looked like her.

"I've changed, I'm not little and pink. They will just think I'm another stranger."

"No," Kekku tried to protest. "It is too dangerous."

"If I'm not with you, they will never know."

"Let us return to our island. I will go to market tomorrow. I will not chain you, now that you know why you can't follow."

Mara barely heard. Her head was full of hope and fear and thoughts of seeing the strangers and riding the rocket with them and seeing where she came from.

She dived into the water. She surfaced and turned to see Kekku staring at her. "Don't leave me here."

Mara pushed the boat, kicking her feet, toward the shallows. When she could stand on the bottom, she looked at her owner.

"How will I find air shells?" Kekku's black eyes didn't leak water, but she knew the Thkili felt the same as she did.

"You still have the net and the digging tool."

They looked at each other for a long time. It was hard for Mara to turn away. When she did, Kekku said, "I will be unhappy that you are gone."

"I might come back."

"No."

Kekku was right. This was it. "I will be unhappy too."

Mara looked at the dark buildings on the horizon, where there were strangers that looked like her and a rocket that might take her far away. She looked back at Kekku for a second.

She slipped into the water and began to swim.

Original (First) Publication
Copyright © 2014 by Robin Reed

Nancy Kress is the winner of 5 Nebulas (so far; she's up for another, but we're going to press before the results are known) and 3 Hugos. We've run her reprints in the past, but this is a brand-new never-before-published Nancy Kress story.

DO YOU REMEMBER MICHAEL JONES?

by Nancy Kress

Carol Kincaid and her husband, whose name began with either J or K, stood across the room, drinks in hand, talking to Dave Bukowski. Dave had put on a lot of weight. Carol had lost a lot. Above their heads drooped the red-and-gold Mylar banner: WELCOME CLASS OF '79! Tiny bits of Mylar hung from the sagging top like bird droppings sliding down a window. I forced myself to cross the room and talk to them, because what was the point of going to your high-school reunion if you didn't talk to anybody. Carol looked up. "Jim! How nice to see you!"

I hugged her, shook hands with Dave and either-J-or-K. Carol's eyes were so sunken in her drawn face that they almost disappeared. She had been our prom queen. A year ago she'd been diagnosed with cancer. That was almost the last thing Maureen had told me before she left.

"Good to see you, too, Carol. How are the kids?"

"Gone. Like everybody's kids. After they leave college, they all move to other states."

Dave smiled. "My sister's son moved clear to another country."

We chatted for a while about kids, me trying not to remember the terrible conversation with Nicole when I'd told her that Maureen and I were separating. Nicole always sided with her mother, her whole life, but of course this time she had reason. Neither Carol nor Dave asked about Maureen, which told me that they'd already heard the whole sorry story. I wished I had stayed home with a glass of Lapharoaig and the last of my smuggled Havana cigars.

Dave said, "Oh, there's that girl from my chemistry class—will you excuse me? I'm going to ask her to dance."

"Sure," Carol said. "Go for it." As Dave hurried off, she shook her head and laughed. "We none of us change, do we? He couldn't get girls to notice him in high school, and he's still trying."

Carol's husband—Jack? Keith?—said, "When I went to my thirty-fifth, none of the people I wanted to see showed up. It was a major disappointment."

"Oh, you," Carol said, "you'd have been just as disappointed if they had. All those old nerds still wearing plaid pants and carrying calculators."

Jude-or-Kevin laughed, and at the glance of real and deep affection that went between them, my heart suddenly hurt as if I'd been kicked in the sternum. Maureen and I had that once, but no more.

Carol said, "You know who I wanted to see here and don't? Michael Jones. Do you remember him?"

"Yes. He was … I think he was at my wedding."

"Really!" The sunken eyes sharpened. She had been so beautiful once, fresh as morning in a blue tulle prom gown. "Did you know that he saved my life once? Literally?"

I shook my head. Carol's husband frowned. 'Sweetheart—"

"No, Ken, I want to tell the story. I do." She looked directly at me. "When you don't have too much time left, the truth of things starts to really matter."

It was said without drama or self-pity. I nodded, not sure what else to do or say.

"It was my junior year. My mother had just died. I was so depressed I'd dropped out of school. I was—well, I was contemplating suicide. You remember that I just disappeared from Honors English."

I didn't remember, even though Carol and I had sat behind each other in class. The things that are so pivotal to one person don't even make a dent on another.

"I'd actually gotten hold of pills. What was I thinking? I'd have missed Ken and the kids and all the. … Anyway, Michael Jones came to my house. He was bringing me my trig assignment, but instead we talked and talked. I cried for the first time about my mother. When he left, I felt so much better. The next week I went back to school. I never told him how much that meant to me—you know how easily

kids get embarrassed. Then he moved to New York and I never got the chance."

"He didn't move to—" I started to say, but Bad-Ass DiMonti came rushing up and threw his arms around Carol.

"Babe! You look like hell!"

"Let me go, you idiot!"

He did. All through high school we called him "Bad-Ass" because he wasn't. Inevitably he did the wrong thing, sometimes subtly wrong and sometimes so monumentally wrong that everyone was left blinking in sheer disbelief. He was our butt, our clown, our sacrifice to an ineptitude so deep that the rest of us felt competent by comparison. Bad-Ass flunked every course, although I suspected he was not stupid. Flunking so much and still knowing the smart kids gave him a weird distinction. He pissed off every girl who might have gone out with him. He let himself be bullied—no, he almost invited bullying. It was, after all, a form of attention.

"Hey, Bad-Ass," I said, to see if he would object, finally, to the ridiculous nickname. He beamed.

Carol said, "We were just talking about Michael Jones. Do you remember him?"

"Remember him!" Bad-Ass shouted, so that several dancing couples turned around, rolled their eyes, and went back to clutching and swaying to Donna Summer. "He got me through school!"

I said, "What? I thought you weren't allowed to graduate."

"Well, not with you losers," Bad-Ass said. He pulled out and lit a cigarette, despite the clear NO SMOKING signs. Still trying to be cool. Still failing. Carol moved slightly away. Bad-Ass said, "I graduated in December the next year. Michael Jones, he really let me have it. Told me I could do it if I tried, and the only reason I didn't try was that I couldn't equal you grinds, but so what? And anyways all of you was gone. So I got a tutor and Michael called me up every week and yelled at me some more and I graduated and that's why Harry Parker gave me that job at the Grease 'n Go, and now I got my own body shop."

"Good for you," Ken said.

"Course, Michael moved away after that, to Atlanta. Sent me a postcard once."

Carol sagged against her husband, and instantly Kevin had his arm around her. "Tired, sweetheart?"

"A little."

"Let's go sit down."

They walked off. Bad-Ass said, "I forgot she's going toes up. Hey, I hear you split from Maureen and got yourself a little tootsie."

"Fuck off, Bad-Ass," I said again, and he grinned. I wish I'd called him "Rick" instead.

The reunion was depressing. I had nothing to say to these people, who had known both Maureen and me and who now, apparently, knew about the middle-aged insanity that had led to the stupid, exciting whirlwind six months with Kayla. I had never known that much sheer, lustful excitement. Now that she'd dumped me, I hoped I never would again.

I only stayed at the reunion because now my curiosity was piqued about Michael Jones. He hadn't moved to New York or Atlanta; he'd been at my wedding. I asked several people about him, because at least it gave me a topic of conversation, "Do you remember Michael Jones?"

They all did. Everybody had a story about some way he'd changed their lives. Mostly in good ways, although Cathy Parminter curled her scarlet lip and said, "That prick. Always sticking his nose in. He told me to break up with Paul before I got preggers. I didn't, and I did, but that still don't mean that smug-doll Michael had any business sticking his blond head in *my* business."

"Michael wasn't blond," I said. "Was he?"

"Sure. Looked like Robert Redford. Don't you remember? The one that got away." Cathy laughed, short and bitter. Her skirt was too short for a woman in her fifties, her top too tight, her hair too yellow. She glanced at my left hand and eyed me speculatively. I decided it was time to go home.

Just as I left to the strains of the Village People, the Mylar banner snapped loose at one end and fell into the bowl of non-alcoholic punch for those whose livers no longer let them drink.

✿

At home, I looked for my high-school yearbook, but I couldn't find it. Maybe Maureen had taken it. She wouldn't have asked; Maureen always just did what she wanted. Our wedding day was the first time I discovered that we had a hundred guests, not the twenty I'd been told about. That we were footing the bill, not Maureen's parents. That Maureen carried goldenrod in her "autumn bouquet," even though I was allergic to it. I sneezed all through the ceremony. My nose ran all night.

In my study, which was where I spent most of my time since Maureen had taken all the living room furniture, I poured a glass of Scotch and lit my cigar. Bachelor freedom: smoking in the house. The Scotch smelled and tasted smoky, an October bonfire.

On the top shelf of the closet, behind a box of golf trophies, I found our wedding album. Picture after picture of family, some of them now dead, and friends, most of them out of touch. In nearly the last picture, a big group outside on the lawn in front of the hotel where we'd had our reception, I found Michael Jones. He stood in the back between my cousins Jared and Fred, his face half-hidden and fuzzy—had he ducked his head at the last minute? Somehow I couldn't even tell the color of his hair. At the reunion people had said red, or black, or blond.

Maureen was clear, though, laughing in the front of the picture, her arm through mine. God, she looked happy. Her full white gown had blown partly across my leg. Her face looked as lovely as her roses.

Roses?

I squinted at the picture, and then looked back at the rest of the album. Yes, Maureen's bouquet was white roses. No goldenrod. Nowhere was my nose running. And then I remembered: She had planned on carrying an autumn bouquet, until I told her about my allergy. That was the very morning of the wedding. She left the goldenrod and chrysanthemums and hydrangeas in the limo, tied up with their white ribbons, and instead she'd carried a few roses her cousin hastily stole from someone's garden.

And those hundred guests—did she really spring those on me that day, or had I agreed, however reluctantly, ahead of time? Did I pay for the wedding, or did she use money left her by her grandmother? Of course, that was "our" money, too, that we could have used for something else … but why did I remember, then, that I had resented and staggered under debt for a too-lavish wedding?

I turned back to the picture of Michael Jones, whom everybody remembered and no one had seen since. Was he really there, or was he—oh, I don't know, it sounds so vague—the *idea* of Michael Jones? Was that all he had ever been, an idea, sprung from somewhere deep in people's best selves and—

No. That was dumb. There stood Michael Jones at my wedding, head down and face fuzzy but undeniably solid in his dark suit and a glimpse of white shirt. As real as Maureen and I, both of us laughing and happy.

I remembered, all at once, that it had been I who urged Maureen to take all the living room furniture. I'd hoped it would assuage my guilt about Kayla. It hadn't.

I finished my drink. I finished the forbidden, fragrant, it-will-kill-you-but-we're-all-headed-for-Carol's-fate-anyway Cuban cigar. I savored that cigar. Its taste, its smell, its simple richness right until the last ash. I made it last nearly another half hour.

When I glanced down at the still open wedding album, I couldn't remember why I'd hauled it down from the closet. Something about my cousins Jared and Fred, standing close together in the back row. I should call Fred. It had been too long since I'd seen him.

Instead I picked up the phone, braced myself, and called Maureen.

Original (First) Publication
Copyright © 2014 by Nancy Kress

⌑ ⌑ ⌑ ⌑ ⌑

Alex Shvartsman is a writer, translator, and game designer, with more than 30 short stories to his credit. He is currently editing the hilarious Unidentified Funny Objects *series of anthologies. This is his second appearance here.*

DOUBT

by Alex Shvartsman

An operative's worst enemy is doubt.

As the town car drove him through the patchwork of narrow streets in the heart of the Russian city of Kursk, the Raptor stared out the window at the ramshackle storefronts, the boarded-up windows, the downtrodden locals hanging around in front of the ugly apartment buildings. If not for the ubiquitous Cyrillic graffiti, it would have looked much like turn-of-the-millennium Camden or Baltimore.

Was coming here the right move? He'd never worked with these people before. On the other hand, their technology was far superior to anything his usual sources could procure. It was worth the risk. The Raptor issued a mental command to his implant chip and the car seemed suddenly filled with a strong smell of tangerines. Activated by the changes in the chemistry of his brain, the computer altered the signals sent by his olfactory receptors. For the Raptor, this deception was as good as the real thing. The scent of tangerines always calmed him down.

The town car stopped in front of a four-story building, chrome and glass gleaming in the afternoon sun. The driver circled the car to open the door for the Raptor. A bald man whose wide shoulders, straight back, and military bearing didn't quite mesh with the white lab coat he was wearing waited by the front door.

"Welcome, Mr. Bauer," he said with a thick Russian accent, his W sounding like a V and his R a little too sharp. "Follow me, please." He headed for the elevator without bothering to check if the Raptor followed.

Something felt off. The Raptor had no evidence yet, couldn't quite put his finger on it, but years of dangerous missions had allowed him to develop a sixth sense about such things. He considered his options. Getting away now might prove messy, and he needed what he came here for. He decided to see how things would play out, and rushed to catch up to his guide.

Once the two of them boarded the lift, the doors closed, the speakers played Tchaikovsky's 1812 Overture, and the elevator descended. It took over a minute for the elevator to reach its destination. The deceptively small building hid a huge installation underneath it.

The Raptor's pulse quickened. He ordered the nanites in his bloodstream to tweak his serotonin levels slightly—enough to keep calm, but not so much that he would be unable to generate a quick adrenaline boost if he needed to fight.

On the inside, the Antey Biorobotics building looked like a military installation. It was cavernous, compartmentalized, and brimming with well-hidden security equipment. The Raptor's cybernetic implants identified every camera, tracked every motion sensor, mapped every potential weak spot. The Raptor was ushered into an ordinary office where a blonde woman in her forties was seated behind the desk.

"Olga Tretyakov, director of operations," she introduced herself by way of greeting. She pointed at the chair across from her.

"Nice to meet you." The Raptor sat down.

Tretyakov gave him an appraising look. "You're older than I expected."

"Beg pardon?"

"Let's dispense with the pretenses, shall we?" She leaned back in her high-backed leather chair. "Your passport may say Chris Bauer, but it's just one of a dozen aliases you use, that we know of. You're the Raptor, one of the world's most effective assassins."

So they knew. Given Antey's security apparatus and reach, the corporation probably knew more about him than most governments, and there was no sense in denying the truth. "Is this going to be a problem?"

She smiled. "Not at all. My superiors are eager to cultivate a working relationship with you. I trust you're amenable to—how do you Americans say it—working something out in trade?"

"I prefer to pay cash," said the Raptor.

"Not an option," said Tretyakov. "You're only here because we have need of your services. You could try our competitors in Taipei or Curitiba, but they're each at least a couple of years behind us." She shrugged. "High-end nano-enhancements are a seller's market."

The Raptor had already explored those other options, and he wanted the best. "All right," he said. "What do you want me to do?"

"First, you'll need to prove yourself. A free sample, so to speak."

The Raptor frowned.

"Don't get me wrong, I'm a fan of your work," she said. "But there are some on our board of directors who might look at your graying temples and your wrinkled face, and doubt your effectiveness."

"What hoop do you want me to jump through?"

"We got word that the Renegade Chemist is in town. Have you heard of him?"

The Raptor's computer implant performed a quick net search. Pictures and text projected onto the inner cornea of his left eye. "He's an up-and-comer in the drug trade," he said, as though he knew about the man all along. "Western Europe, mostly." He focused back on Tretyakov. "He has good security."

"Our intel suggests he's in town for a quick meeting, with only a handful of bodyguards, nothing you can't handle. We want you to take them all out, a message to any syndicate that contemplates setting up shop in our backyard."

"Fine," said the Raptor. "That's the free sample. What's the real job?"

"One thing at a time, Raptor," said Tretyakov. "One thing at a time."

✿

The car pulled to a stop at the edge of town, where affluent Russians had their summer homes.

"The Renegade Chemist and his men are in the yellow dacha up the road," said the driver.

"I don't have a gun," said the Raptor.

The driver looked at him impassively and didn't reply. The Raptor shrugged and got out of the car.

His body went into fight mode as he approached the dacha. The nanites in his bloodstream activated chemical reactions which released perfectly measured amounts of adrenaline and dopamine. He felt sharp and focused and in control.

The Raptor circled around and approached the dacha from the back. He jumped, cybernetic implants in his leg joints allowing him to clear the eight-foot fence. The Raptor landed on his feet and ran toward the house.

Utilizing both the mechanical and chemical enhancements to his body, he moved with incredible speed. In contrast, the first pair of bodyguards he discovered seemed like they were treading water. The Raptor snapped one's neck before the man's gun was out of the holster. He jump-kicked at the second man, who fell backward. By the time the second opponent got back on his feet, the Raptor already held the first man's gun. He shot the bodyguard once between the eyes and moved on, hunting for others.

Several minutes later the Raptor approached the inner sanctum of the dacha, reloaded gun in hand, the nanites still pumping adrenaline into his bloodstream. All seven of the Renegade Chemist's bodyguards were professionals. They fought and died well. Would the Chemist fight until his last, or would the Raptor find him rolled up in a fetal position, begging for his life? The Raptor had seen plenty of both in his career. Men who were about to die always revealed their true selves to him; there was no time for pretenses in their final moments.

He slipped into the room to find the Renegade Chemist making tea.

The drug lord was in his sixties, dressed in a thick bathrobe worn over a plain white undershirt and linen pants, his gray hair and beard neatly trimmed. The Chemist filled a porcelain cup with steaming liquid from a vintage samovar and gently set it onto the matching saucer. Only then did he look up at the Raptor.

"Are my men dead?" The Chemist spoke with a faint German accent. His voice was even and his face serene.

The Raptor nodded, his eyes darting around the room. It was sparsely furnished, and he detected no traps.

"Pity," said the Chemist. "They were competent and loyal, a rare combination these days." He picked up another cup and filled it from the samovar. "Would you have some tea with me before you kill me?" When the Raptor hesitated, the Chemist smiled and took a small sip from the cup he offered to his assassin. "See? Perfectly safe."

The Raptor scanned the table area. There were no hidden weapons. He approached and accepted the cup. "You're taking this remarkably well," he said.

"There's a fable about an Emperor who knew that one of his generals was about to assassinate him," said the Chemist. "The Emperor invited the General over to a meeting in a garden, alone. The other man was so impressed by this show of trust that he didn't strike, and ultimately became one of the Emperor's most loyal supporters." The Renegade Chemist drank from his cup. "Some people think the moral of this story is to throw yourself at the mercy of your enemies. I think what really happened is that they had the time to negotiate, and the general got himself a better deal. Perhaps we can negotiate, too."

The Raptor took a sip. The tea was aromatic and rich. "I doubt it," he said.

"Why not? You have no personal grudge, do you? You're here doing a job?"

The Raptor nodded again.

"Then it's only a matter of price." The Chemist smiled.

"I have enough money," said the Raptor. "You can't give me what I want."

"Try me," said the Chemist. "Information? Resources? I have both in abundance."

"What do you know about the Antey Corporation?" asked the Raptor.

"Ah! It does make sense. I am in Kursk to meet with my contact from Antey. Most of my other enemies wouldn't even know I was here. They are one of my suppliers. They manufacture synthetic drugs of better quality than most of the crap sold on the streets." The Chemist swirled the tea in his cup and stared at the liquid. "We made good money together, but they've been growing fast. Perhaps they got too big to be making a few extra million on the black market. So they're sweeping old embarrassments like me under the rug."

"What do you know about their nano-robotics operation?"

The Renegade Chemist shrugged. "Antey started out as a defense contractor for the Russian army and grew from there. They're a huge multi-national conglomerate that makes everything from nanites to baby formula." The old man glanced at the clock on his desk. His voice remained even, but the Raptor could see beads of sweat forming on his forehead.

"If I wanted an overview, I'd read their Wikipedia entry. You've got nothing I can use." The Raptor set down his cup and aimed the gun at the old man's head.

"Wait! I can get you dirt on Antey. Let me just make a few phone calls." The Chemist's hands were shaking now, sweat rolling down his face.

"You're stalling for time, but you already know that your tactic has failed," said the Raptor. "I should have been unconscious on the ground less than a minute after I took a sip of your tea, but my body is at least as adept at neutralizing the toxins as yours."

"We can still make a deal!" There was fear on the drug dealer's face, his calm façade completely demolished.

"The difference between you and the Emperor from your story is that he did negotiate in good faith," said the Raptor. "He didn't try to poison his rival."

The Renegade Chemist managed a weak smile. "Would good faith have made any difference at all?"

The Raptor contemplated this for a moment. "No," he said.

He fired two bullets into the Renegade Chemist's eye and walked out without looking back.

☼

"The board is suitably impressed," said Tretyakov.

"That was amateur hour," said the Raptor. "No preparation, no weapons, and a crime scene that gives the local press plenty to report about. The truly impressive operations are the ones where the general public never finds out."

"The publicity suits our needs." Tretyakov didn't elaborate.

"Why don't you tell me what you really want from me?" asked the Raptor.

"We have reason to believe this site is going to get hit by Mercury's team," said Tretyakov. "We want you to stop her, with extreme prejudice."

"You want me to go up against the second-best assassin in the world? Your nanites aren't worth that."

Tretyakov chuckled. "Aren't they? Every day, you are getting a little bit slower, your aim just a bit less steady. You are getting older, Raptor, and age is an enemy even you can't defeat. At this rate, Mercury isn't going to remain second-best for long."

Tretyakov rested her palms on the table and leaned toward him. "Antey Corporation has the most advanced nanite technology in the world. Do you want to roll the dice and wait a year or two, hoping that one of our competitors catches up soon, or do you want them now? Millions of tiny robots working tirelessly to keep you at the top of your game?"

The executive and the assassin stared each other down.

The Raptor thought back to the decades of surgery he had endured to make him more than human. Implants to improve his body's various functions well beyond the norm. Servos grafted onto his joints to give him a boost in strength and speed. Generations of nanobots floating in his bloodstream, from the crude early technologies to the latest and most sophisticated miniature machines.

All of that allegedly made outdated by Antey's latest advances. If their tech was all it was promised to be, he could be even faster, stronger, more lethal than ever. And if not, there was always the emergency protocol.

"I'll do it," said the Raptor.

A self-satisfied smirk spread over Tretyakov's face. "There's a catch," she said. "The nanites fuse themselves directly into the host's nervous system. This procedure is extremely painful." She gave the Raptor an appraising look. "Then again, I heard you enjoy pain. Certainly explains the countless elective surgeries you've had."

The Raptor didn't reply. His face betrayed no emotion. He just stared at Tretyakov impassively, until she shrugged and summoned an assistant to schedule the procedure.

☼

The sparse room where the procedure was to take place reminded him of a similar space, half a world away and twenty-seven years ago.

Back then he'd had another name, another job, another life. He was a junior CIA agent assigned to the U.S. embassy in Jakarta. He was there when the bomb went off. He remembered no details of that. One minute he was going over paperwork at his desk and the next he woke up in a hospital bed. There were burns and bruises all over his body; his head was bandaged in layers of gauze, leaving only a thin opening for his eyes. And yet, he felt no pain.

"I've never seen anything like this," a doctor told him later. "There is a small bit of shrapnel lodged deep in your brain tissue. It's beyond our ability to surgically remove safely and, by all rights, it should have already killed you." The doctor leafed through a pile of scans and blood tests. "You seem totally fine; it hasn't even impaired your motor functions. Are you a religious man? I'm an atheist myself, but this is the closest thing I've ever seen to a miracle."

The doctor was wrong—he wasn't fine at all. He tasted nothing when he ate his food, he couldn't smell the anesthetics, or anything else, around him. And he still felt no pain.

Alone in his hospital room, he used manicure scissors to cut into the skin on the back of his hand. He watched with fascination as the blood swelled from the gash. When he made the cut, he felt only the dull pressure of metal against skin.

He was scared, which is why he made the mistake of telling the doctor. The man was incredulous. He ran a series of tests, but had no answers. The next day, a CIA official arrived and said they would be transporting him stateside, effective immediately.

He didn't want to become a guinea pig, a lab rat for the agency doctors to poke and study. So he ran, abandoning his wife and daughter, leaving behind his life and even his name. Chris Bauer was born.

It wasn't until a few years later that he earned the nickname of the Raptor. Cold-blooded and vicious, they said. He merely wanted to raise enough money to get cured, and his CIA-trained skill set was always in demand on the black market.

The Raptor had discovered no cure for his condition, but he'd never stopped working. The freak accident robbed him of both pain and pleasure—all his feelings dulled to the point where no external stimulation was meaningful. But he could still feel pride, the satisfaction of being very good at what he did.

He performed well and was getting progressively more dangerous jobs, missions that paid handsomely but required more of him than merely the ability to shrug off pain. That's when the Raptor had discovered cybernetic enhancements, the edge they gave him, and the ease with which his body handled even the most invasive surgery. A string of procedures followed.

The Raptor was in an arms race against other operatives, against the ever-more-sophisticated security systems, and against time itself.

One of his most recent acquisitions was a batch of nanites that fooled his brain into thinking he once again had the sense of smell. It simulated any scent he desired on demand, which for him usually meant tangerines. The Raptor thought this was even better than regaining his natural olfactory functions.

The Raptor wondered at what other things he might gain through technology that would allow him to further surpass his humanity. He nodded to the men and women in surgical masks who towered over him, and allowed the general anesthesia being delivered through the IV drip to put him to sleep.

✿

When the alarms went off announcing the attack, the Raptor was glad the waiting was finally over.

The Antey Corporation had installed him in the ground floor office stuffed with surveillance equipment. Officially, he was recuperating from the procedure. The new nanites were already doing their job. The Raptor felt sharper, stronger, more alert than ever. A bottle of painkillers sat unopened in his desk drawer.

He'd been frustrated by days of pointless waiting, by the passive nature of the mission. He'd roamed the building checking and rechecking the security systems and coming up with plans of attack he'd deploy were he in Mercury's shoes, then figuring out the way to counter them. He'd been reasonably sure that he'd prepared for any stratagem his rival might attempt.

In the end, Mercury failed to surprise him. By the time her team took out the perimeter guards and entered the building, he was in fight mode. He moved impossibly fast, taking out her team one by one.

They were good, far better than the Chemist's bodyguards. Some were even augmented with a handful of cyber-implants of their own, but their frail human bodies were no match for the Raptor's nano-enhanced perfection. He killed them quickly and efficiently, until only Mercury was left.

She moved toward him, her reflexes faster than any opponent he'd ever faced. He came at her, knocking the gun from her hand. When she saw him up close her eyes went wide and she stopped fighting. The Raptor trained the gun at her but didn't fire, surprised by this move.

She stared at his face. "Dad?"

The Raptor staggered back, shocked. He studied Mercury. She was five foot ten, of slight build, comely but not beautiful. Non-threatening and not memorable. Perfect for covert work. He could see a patchwork of tiny telltale scars on her upper neck—she had an implant chip of her own, a brutally painful upgrade for someone without his unique condition.

Could it be? The facial features, the age … The Raptor thought back to his family, to the little girl he was forced to abandon. It had been so long. Was this a trick? He retreated several steps, kept his expression neutral and his hand steady, the gun aimed at her heart.

"It's me, Leigh. Don't you recognize your own daughter?" She took a step forward. "I've been looking for you for a very long time."

Whoever this stranger was, she knew his daughter's name.

It's a deception, a trick to make you lower your guard, said the voice inside his head.

The Antey nanobots let the Raptor's new employers talk to him whenever they pleased. It was perhaps the least palatable new feature, and he looked forward to disabling it as soon as this contract was fulfilled. Although the communication was one-way, they also monitored the security feeds.

Take her out now, before it's too late.

"You're such a bastard," said Mercury.

Kill her now.

The Raptor stared at her, motionless.

"I've been playing out this scene in my head for years," said Mercury. "What I'd say when I finally met you. How I'd eloquently convince you that it was wrong of you to run. How it devastated Mom and almost screwed me up. How you might react to all this. Dozens of scenarios, playing over and over

again." She looked at the Raptor, waiting for him to say something.

It's psychological warfare. She's softening you up.

"I'm sorry," he said after a long pause. "The Agency wasn't going to let me come home anyway. They would have locked me away in some lab and experimented on me for the rest of my life. Running was the only option."

"Lock you away? The Agency takes care of its own. We would have trained you, protected you, made you better. They said you were a good agent before your accident. I'm not at all certain that losing your ability to feel pain made you a better one, but we could have worked with that."

So that's how you tolerate the procedures so well. Very interesting.

The Raptor was angry at Mercury for carelessly spilling his secret, but the ramifications of that could wait.

"You're CIA?"

"Yes," said Mercury. "I joined up partly because they offered me the resources to look for you." She took another step closer. "You lost more than you know in that explosion. You lost your humanity. Have you ever bothered to learn about what had happened to your family? Did it even occur to you to try?"

Don't let her get too close!

"Some faint echo of my father is still inside you, or you would have pulled the trigger. It's never too late for redemption. Come back into the fold."

He stared at Mercury, trying hard to see the grown-up version of his Leigh. Did she have his eyes? Her mother's cheekbones? He couldn't be sure.

"Why are you here?"

"I'm here to save you, among other things." She lifted up a small backpack. "There's an EMP grenade in there. I have to get inside and wipe out Antey's nanite lab."

"Save me? You didn't even know I'd be here."

"It adds up," said Mercury. "They are aware of your quest to … better yourself through science. They must have lured you in with a promise of superior technology, but it's a trap. Their new nanites are a Trojan horse. Once they're activated, Antey will literally own you."

She'll say anything to complete her mission.

"Help me do this," said Mercury. "Help me, and come back home."

An operative's worst enemy is doubt. He stared into Mercury's eyes while he was trying to decide. Eyes that looked so much like his own.

The Raptor lowered his gun.

We didn't want to do this, but you've left us no choice.

The Raptor's body tensed up as millions of nanites fused to his nerve endings activated at once, wresting control of his motor functions away from his own mind. The Raptor twitched once, twice, fighting for control.

"What's happening?" Mercury frowned and took another half-step forward. Then her eyes widened. "You already did it, didn't you? You already had the procedure?"

The Raptor wanted to speak, but his body wasn't responding. He felt like a marionette on strings, the puppet masters forcing his body to make sluggish, jerky moves.

The Antey nanites controlled his nervous system, but not his brain chemistry. He could still issue commands to his implant chip. The Raptor activated the emergency protocol.

He never expected to use the failsafe like this. It was a way to remove a batch of nanites with faulty design or programming. Millions of pre-existing, self-replicating nanites in his blood stream activated with the sole purpose of finding and destroying every microscopic robot that didn't share their digital signature. They would purge the Antey tech from his body and spare the older, more reliable upgrades, but it would take time.

"We can still help you," said Mercury. "Let me complete my mission. The EMP blast will take out all the nanites they cooked up here, including the ones inside you." She reached into the backpack.

The Antey nanites pulled on the marionette strings. In one fluid motion the Raptor raised the gun and fired several bullets into Mercury's heart. She gasped and fell backward.

The operative's worst enemy is doubt. The Raptor couldn't be sure if the woman sprawled on the linoleum tile floor of the lobby was really Leigh, or perhaps a competent agent who sought to take advantage of his Achilles' heel. All he could think of was the last day he spent with his family. The three of them sat on the couch, watching cartoons and peeling tangerines. Seven-year-old Leigh laughed, her little hands covered in citrus juice. The scent of tangerines filled the living room.

She was an impostor. She would have said anything to get you to lower the weapon.

After all these years it was difficult to be sure. Was the Raptor feeling pain, or just turmoil? He couldn't be certain.

You were wavering. We had no choice but to take charge.

The Raptor wiggled his fingers. He was slowly regaining control as the nanites in his bloodstream exterminated their unwelcome brethren. In a few more minutes, the purge would be complete. Then, all too quickly, he found himself able to move again.

We've released you. Take a few minutes. Then come inside.

He took small steps toward the body. Should he hug her? Was that the appropriate—the human—thing to do? He settled for reaching out and touching her forehead. He listened to his heart but it remained numb, like his fingers against Mercury's skin.

He reached for the backpack, and took out the EMP grenade. He held up the sleek device the size of a shoe box and studied it.

Somewhere, faceless Antey executives watched his every move, ready to press the button and to steal his body again at the first sign of trouble. They didn't know that their nanites were all but wiped out by now. The Raptor could carry the EMP right into the heart of their precious lab and press the button, and there was no one around who could even slow him down.

But then, his nanites would be destroyed too, along with most of his cyber-implants. Nearly three decades of surgeries, enhancements, and upgrades would be negated with a single click. He would lose his advantages, his speed, and his strength. He would become nothing more than a damaged human.

The Raptor dropped the device onto the floor and stepped on it hard, grinding it into the ground with his heel. "I'm coming in," he said to the cameras. Then he walked to the elevator. Behind him, the puddle of Mercury's blood was pooling toward the broken mess of plastic and microchips.

He stepped inside the elevator. The sound of Tchaikovsky's 1812 Overture from the speakers mixed with the scent of tangerines the Raptor had allowed himself. The medley filled the elevator cabin as it descended into the bowels of the building.

An operative's worst enemy is doubt but, for once, the Raptor was certain of his next move. Secure in their belief that they could control him, the Antey officials would let him get as close as he needed. EMP wasn't the only way to destroy a lab. He wondered what truths about herself Tretyakov would reveal in the final moments of her life.

The elevator came to a stop and dinged, the doors sliding open. The Raptor tightened the grip on his gun and stepped outside.

Original (First) Publication
Copyright © 2014 by Alex Shvartsman

✧✧✧✧✧✧

Joy Ward is the author of one novel. She has several stories in print, at magazines and in anthologies, and has also done interviews, both written and video, for other publications.

THE *GALAXY'S EDGE* INTERVIEW
❧ GENE WOLFE ❧

Joy Ward: *We're here with Gene Wolfe, Grand Master of science fiction and a grand person as well. Gene, how did you get into writing science fiction?*

Gene Wolfe: My wife and I married. We had no money at all. We were living in a furnished apartment that had once been an attic. All the rooms were pointed at the top, if you know what I mean, and we needed money for furniture. I came across a notice in a magazine somewhere, mentioned in a magazine, that said Gold Medal books was paying a guaranteed $2000 (which was much more in those days than it is today) for any book they would accept. I thought, "I will write a book for Gold Medal books and we will have money to buy furniture." So, I tried and it was not a saleable novel but I got the bug that way and I kept writing all sorts of stuff, frankly, and the stuff that sold was science fiction or fantasy. The first thing that I sold was a story called "The Dead Man," which was basically a ghost story. It's about a man who discovers that his body is in a crocodile's cave. Crocodiles dig lairs under the river bank and they stash bodies in there until the bodies get ripe enough to eat. Crocodiles can't chew by the way. Anyway, that was my first sale and my second one was a science fiction story that I sold to *Galaxy* … no, pardon me, it wasn't *Galaxy*, it was *Worlds of If*. I sent it to *Galaxy*. I was going down an alphabetized list of markets and it was sent back with a form rejection slip, which is how all my stories came back. I then sent it to the next magazine on the list, which was *Worlds of If*, unaware that they were being edited by the same man, who was Frederik Pohl. This time I got a letter from Frederik Pohl that said I think the rewrite has really improved this (and there had been no rewrite) and I will buy it if you will accept one cent a word. And, God knows I have been stupid all my life but I wasn't so stupid as to say I would not accept one cent a word. I said I would be happy to accept one cent a word. Sold! And so he bought it. I thought, the first thing that sold was a ghost story and the second thing that sold was a science fiction story, so maybe that should be telling me something. I started writing that type of story more than other types of stories. I had written some things like straight love stories and some detective mystery stories, and what do you know, I could not only write those stories but I could sell them if I wrote fantasy or I wrote science fiction. So that's what I wrote.

JW: So which type of story did you enjoy writing most?

GW: I enjoyed writing both. I still do and I kind of ping-pong back and forth between the two. I wrote a number of fantasies recently. Then I wrote *Home Fires*, which is a straight science fiction novel. Then I wrote *A Borrowed Man*, which I just sent to the agency. That is a straight science fiction novel. So I'm kind of correcting the deficit of writing so much fantasy and I'm writing more science fiction.

They are both interesting forms in themselves. Fantasy has the danger that you will play so fast and loose with it to make things easy for yourself, which you must not do.

I teach creative writing sometimes. When I read students' stories I often get stories in which things change simply because it is convenient for the author. I have read some stories written by good established authors who have done the same thing. The man is rich when it is convenient for the author that he be rich and he is poor when it is convenient for the author that he be poor, and so on. A character is helpless at one point in the story and far from it at another point in the story. Supposedly it's the same person because that's convenient, too. This is not realistic and it's not artistic. You shouldn't do it. When you say so and so is a wizard you're in danger of saying he can do anything and that's not interesting.

JW: What's bad about that for both the reader and the writer?

GW: It's unrealistic and it's obviously cheating for the writer. It's like the story I was talking about earlier where the author is plainly working out a grudge. He has this rather ordinary woman whom he hates and it comes through all the time … I hate this damned character and I'm going to tear her to pieces in my story and it will feel so good. And that's not art. It's not literature. It's not anything that a reader is going to enjoy. You tend to look at this poor woman and pity her because you know that the author hates her and is going to do really ugly stuff to her. You think she doesn't deserve this. Come on. Why do you hate her so much? Put it down. And of course he doesn't, and the reason he hates her so much is some stupid trivial thing like she doesn't want to watch football with him or something. Come on. Grow up.

JW: Who as an author has really had an impact on you?

GW: Lots and lots of people have. G. K. Chesterton … Rudyard Kipling. I'm not deliberately sticking to Englishmen. It just so happens that those are people who had a real impact on me. Earlier than that, a woman named Ruth Plumly Thompson who continued the Oz series after the death of Frank Baum. As a kid I liked the Plumly stories better than I did the Baum stories, although I liked the Baum stories … They just appealed to me more. There was more an open, pleasant feeling to them than there was to the Baum stories as far as I was concerned.

JW: Who else has had a real impact on you?

GW: H.G. Wells, for one. H.G. Wells for me started with his *History of the World* … I had the odd experience of having a father who had been one of the really early science fiction fans. He was an H. G. Wells fan. As a result I would not read H. G. Wells because I was a kid and kids are that way … He put H.G. Wells' *History of the World* into my hands and I kind of skipped around in that. I looked up things I was interested in and all that sort of stuff. Then I was reading pulp magazines and Famous Fantastic Mysteries came out with *The Island of Dr. Moreau*. I failed to notice that it was H. G. Wells, the author that my dad was so fond of. I read it and it was wonderful! And it's still wonderful after 100 years now. It has to be close to 100 years old and it's still a terrific book! So he was certainly early science fiction. The first downright science fiction story I ever read was

"A Microcosmic God" by Theodore Sturgeon. I had been reading Flash Gordon and Buck Rogers in the Sunday funnies. I was a Sunday funnies reader at that age. I fell off my bicycle and injured my leg sufficiently badly that I could no longer ride my bicycle to school, so my mother was taking me in the car until my leg healed. And she was waiting outside the school one time for me to come out so she could drive me home. She had a mass market paperback on the car seat beside her. My mother was a fanatical mystery reader. She had been reading those and I had been reading them behind her … So here she had this book and I could tell from the cover that this was something like Buck Rogers because it was a futuristic city with space ships coming out of it. I said, "Can I read that after you when you're finished?" She said, "Well you can read it now because I don't much care for it." So I read it and the first story I read was "A Microcosmic God" by Theodore Sturgeon. That just turned me on to science fiction and blew my mind. I thought, "This is marvelous stuff." And I was right. It is marvelous stuff. And I would point out to those who insist on rocket ships, ray guns, and robots, that "The Microcosmic God" has no rocket ships, no ray guns and no robots in it but it is science fiction and it is really, really good science fiction.

JW: If you could set up a writing school now, and include any writers from the past and any who are currently writing, who would you put in it?

GW: That would be a neat idea! I would of course have Wells. I would have Sturgeon, Chesterton, and Kipling, if I could get them. I think I would take Dickens although I would have to give him a lecture, seriously, on the uses of punctuation. Dickens writes correct punctuation for the period in which he was writing, and correct punctuation has changed considerably since his books and stories were written. So he needs modernization on the punctuation. Nobody, I think, could resist the temptation to get William Shakespeare to teach. He was so good and so versatile.

JW: You've obviously had a lot of students, many of whom have gone on to become excellent writers. What does that do for you?

GW: It doesn't do anything for me except make me feel happy and proud and feel like I have not wasted my time.

If you can pass on the flame, hand on the torch, you like to do be able to do that. As far as I had a mentor, my mentor was Damon Knight, and Damon taught me a heck of a lot. The one I always remember … he used to say he grew me from a bean. I had written this crazy story in which everything was in two panels, two parallel columns, one by an earth man and one by an alien, describing the same events; one from the earth man's viewpoint and one from the alien's viewpoint. And what Damon said we needed to do was cut this thing so that we would go from the earth man to the alien and then back and forth. He said, "I have tried cutting it up. See how you like this." And I spent the evening after I got that trying to cut it up better than Damon had, and I couldn't. Everything he did was right and I couldn't do anything righter than he had done. But I learned a hell of a lot in going through that story and seeing how he had divided things. The story is "Trip Trap," for anyone who wants to find the story and go after it.

JW: Are most of your stories still in print? I know there have been collections.

GW: A whole lot of them are still in print. Yes. I am primarily published by Tor Books and Tor Books has been very good to me about keeping my stuff in print. I know that … (some) writers I could name who have been prolific are now getting no royalties at all from some of the things that they have written; books they have written. You don't normally get royalties from short stories although occasionally somebody pays you money to reprint the thing. But you do get royalties from books if the books are still out and available from the publisher. Theirs aren't. The publisher is not keeping these books in print. So they bellyache about it and they do what they can to try and get them back into print. I was very, very lucky because *The Book of the New Sun* was sold to a publisher who did not keep it in print but would not revert it because my contract said that the book did not have to be reverted as long as it was in print from any source licensed by the publisher. It was in print from Science Fiction Book Club, licensed by that publisher. So, the publisher could have the book out of print but not revert it because it was still available from Science Fiction Book Club. And what happened then was that my then son-in-law worked for the company that had published the book, and the president of the company was leaving for a new job and they threw him a party. At the party my then son-in-law went up to the president and said, "Would you do me a favor, please, Mister? Revert my father-in-law's books." And the president said, "Sure, I'll be happy to," and he did. On his last day, just before he cleaned out his desk, he reverted those books. And the result was that my agent got to sell them again, this time to Tor Books. I got more money and they are still to this day in print from Tor Books.

JW: Any advice you would give newbie writers who are facing the great crocodile of publishing?

GW: In the first place, write short stories. I'm assuming, you say newbie writers. I'm assuming these are writers who are interested in writing fiction. If they are interested in writing non-fiction the answer is write magazine articles. But for the fiction writer, the advice is write short stories.

JW: Why start out with short stories?

GW: Because that is the easy way to learn to write. It takes you so much less time and less effort to make your mistakes in short stories and realize, one hopes eventually, what you have done. I know a lady, a friend of mine, who wrote some good short stories and also wrote six novels, none of which ever sold. I have never read her six novels so I don't know what she was doing wrong, but I know she wrote some good short stories and she should have been able to look at those novels and see what she was doing wrong. But she was not a person who accepted teaching from someone else.

I had a male friend who was the same way. He was a wonderful person. He was extremely intelligent. He had all sorts of talents, and he wanted to write. But when you said, "Don't do this," instead of learning from what you said he argued with you that what he did was right and acceptable and so on. He was wrong; just plain wrong. He used solecisms and

things that are not found in good writing, except when a character is speaking. If you want to characterize a character you can have him do all kinds of things and make grammatical mistakes. Sometimes that is what you want to do but when you are just writing the text you don't do that. You write literarily acceptable English, and that is what he would object to.

I tell my classes, "Look, if I tell you to take X out of your story, I could be wrong. I'm often wrong. I'm just one person. And if so and so also tells you to take X out of the title we could both be wrong. But if everybody is telling you to take X out for God's sake don't screw around with it, TAKE X OUT! Throw it away!"

Don't be so stubborn that you kill yourself! The person who insists on driving at 80 miles an hour, icy roads or no icy roads, ends up dead.

JW: Any other rules or suggestions you would have for newbie writers that maybe you would have even told yourself when you were starting out?

GW: Read good writing of the type you want to do. If you want to write mystery, read good mystery stories. If you want to write fantasy, read good fantasy. That doesn't mean just pick out a few books because you like the covers. Try to find out what has reputation, what is well thought of in the field, and read some of those books and look at them. Insofar as you can, read them as a writer. How is this written? How does the book open? And does the book's opening really draw the reader in? And if I'm really drawn in by this opening, what is it the writer has done in that opening that draws me in?

I used to workshop often with Kate Wilhelm. Kate Wilhelm would always bring a red pen to her workshops. One thing that she did frequently to a story was to take her pen and draw a line half way down page three or wherever it was, and say, "This is where the story starts. This stuff before is stuff you have written to get yourself into it. It's for you. Take it off of the story that you are going to submit. Start your story here."

I read advice from a western writer one time who said, "Shoot the sheriff on page one." Of course he didn't mean that to be taken literally, but he meant to do something significant on page one. Don't begin your story or book with twenty or thirty pages of scene setting and ranch life, and what it's like at the spring roundup and so on and so forth. Shoot the sheriff on page one. Get it going. The rest of that stuff you can put in later as needed.

I taught Clarion West at one time. There was a man there who, I thought from his background, was likely to be one of the best students. He sure as heck wasn't. I'll call him Bob. At the end of your week teaching Clarion West you had one-on-one interviews with each of the students, talking about their work and trying to help them. When Bob came in, I said, "Bob, I have your most recent story here. Whenever you introduce a new character you stop the story dead and give us anywhere from half a page to two and a half pages on what this character is like; what he looks like, how he dresses, what he enjoys doing, what he likes to eat, what he does for a living, what he used to do for a living, how he treats his wife, and so on and so forth. Now I know I'm the sixth and last instructor on this six-week course. I know who the other instructors are. You had four good writers and you had a good editor who were your instructors in the earlier weeks. I know damned well that those people have been telling you not to do this and I've been telling you not to do it all week and Bob, you're still doing it! Why the hell are you still doing it?" And he said, "Well I think we need that." What can you do?

JW: So how did you get him out of that?

GW: I didn't get him out of it. I've never seen his byline anywhere so he probably is if he's still writing.

I read a while back and probably you did too, about a man in Australia who has written 15 novels and none of them have sold. I told you about my female friend, she's now dead, who wrote six novels none of which sold, and there are people like that and they write for 20 years and they never have any success because they are doing something or some things wrong and they never catch on to it. Read other people's writ-ing. If you are doing something distinctly different from what those other people are doing, look at the thing really hard because it may not be what you want to do.

JW: Switching gears here a bit. Obviously, you are a grand master of science fiction. In the future, how do you want to be seen?

GW: I was trying to remember the little rhyme, about, "When I die, may it be said that his sins were scarlet but his books were read."

Copyright © 2014 by Joy Ward

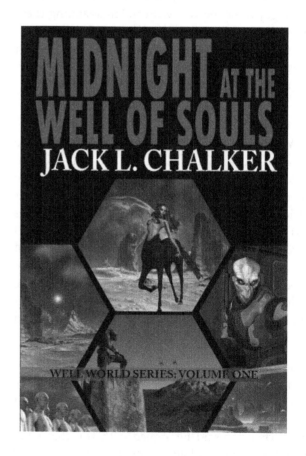

Paul Cook is the author of 8 books of science fiction, and is currently both a college instructor and the editor of the Phoenix Pick Science Fiction Classics line.

BOOK REVIEWS

by Paul Cook

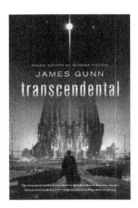

Transcendental
by James Gunn
Tor - 2013
ISBN-13: 978-0765335012 (Hardcover)

James Gunn has already established his *bona fides* as one of science fiction's most astute scholars and critics, as well as one of its more daring writers. His bibliography of both fiction and non-fiction is as extensive as it is impressive. If anything, he will be known for his extraordinary five-volume collection of classic science fiction stories detailing the history of science fiction. I have used volume three of *The Road to Science Fiction* in my science fiction classes at Arizona State University for years and can't imagine life without it. As the song says, nobody does it better.

Gunn's latest novel, *Transcendental*, concerns a gathering of religious pilgrims on a very long interstellar voyage to seek transcendence through a mysterious machine that is rumored to offer release from earthly woes. The main character is a former soldier of fortune named Riley who is both bitter and disillusioned, but who has been "enlisted" to go on a pilgrimage with a number of unique aliens, all of whom have very checkered (and violent) pasts. All claim, though, to be reformed and desirous of transcendence. Also rumored on the voyage is a Prophet who is connected with the transcendence machine in some way, and Riley's mission is to kill the Prophet (among other things) and prevent the aliens from transcending.

Transcendental is very well-written and it's a pleasure to read a work of fiction by Gunn once again. Unfortunately, Gunn has chosen a narrative strategy that bogs down the flow of the narrative and inserts jarring, extra-literary inferences into the novel that the book does not need. Basically, *Transcendental* is a re-telling of *The Canterbury Tales*. Perhaps not quite a retelling, but the novel uses *The Canterbury Tales's* narrative strategy of letting one pilgrim at a time tell their story as the larger narrative moves along. *Transcendental* starts out in a traditional narrative mode common to science fiction, and moves quite well for several chapters until the book comes to a dead stop as Gunn begins to tell the tale of a pilgrim and how he-she-it got to the ship and the pilgrimage. The narrative picks up for a chapter or two—then comes to a dead stop for dozens of pages as yet another character speaks.

The aliens are interesting, but I would have preferred each being's tale to be inserted or revealed in the general flow of the novel's narrative because the overall story is quite passable. It's just getting there that's the problem. Others may like this; I did not. I'd much prefer to read Gunn, not Chaucer. The conceit did not work for me because I wanted Gunn to get on with telling the story—mostly because he starts out telling it in a traditional manner. The novel consequently moved in pulses and jerks, and each time something interesting happened, Gunn suddenly stopped and told, at length, another pilgrim's story.

My other complaint was the lack of mystery about the pilgrims. None acted or behaved as if they were truly religious and on a religious pilgrimage in the beginning, and that's a dead giveaway. Even if none of them were, it would have added to the mystery and dramatic tension if we could have believed that this was indeed a religious pilgrimage. Mostly they're scoundrels. But by the time several of the novel's puzzles are revealed regarding the pilgrims' various pasts, the reader is thirteen steps ahead of where the novel is going and that's not a good thing.

Gunn has written better and he's written better as *James Gunn* and not Geoffrey Chaucer. The novel would have been quite the success without the fall-back on a very cliched trope—a trope that was, even when Chaucer used it, already a cliche. We don't need the retelling of any novel, epic poem, or play. We just need well-told, interesting stories.

The Teleportation Accident
by Ned Beauman
Bloomsbury USA - 2013
ISBN-13: 978-1620400234 (Trade paperback)

I purchased this book on my own because the cover intrigued me—and the title. I knew that this was a book of "literature" and not science fiction, but I'm reporting here that it's safe to buy this wonderful, bedazzling, silly—and yes, "literary"—book just because it has so much fun with both literature and a very famous science fiction trope: teleportation.

True, *The Teleportation Accident* is not exactly written as, paced as, or presented as science fiction, but like the novels of Thomas Pynchon, Philip K. Dick, and J.G. Ballard (especially his later novels), *The Teleportation Accident* involves quirky, non-heroic heroes caught up in the gyrations of the historic moment, including advancements in science and technology before World War II. The novel starts out in Germany in the early 1930s and follows the dreams and idiotic obsessions of Egon Loeser, a failed theater set designer as he pursues the affections of a now-grown-up former pupil named Adele Hitler. (If that doesn't bring a chuckle, then you're incurable.)

Egon Loeser is also obsessed with an earlier Italian set designer by the name of Lavicini who in the 1600s had developed a device for moving actors across the theater stage instantaneously: a teleportation device. A *real* teleportation device. The novel's action swirls around the decadent theater-going crowd of Depression-era Germany with the Nazi Party on the rise (with many of Loeser's friends being the sycophants of Bertolt Brecht, whose evasive presence informs much of the absurdity of this novel). Inspired by his own lunacy, Loeser tries to build his own teleportation device, but it's nothing more than a strap-on vest an actor wears attached to invisible piano wires that yanks him up into the air above the stage and whisks him over to the opposite side of the stage. The results of a test run are hilarious, involving a stretched spine and dislocated arms and legs of the test subject.

The action moves to Hollywood and Hollywood's own decadent culture of the late 1930s, where Loeser meets an actual inventor of a teleportation device who turns out to be one of literature's classic mad scientists. (He might also have been the prankster who put a Model T on top of one of the buildings at Cal Tech. How, possibly? Teleportation, maybe? Loeser is intrigued and so are we!) This scientist actually reminded me of Emilio Lizardo from *The Adventures of Buckaroo Banzai*.

Beauman's writing is light-hearted and light-handed and *The Teleportation Accident* should be read by anyone who wants to see what someone outside the science fiction field can do with many of the standard tropes and conceits that science fiction has to offer. If you've read Thomas Pynchon, then this novel should be a cinch. It has many of Pynchon's weird characters but it's not nearly as complex, culturally referential, or as literarily adroit as Pynchon's narratives. But I think you'll like it. This is one of the best books—of any caliber—that I've read in a long, long time.

And what happens to the mad scientist in the end will make you laugh.

The Goliath Stone
by Larry Niven and Matthew Joseph Harrington
Tor - 2013
ISBN-13: 978-0765333230 (Hardcover)

Because of the moderately satisfying ending of this rather congenial (and successful) novel by science fiction veteran Larry Niven and newcomer Matthew Joseph Harrington, *The Goliath Stone* is probably the beginning of a new trilogy. If so, then I'm there.

Larry Niven lately has embarked on several collaborations with rather spotty success. This book, *The Goliath Stone*, emerges as a fun read and a throwback to what Niven has really done best: take a basic idea (or conceit) and milk it for all it's worth. The focus here is quite narrow (as opposed to the wildly-out-of-control scatter-shot of ideas in his last collaboration, *The Bowl of Heaven* with Gregory Benford). In *The Goliath Stone,* nano-scientist Toby Glyer has given the world all kinds of miraculous cures through his scientific wizardry. Unfortunately (as in Greg Bear's "Blood Music"), the nanobots emerge as a new kind of "life," one that has ideas of its own. It turns out that the nanobots were used to divert an Earth-crossing asteroid. The idea is to return it to Earth orbit and mine it. The problem is that the nanobots have commandeered a larger asteroid and Armageddon looms as humans and nanobots collide (metaphorically speaking).

Unlike *Bowl of Heaven*, this novel is highly polished and very readable and neatly focused around the activities of the humans who attempt to stop the asteroid and the nanobots, and the nanobots themselves. In fact, the writing around the nanobots and their manner of thinking (and conspiring) is very engaging. And as is typical of most science fiction novels, the nanobots emerge as more "human" than the humans.

It's clear that much of the imaginative backbone of this novel is from Larry Niven's ever-fertile imagination. But the writing itself shows the clear presence of "someone else." That someone would be Matthew Joseph Harrington. It's his touch that guides this book—all to its credit. My only quibble has to do with Niven's constant referencing of other science fiction novels and novelists. This is clearly a "wink-wink-nudge-nudge" to the fans, but I found it very intrusive. Engineers and astronauts don't spend their time talking science fiction—except in science fiction novels. But when our human heroes in *The Goliath Stone* get down to the business of stopping the asteroid and making contact with the nanobots, the novel transcends Niven's occasional silliness.

As I mentioned earlier, this does seem to be the first novel in either a series or a trilogy, though it does stand alone. But I would add here, in conclusion, that I'll read any collaboration by these two authors any time. Niven has always needed an editor. He had one in Steven Barnes; he now has one in Matthew Joseph Harrington.

Horse of a Different Color
by Howard Waldrop
Small Beer Press - 2013
ISBN-13: 978-1618730732 (Hardcover)

Howard Waldrop is the last of our great clowns. His work has constantly reminded me of the fun I had reading Robert Sheckley's stories from the Fifties and Sixties as well as those by Eric Frank Russell (as well as half a dozen others). Waldrop's writing style is part autobiographical and part whimsy—and all science fiction. His novelette of human stupidity, "The Ugly Chickens," won the Nebula in 1981 and should be read by everyone. The one story—from a writerly perspective—that enamored me to Waldrop was his "Do Ya, Do Ya, Wanna Dance?" whose ending has never been rivaled by any story I've ever read. He is our one true magician.

Horse of a Different Color is his latest collection, published by one of our best publishers of short science fiction and fantasy, Small Beer Press. The stories with this latest edition are typical Waldrop fare. Waldrop takes much of his inspiration from recent American history, much of it from movies, and he tends to look at how things might have turned out differently. For example, in "The Wolf-Man of Alcatraz," he looks at the Wolfman actually being in prison. He tackles the polio epidemic of the 1950s (a favorite "realm" of Waldrop exploration) in "The King of Where-I-Go." In "The Bravest Girl I Ever Knew," King Kong is actually real, and a bit actor at that. Waldrop even rewrites the Hansel and Gretel children's fairy tale and re-envisions it and returns it to its true medieval, and very horrific, context. For all his fabular imagination, Waldrop can be quite brutally honest.

One of the best stories is "Thin, On the Ground," where two high school chums go to Mexico in 1962 and experience just about every urban legend you can imagine (as well as an invisible man!) in a small town out of the magical realism stories of Gabriel Garcia Márquez or Jorge Luis Borges. (I suspect the story had much inspiration from the movie *The Last Picture Show* as well.) Another gem is "Frogskin Cap," which is set in the very, very far future set in Jack Vance's *Dying Earth* realm. Though it's short, it manages to evoke the extreme limit of human history where most of it is barely a memory—except for one man recording his moment in time, which might be the earth's very last.

The stories are short, to the point, and each one is a delight. Waldrop provides excellent afterwords for each story which are themselves a delight. (I normally ignore forewords and afterwords, but as in the

case of Harlan Ellison, I make an exception every now and then and Waldrop is one.)

I highly recommend this engaging collection to you. Waldrop's humor and joy in writing (and playing with diverse and even divergent ideas) can be found in every story. He's a man who has engaged our culture (and pop culture as well) and has wrung gems from it. Find this book. It belongs in your collection.

✧

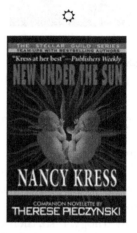

New Under the Sun
by Nancy Kress and Therese Pieczynski
Phoenix Pick - 2013
ISBN-13: 978-1612421230 (Trade Paperback)

New Under the Sun by Hugo and Nebula Award-winning Nancy Kress and newcomer Therese Pieczynski is part of Phoenix Pick's Stellar Guild Series wherein a veteran of the science fiction world teams up with an up-and-coming writer. The series so far has been a rousing success and reminds me often of the Ace Doubles of yore or the novellas Tor used to publish. There clearly is a place for publishing two novellas or novelettes together, and series editor Mike Resnick is having a good time with his choices.

Some pairings in this series are meant to go together, such as *When the Blue Shift Comes*, which couples Robert Silverberg's novelette "The Song of Last Things" with a companion story by newcomer Alvaro Zinos-Amaro, who completes the narrative. *New Under the Sun* begins with a novelette by Nancy Kress called "Annabel Lee" but the follow-up story by Therese Pieczynski, "Strange Attraction," is a different story entirely. It is, however, written in a style close to Kress' and makes for a pleasant reading experience. (The Ace Doubles also had disjointed duos.)

"Annabel Lee" is another of Kress' stories of biological change. A young Annabel Lee is exposed to a self-replicating symbiote that takes a lifetime to reach maturity in Annabel Lee. The story's background is one of religious suppression and tyranny, and as usual with Kress, she handles both the public and private worlds of her characters with grace and aplomb and a great deal of sympathy. Kress, more so than any other author I can think of, has a way of making her characters seem human. She does this through emphasizing how connected people are to their parents or their siblings or their communities. But Kress is also a ruthless explorer of the ways in which technology (or in this case an alien parasite) can change the outer world. The story is a stand-alone and I wouldn't be surprised if it won either a Hugo or Nebula or both for Ms. Kress.

The follow-up story, "Strange Attraction" by Therese Pieczynski, takes place in Nicaragua in the late 1980s and will remind the reader of some of Lucius Shepard's science fiction tales about guerilla warfare in the jungles of Central America. Here the central character is witness to a demon of some mysterious kind that appears and wreaks havoc. It's a much less ambitious story, but as I said earlier, Pieczynski's writing style dovetails nicely with that of Ms. Kress. The Stellar Guild Series is served well by this entry, though clearly Nancy Kress' name will be the big attraction here. It will be interesting to see how Ms. Pieczynski's career evolves from here. Clearly, she's an able wordsmith. Now we just have to see her imagination soar.

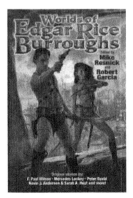

Worlds of Edgar Rice Burroughs
by Mike Resnick & Robert T. Garcia (editors)
Baen - 2013
ISBN-13: 978-1451639353 (Trade Paperback)

If you're looking for a great read, you need look no further than Mike Resnick's and Robert T. Garcia's *Worlds of Edgar Rice Burroughs*. The Burroughs estate has graciously allowed some of our best story-tellers to add their two cents to the Burroughs canon by updating or extrapolating on various characters in the Burroughs fictional universe. Tarzan, of course, dominates. There are three stories featuring Tarzan, the best of which is "Tarzan and the Great War" by Kristine Kathryn Rusch, which puts the ape man in the broader context of the war in Algiers. Mercedes Lackey tackles a Pellucidar story; Richard Lupoff, himself a Burroughs scholar, pens a Carson Napier story on Venus ("Scorpion Men of Venus"); Peter David updates the Moon Maid story in "Moon Maid Over Manhattan"; Kevin Anderson and Sarah A. Hoyt put Tarzan up against a Martian scout ship in "Tarzan and the Martian Invaders." The one John Carter story is a reprint by Mike Resnick written in 1963 called "The Forgotten Sea of Mars." Burroughs also wrote action/adventure stories that did not take place in or on fantastic worlds. Those are here as well. "Apache Lawman" by Ralph Roberts returns us to a robbery at the Billing Ranch. There's a Mucker story in "The Two Billys, a Mucker Story" by Max Allan Collins & Matthew Clemens.

The story I found the most engaging that combines two of Burroughs' creations was "Tarzan and the Land That Time Forgot" by Joe R. Lansdale. In "Tarzan and the Land That Time Forgot," Tarzan journeys to that strange island in the Pacific that made the Caspak Series so memorable. Oddly, that island became—at least to me—one of Burroughs' most dangerous locales. Landsdale, though, ramps up the element of the danger, giving the story a more modern edge. For all that, he still captures Burroughs' flair for fun.

If you're a Burroughs fan, you'll find a lot here to satisfy your palate for adventure. I am also very pleased that the editors chose to include the westerns that Burroughs wrote. (Let us not forget he wrote mainstream and romance novels as well.)

Despite the fact that they aren't as popular as Burroughs' novels of Mars, the Moon, Venus, and Pellucidar—and the Africa of Tarzan—they are still exciting nonetheless. Burroughs set the standard for all pulp writing, at least for the first half of the 20th century, and our current crop of science fiction and fantasy writers have made excellent students. I highly recommend this book to you.

Copyright © 2014 by Paul Cook

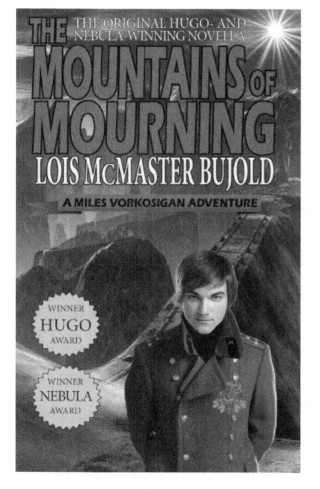

Views expressed by guest or resident columnists are entirely their own.

Greg Benford is a Nebula winner and a former Worldcon Guest of Honor. He is the author of more than 30 novels and 6 books of non-fiction, and has edited 10 anthologies.

WHY DOES A SCIENTIST WRITE SCIENCE FICTION?

by Gregory Benford

Speech delivered at UC San Diego Reunion, 1985

I remember very well the days when I was first here as a graduate student. What struck me at the time was how much communication there was among the graduate students and, even better, between the faculty and the graduate students. Somebody remarked at that time that the principal job hazard of being a student at San Diego was getting sunburned tongue—because everyone talked so much. I found it such a fascinating place that it stuck in my mind, and I eventually wrote a whole damn novel about it. It had struck me, in fact, that La Jolla was a unique place. It seemed to be invested heavily in the future—using, of course, as we all do, the taxpayer's dollars. Also, La Jolla was about the future as vision more than any place I had ever been—particularly if you come from Alabama, which is fundamentally about the past.

Another place basically about the past is Cambridge, England. The reason I chose the strategy in *Timescape*—based half in UCSD in 1962 and 1963, and the other half set in Cambridge in the late 1990s—was to talk about the difference between the two societies. The novel is based on the experience I had in Cambridge when I was there in 1976, on sabbatical leave. One evening I went to dinner at King's College—the whole high table ritual, with the cracked walnuts and the port wine and the obsequious behavior. Someone told me a story I have never forgotten. They had gotten a large bequest to the College and were trying to decide how to invest it. The bursar said, "Certainly we ought to invest it in property, real property. That has stood the college very well for the last thousand years." But the oldest senior fellow in the room shook his head and said, "Well, that is true enough. But the last thousand years have been atypical."

Well, I feel the same way. It has been atypical, this last millennium, and one thing I am sure of is that the next thousand years are as sure as hell going to be atypical, too. Fundamentally, that is the message science fiction has to say in literature.

To my mind, most literature is focused very much upon the immediate past and acute personal experience, without realizing what is going on in society as a whole, over the long run. So I was drawn to write science fiction (although I don't write only science fiction) because it tries to talk about the impact of everything on society, not just the individual experience. But, of course, fiction has to be about individuals. The trick, you see, is that science fiction talks about science. You might even guess that from the name, although you wouldn't guess that necessarily from reading a lot of it. You know these statements at the beginning of books where they say, these characters bear no resemblance to any person living or dead? Well, that is the problem with them, usually. There is no semblance of real human beings, and that is the trouble with science fiction novels frequently. One of the things that I have tried to do is counter that all-too-frequent fact.

And indeed, scientists are like ordinary people, only worse.

Science is the mainspring in this century. Historians will call this the century of science, more than any other century, because this is where it became obvious that the big driving term in the equation of society is science. In the past, for example, it may have been whatever crank religion was on the scene, or something like that—lately, millennial politics, a la Marxism, Fascism and other faiths. Science has really started to drive human society right into the nonlinear phase—one I spend a lot of time with in plasma physics—for plasmas are pesky and nonlinear as hell. Now society is clearly in that regime, also. And coming at us fast.

✿

As a scientist the first thing you have to counter is the cult view of us; this lab smock image. You see, we have become the emblem of truth. If you don't doubt it, just look at commercials. If they really want to say something is undeniable, they say it is scientifically proved—which means they took a poll, they asked six people. And the opposite of that, of course, is lies. Another synonym for lies is, as we know, fiction. So, how can you construct a thing that is called science fiction? What does it mean? Fiction is nice, it is pretty, it is poetic, exciting, informing, maybe even enduring, but fundamentally it is lies. So what is science fiction? Is it lies about the truth, or is it the truth about lies? Either way you choose, it looks like a mug's game. The right answer to this is none of the above. Science fiction is supposed to be literature that tells us what the hell science is doing in society. One of the things that bothers me about SF is that it doesn't seem to be able to talk concretely about scientists themselves very frequently. Instead, it is about people like star ship captains and other riffraff who will land on alien planets, or world dictators who pretend to see the future, and other figures apparently close to our hearts.

I should answer the question in my title. When Brian Maple—my classmate so clearly bound for better things, even then—called me, he said, we want you to talk. We are having people discuss history and research and so on. Oh, I said great, Brian—you want me to talk about relativistic jets from galaxies? He of course said, "No." And I asked, you want me to talk about plasma physics? He said, "No, uh …" I said, you want me to talk about surfing, don't you, Brian? He said, "No, no." "So it's going to be the old SF talk again, right?"

So, to give the same old answer: The basic reason I write SF is that it is fun. I don't think you should write anything unless it is fun. So why do people have so much trouble writing scientific papers? The doing of science is fun. Writing it up, though—particularly this Germanic way we have evolved—then the scientific paper is not fun. I did a parody once called, " How to Write a Scientific Paper," published in *Omni*. It was supposed to be a paper written the way scientists actually read them. So it opened with the references. Yes, you see, you all understand! That's our tribe, writ true. Then there came the acknowledgment. Then the title, then some figures. That is where the paper ended!

You see, if you put that in a book, no nonscientist would understand it unless you explained—and then you would kill it. That is one purpose of art. Art is often the embalming of what was once lively. That is largely what I tried to do in *Timescape*—particularly, in the UCSD portions—to write about our experience. What it is like to come to this blissfully beautiful place, full of gigantic minds, many quite distracted and irritable—sorry!—and with similarly sized egos—ah, the atmosphere as it was then! Because, as you have probably noticed, it ain't that way now. It is a big, calcified University with an apparatus in place, and reputations to protect. It is not the same experience we had. I thought that was such a wonderful time, I decided to write about it. I also wrote a fair amount of the stuff set in England. My sister-in-law, Hilary, wrote the point of view of the English housewife, which I felt unqualified to talk about. I wrote about physicists in the English environment and tried to talk of what I think is going to happen to England—and some other places, like the United States, too, if we don't change.

A lot of things happen when you are trying to write about science. Of course, I know you find our profession absolutely fascinating. Seen from the outside, stylistically, watching scientists work is essentially on the same par with watching paint dry. But, at not quite the same pace. And in the SF media, of course, we have things like "Star Wars" and high camp SF. That doesn't have anything to do with science. What does sometimes have to do with science are films like "2001" on a higher plane. *Timescape* was the first major novel in which I really tried to just talk about scientists. This new one, *Artifact*, is another such novel, although written with a much faster pace about other kinds of scientists. I got bored with physicists after a while and did a lot of work on archeology. *Artifact* is mostly about how archeologists work, and the fact that it intersects politics a great deal. As many of you have noticed, in *Timescape* I went around, and, as every novelist does, copied a lot from real life. There is a person in this room, I stole this gesture from [leans back, puts a foot flat against the wall]. Laurie Littenberg! I noticed that when I ran into Laurie here the other night; within

three minutes he repeated this gesture. It was heartwarming. I stole a whole lot of things from a whole lot of people. There is the character that everybody always asks me about, Gordon Bernstein, who is not a copy of Herb Bernstein, although I took some stuff from Herb Bernstein. And, you know, until I finished the novel I did not realize at all—at least did not realize consciously—that the life profile of Gordon Bernstein is exactly that of—is anybody recording this?—Shelly Schultz. Shelly is not here, is he? Oh, he sent you. Yes, well, in the story, Gordon Bernstein is having an affair with a woman of another faith—there is a word for that and there are a lot of things in there that are not true of Shelly, I think. But many things are.

He went to Columbia University, he is Jewish, he was an Assistant Professor, he was coming here to try to get some papers out so he would get tenure. We remember that, don't we? Things of that sort, but the rest of the thing, of course, was invented entirely. I stole bits of stuff from diverse people like Bud Bridges. Roger Isaacson appears in somewhat transmuted form in the book, and for a small sum I can tell you who that is. Maybe not a small sum! And there are a lot of real walk-on people. People like Herb York, for example, is mentioned in passing. In the Department often that was what he was doing, passing through on his way to the Test Ban Treaty or Camelot or someplace. And lots of people are in there who were on the faculty. It was not their fault, they just happened to be on the faculty and so I used their names. Gordon Bernstein, the character falls asleep in a Colloquium given by, yes, by Norman Rostoker. That's right. Can't figure why I said that.

But I take from a paper on Norman Rostoker's wall a list of the evolution of the laser fusion program. I used that as a parody of what happens to scientific programs. You can find it in the book; I can't repeat it offhand. I took lots of things from graduate students—most of them unsuspecting. There was only one person whom I really felt that I had to take material from, and use as a foreground character and assign lines of dialog. I had a very clear memory of what this person had said, but nonetheless I wanted to OK it. Freeman Dyson read it, thought it was great and said fine, go ahead and use it. I Xeroxed that and sent it to the publisher because he was worried about people taking the wrong idea about themselves being presented in novels. I wasn't worried about it—scientists don't have the time to sue anybody. The person whom I did decide to disguise quite well was a person who is called in the book Saul Schriffer. Now the real life stand-in for Saul Schriffer was not on the faculty here. He occasionally passed through, like many of the self-luminous objects in our universe, giving off a lot of radiation. I was giving an invited talk at the American Association for the Advancement of Science about three years ago. I sat in the preparation room with this guy and he said, "You know, I just read *Timescape* because I have just sold a contract for a two-million-dollar novel with Simon and Schuster, and I was trying to figure out how to write it." We had a discussion, over an hour long, about how you present scientists, what you do about covering up your tracks, how you decide to portray people in just the right way so you get the essence of them without all the messy details—a technical discussion, how you cut scenes, all this kind of detailed stuff. He had not thought about many of these things before; you don't, in nonfiction. (Note that we don't have a term for all writing that's supposedly true—it's just not fiction.). He discussed the book in detail—this aspect and that. Nowhere in this conversation did he give the slightest hint that he thought he might be portrayed in the book. And I am convinced that he is not at all aware that he was in the book. This was to me a revelation. Someone had said to me long ago—I think Arthur C. Clarke—that if you change the appearance of a character from that of the actual person, he will almost never recognize him or herself. I think it is actually true, because Saul Schriffer has no physical resemblance to Carl—what's his name? I learned a great deal from that. So if you are ever thinking about writing a book about UCSD you can go ahead and just do anything—simply change the color of the eyes or something, and you're on safe ground.

One thing I particularly liked about writing *Timescape* was that it put me back in touch with a lot of people who were here at that era. So many of the people who figured—sometimes only indirectly—in the book are here this weekend. It is quite possible that somebody else could write another novel about UCSD in that era, but it ain't going to be easy—because there is a limited market for these things you know.

I don't think I'll ever write anything about UCSD again. It was a unique era. *Timescape* talks about time and the fact that our physical theories are not complete. There are many hidden assumptions in physics which, as Einstein showed, have to be reinvestigated. So I think scientists should try to write fiction—to convey that science is not what most of those people out there think—that is, a set of received opinions, a set of frozen data. Science fiction is also about the future, seen through the changing lens of science. Just having a perspective above the flow of the daily news helps to fathom that future. For example, we're here in the middle of the Reagan years, and those will pass, but the larger landscape is visible. I spent a lot of time thinking about the Soviet Union these last few years, spent three chilly weeks there last year, 1984—and I don't mean the temperature. What's next? Clearly, the Soviet Union is doomed. This will surprise some; we tend to think big institutions last. After it falls, we'll see a sudden world realization that freedom and free markets work—big shock, for some. Technology will open doors for us—computers and the internet particularly. But then new enemies of reason and science will arise, and we'll have to fend them off—by making the experience and wonder of science dwell in people's minds, not as spectacle (which too often science fiction is, merely), but as insight.

Science is a giant slugfest of always provisional ideas. What they don't get out there, is science as partial, provisional knowledge. Often they want to turn it into a faith. That is why there is the Jonas Salk lab smock image. We have become the emblem of certainty to them. "Scientifically true! Scientifically proven!" And they don't get it when we say, "Hey, but that can be changed at any moment." One new fact can destroy the oldest theory on earth. They don't understand that. And yet that is the most simple thing about science.

I feel that we have an obligation as scientists to continually remind people that we are not the mandarins of some Byzantine, complex, nonunderstandable, great set of facts. Instead, we are explorers trying to find out what is going on. Often in the physical sciences, as you know, it is like trying to take a drink out of a fire hose. It is often trying to find a fact which will reveal something, against the blizzard of facts that roars through your life all the time.

There is so much complexity in science. They can't understand the difference between that surface complexity and the simplicity underlying it. Simplicity is the only way we are going to reach people. Complexity just makes them think it is another faith. They just think the physical world is a big, complicated machine with no hope of them ever understanding it. How many people do you know who are afraid to get on airplanes and have no understanding of how they work? They know nothing of Bernoulli's Law, fluids, forces. They can't understand what holds it up, so they are afraid it will fall down. That is a simple example, but it expresses a great deal of what people feel about science in our society. Anything we can do to contradict that, to undermine that, to falsify that as their view of science—is a very good idea. So I would urge all of you to communicate—in whatever ways you want. Writing articles for high-paying magazines like *Scientific American*, or appearing at the Rotarians and preaching a "faith"—anything you can do to tell people about science as she really is, is a good idea. All these tax dollars supporting the expansion of our knowledge do have to come from someone. If they don't get the spirit of science, ultimately we are not communicating and they are not going to fund us. That is the bottom line. So I would say you all ought to be communicators of science, because the alternative to popular science is unpopular science!—and we don't want that, do we?

Copyright © 2005 by Gregory Benford

FROM THE HEART'S BASEMENT

by Barry Malzberg

Barry N. Malzberg won the very first Campbell Memorial Award, and is a multiple Hugo and Nebula nominee. He is the author or co-author of more than 90 books.

A FINAL COMPILATION OF PEOPLE, PLACES AND THINGS WHICH WILL NEVER BE OTHERWISE NOTED

1) "The Circuit Riders," by R.C. FitzPatrick. *Analog*, 1962. The entire urban population is biologically online through computer chips. Police monitors at ominous machines observe biological tracings, note the location, all data on those whose circulatory or respiratory functions appear to be approaching peaks or shallows of emotion. These are infallible signs to the Circuit Riders of a crime about to occur. The unfortunate spikers are apprehended by roving police, taken direct to the slammer. A little girl who would have been the victim of a vicious crime never knows how technology has enabled her to be spared.

Same device as in Phil Dick's "Minority Report" six years earlier (maybe FitzPatrick knew that story) but much cooler, inexorable, logical in that ever-so-definable *Analog* fashion. The technology and its employment by the Circuit Riders regarded as an unmixed blessing. Issues of civil rights or privacy are never evoked. (They weren't in the Phil Dick story either.) What the FitzPatrick has is a kind of breathless coolness, a civility of absolute assumption: the technology is infallible, the potentially bad people are apprehended and imprisoned, society so blessed rolls on. The story was in Merril's best of the year, anthologized by Campbell in his own series, *Analog* rolled right on toward Campbell's endorsement (in an editorial in the November 1968 issue) of Wallace's Presidential run. "F--- control base!" the Captain in the capsule screams in *Beyond Apollo*. "They're only a bunch of pimps for the politicians anyway."

Phil Dick, that advocate of individual defiance, was writing letters, some anonymous, to Hoover in the '50s, ratting out various friends and acquaintances as possible Commies.

☼

2) The packed elevator in the Sheraton Hasbrouck Heights Hotel in 1978. Lunacon. About twelve hundred attendance in that place in those years. Girl fans and boy fans and a couple of older fans are almost cheek to cheek, the girls in Princess Leia costumes jumping with anticipation. "Party!" one sixteen-year-old cries, "Party party!" The elevator stops at the upper mezzanine to admit lady and gent in their 50s, well-dressed suburbanites on a Saturday night, obviously to ascend to the expensive rooftop restaurant. "Party party!" cries Princess Leia again. The suburbanites regard her with mingled fear and revulsion. Maybe a tiny bolt of envy illuminating the woman's features like the little green shoots of thought parading over the idiot bride's face in O'Connor's "The Life You Save Must Be Your Own." Then she and her husband, spotting me in the car—black suit and grey tie, an apparent suburbanite in his early forties, a kindred trapped soul—stare at me, obviously seeking a nod of companionship from this other trapped person. I realize, looking at them, and then looking at the kids, that I have achieved the status of Robert Park's Marginal Man who I had studied two decades earlier in Sociology 101 ... the guy who was absolutely comprehending of two disparate (but adjoined) cultures but a part of neither. To the kids I was the third mundane fool in the elevator, to the couple I was an apparent peer who simply did not understand the situation.

"Go on," I thought. "Just keep on writing work like *Beyond Apollo* in your mortgaged house in Teaneck, take the kids to ballet lessons, and do panels at Lunacon. See where it's getting you? Big Noise in Winnetka.

☼

3) R.A. Lafferty, drunk beyond observation or redemption, wandering the mezzanine of the huge Boston Hotel in the hour after completion of the Hugo ceremonies in the adjoining Municipal Auditorium. From one wall to the opposite wall and return and then again to the opposite wall and then, to liven up matters a little, a complete circuit of the enormous, crowded room. I am sitting back against the wall, talking to my Three Wise Men, numb after the presentation which I had observed seated alone in the fourth room, close enough to see George Martin trembling with joy as he accepted first one and then the other of his two Hugos, close enough to see the curious pain in Barry Longyear's aspect as "Enemy Mine" won for novella.

Now, aided by my Wise Men I am trying to make some sense of a genre which I suspect I will never understand, when R.A. Lafferty's travels or travails carry him in my direction. As I see him, he sees me and I lurch to a standing position no less gracelessly than he has been monitoring the lobby. "Barry Malzberg," he says, pausing to regard me. "Barry Malzberg. I don't understand a f---ing word you have ever written." Not waiting for a reply, he departs.

☼

4) The pretty 17-year-old, Renee, who is somehow at a party after the Campbell Awards dinner at the University of Kansas in 1989. Maybe she is someone's daughter. James Gunn introduces us. "I know you would be interested," he says, "She's a very serious violin student." "Oh, great," I say to her, "What are you playing now?" "I'm studying the Bruch Concerto," she says. "Which one?" I ask. "Oh, I suppose the first, that's the famous one." She nods. "Really difficult," I say. "Of course for me everything is difficult, a C Major scale in tune, a harmonic on the E String. Do you want to play professionally?" I ask. She shrugs. "I don't know," she says. "I love it, though." "I know you won't believe this," I say, "but I would give up all the reasons I am this distance from home tonight if I could play the Bruch G Minor Concerto to any concert standard."

Later I talk to Fred Pohl, a standard at the Campbell Conference, who I only learned a few months ago (from an *Analog* profile) is a collector and aficionado of violin concerti, from the standard repertoire to the obscure like the Bruch Third or the Rakov. "She's a violinist. She's studying the Bruch G Minor," I tell him. He reflects no interest. This is a science fiction crowd and Fred has always studied, assessed and dealt firmly with the market.

Renee would be 40 now. Maybe she is in the Pittsburgh Symphony or playing backbench with the Kansas City Philharmonic. I still think it a better outcome than making sardonic on Lunacon panels.

✡

5) Anatole Broyard, adroit and basking in his own reflected light, Broyard that dancer saying to the first session of his New School Creative Writing class in June 1963, "I'll read anything you want to turn in but I want to give you fair warning right now: I hate science fiction."

Fine with me, I think, sitting two rows behind the young woman to whom I have not yet said a word but who will be my wife of 50 years in less than two months, that's a good policy. I don't want to write it. I outgrew all that. I want to be a serious writer. A serious literary writer. Like Bernard Malamud. Like you.

April 2014: New Jersey

Copyright © 2014 by Barry N. Malzberg

SERIALIZATION

Lest Darkness Fall

Part 2

LEST DARKNESS FALL & RELATED STORIES
(only Lest Darkness Fall is being serialized)
by L. Sprague de Camp
Phoenix Pick, 2011
Trade Paperback: 290 pages.
ISBN: 978-1-61242-015-8

Lest Darkness Fall (in a shorter version) appeared in the December 1939 issue of *Unknown*. Copyright © 1939 by Street & Smith Publications Inc. Lest Darkness Fall Copyright © 1941 by Henry Holt and Company. Copyright © 1949, 1977, 1996 by L. Sprague de Camp.

L. Sprague de Camp came pretty close to being the compleat science fiction writer. His work included novels, short stories, science fiction, fantasy, poetry, criticism, history, you name it. He won the Hugo and the International Fantasy Award, was the Guest of Honor at the 1966 Worldcon, won the World Fantasy Lifetime Achievement Award in 1984, became a Nebula Grand Master (the fourth ever) in 1979, and was given a Special Achievement Sidewise Award for Alternate History in 1996. He also edited and continued Robert E. Howard's Conan saga.

De Camp's career lasted for more than 60 years, and he authored more than 100 books, alone and in collaboration with his wife Catherine, and also with Fletcher Pratt (the Incomplete Enchanter and Gavagan's Bar series) and Lin Carter (the Conan series). His other series include the Viagens Interplanetarias, Reginald Rivers, Pusadian, Novaria, Marko Prokopiu, and The Incorporated Knight.

LEST DARKNESS FALL
L. Sprague de Camp
(continued from issue 7)

CHAPTER IV

Padway had resolved not to let anything distract him from the task of assuring himself a livelihood. Until that was accomplished, he didn't intend to stick his neck out by springing gunpowder or the law of gravitation on the unsuspecting Romans.

But the banker's war talk reminded him that he was, after all, living in a political and cultural as well as an economic world. He had never, in his other life, paid more attention to current events than he had to. And in post-Imperial Rome, with no newspapers or electrical communication, it was even easier to forget about things outside one's immediate orbit.

He was living in the twilight of western classical civilization. The Age of Faith, better known as the Dark Ages, was closing down. Europe would be in darkness, from a scientific and technological aspect, for nearly a thousand years. That aspect was, to Padway's naturally prejudiced mind, the most, if not the only, important aspect of a civilization. Of course, the people among whom he was living had no conception of what was happening to them. The process was too slow to observe directly, even over the span of a life-time. They took their environment for granted, and even bragged about their modernity.

So what? Could one man change the course of history to the extent of preventing this interregnum? One man had changed the course of history before. Maybe. A Carlylean would say yes. A Tolstoyan or Marxist would say no; the environment fixes the pattern of a man's accomplishments and throws up the man to fit that pattern. Tancredi had expressed it differently by calling history a tough web, which would take a huge effort to distort.

How would one man go about it? Invention was the mainspring of technological development. But even in his own time, the lot of the professional inventor had been hard, without the handicap of a powerful and suspicious ecclesiasticism. And how much could he accomplish by simply "inventing," even if he escaped the unwelcome attentions of the pious? The arts of distilling and metal rolling were launched, no doubt, and so were Arabic numerals. But there was so much to be done, and only one lifetime to do it in.

What then? Business? He was already in it; the upper classes were contemptuous of it; and he was not naturally a businessman, though he could hold his own well enough in competition with these sixth-century yaps. Politics? In an age when victory went to the sharpest knife, and no moral rules of conduct were observable? *Br-r-r-r!*

How to prevent darkness from falling?

The Empire might have been together longer if it had had better means of communication. But the Empire, at least in the west, was hopelessly smashed, with Italy, Gaul, and Spain under the muscular thumbs of their barbarian "garrisons."

The answer was *Rapid communication and the multiple record*—that is, printing. Not even the most diligently destructive barbarian can extirpate the written word from a culture wherein the *minimum* edition of most books is fifteen hundred copies. There are just too many books.

So he would be a printer. The web might be tough, but maybe it had never been attacked by a Martin Padway.

✿

"Good morning, my dear Martinus," said Thomasus. "How is the copper-rolling business?"

"So-so. The local smiths are pretty well stocked with strip, and not many of the shippers are interested in paying my prices for such a heavy commodity. But I think I'll clean up that last note in a few weeks."

"I'm glad to hear that. What will you do then?"

"That's what I came to see you about. Who's publishing books in Rome now?"

"Books? Books? Nobody, unless you count the copyists who replace worn-out copies for the libraries. There are a couple of bookstores down in the Agiletum, but their stock is all imported. The last man who tried to run a publishing business in Rome went broke years ago. Not enough demand, and not enough good authors. You're not thinking of going into it, I hope?"

"Yes, I am. I'll make money at it, too."

"What? You're crazy, Martinus. Don't consider it. I don't want to see you go broke after making such a fine start."

"I shan't go broke. But I'll need some capital to start."

"What? Another loan? But I've just told you that nobody can make money publishing in Rome. It's a proven fact. I won't lend you an as on such a harebrained scheme. How much do you think you'd need?"

"About five hundred solidi."

"*Ai, ai!* You've gone mad, my boy! What would you need such a lot for? All you have to do is buy or hire a couple of scribes—"

Padway grinned. "Oh, no. That's the point. It takes a scribe months to copy out a work like Cassiodorus' *Gothic History* by hand, and that's only one copy. No wonder a work like that costs fifty solidi per copy! I can build a machine that will turn out five hundred

or a thousand copies in a few weeks, to retail for five or ten solidi. But it will take time and money to build the machine and teach an operator how to run it."

"But that's real money! God, are You listening? Well, please make my misguided young friend listen to reason! For the last time, Martinus, I won't consider it! How does the machine work?"

If Padway had known the travail that was in store for him, he might have been less confident about the possibilities of starting a printshop in a world that knew neither printing presses, type, printer's ink, nor paper. Writing ink was available, and so was papyrus. But it didn't take Padway long to decide that these would be impractical for his purposes.

His press, seemingly the most formidable job, proved the easiest. A carpenter down in the warehouse district promised to knock one together for him in a few weeks, though he manifested a not unnatural curiosity as to what Padway proposed to do with the contraption. Padway wouldn't tell him.

"It's not like any press I ever saw," said the man. "It doesn't look like a felt press. I know! You're the city's new executioner, and this is a newfangled torture instrument! Why didn't you want to tell me, boss? It's a perfectly respectable trade! But say, how about giving me a pass to the torture chamber the first time you use it? I want to be sure my work holds up, you know!"

For a bed they used a piece sawn off the top of a section of a broken marble column and mounted on wheels. All Padway's instincts revolted at this use of a monument of antiquity, but he consoled himself with the thought that one column mattered less than the art of printing.

For type, he contracted with a seal cutter to cut him a set of brass types. He had, at first, been appalled to discover that he would need ten to twelve thousand of the little things, since he could hardly build a type-casting machine, and would therefore have to print directly from the types. He had hoped to be able to print in Greek and Gothic as well as in Latin, but the Latin types alone set him back a round two hundred solidi. And the first sample set that the seal cutter ran off had the letters facing the wrong way and had to be melted up again. The type was what a twentieth-century printer would have called fourteen-point Gothic, and an engraver would have called sans-serif. With such big type he would not be able to get much copy on a page, but it would at least, he hoped, be legible.

Padway shrank from the idea of making his own paper. He had only a hazy idea of how it was done, except that it was a complicated process. Papyrus was too glossy and brittle, and the supply in Rome was meager and uncertain.

There remained vellum. Padway found that one of the tanneries across the Tiber turned out small quantities as a side line. It was made from the skins of sheep and goats by extensive scraping, washing, stretching, and paring. The price seemed reasonable. Padway rather staggered the owner of the tannery by ordering a thousand sheets at one crack.

He was fortunate in knowing that printer's ink was based on linseed oil and lampblack. It was no great trick to buy a bag of flaxseed and run it through a set of rolls like those he used for copper rolling, and to rig up a contraption consisting of an oil lamp, a water-filled bowl suspended and revolved over it, and a scraper for removing the lampblack. The only thing wrong with the resulting ink was that it wouldn't print. That is, it either made no impression or came off the type in shapeless gobs.

Padway was getting nervous about his finances; his five hundred solidi were getting low, and this seemed a cruel joke. His air of discouragement became so obvious that he caught his workers remarking on it behind their hands. But he grimly set out to experiment on his ink. Sure enough, he found that with a little soap in it, it would work fairly well.

In the middle of February Nevitta Gummund's son wandered in through the raw drizzle. When Fritharik showed him in, the Goth slapped Padway on the back so hard as to send him halfway across the room. "Well, well!" he bellowed. "Somebody gave me some of that terrific drink you've been selling, and I remembered your name. So I thought I'd look you up. Say, you got yourself well established in record time, for a stranger. Pretty smart young man, eh? Ha, ha!"

"Would you like to look around?" invited Padway. "Only I'll have to ask you to keep my methods confidential. There's no law here protecting ideas, so I have to keep my things secret until I'm ready to make them public property."

"Sure, you can trust me. I wouldn't understand how your devices work anyhow."

In the machine shop Nevitta was fascinated by a crude wire-drawing machine that Padway had rigged up. "Isn't that pretty?" he said, picking up the roll of brass wire. "I'd like to buy some for my wife. It would make nice bracelets and earrings."

Padway hadn't anticipated that use of his products, but said he would have some ready in a week.

"Where do you get your power?" asked Nevitta.

Padway showed him the work-horse in the back yard walking around a shaft in the rain.

"Shouldn't think a horse would be efficient," said the Goth. "You could get a lot more power out of a couple of husky slaves. That is, if your driver knew his whip. Ha, ha!"

"Oh, no," said Padway. "Not this horse. Notice anything peculiar about his harness?"

"Well, yes, it *is* peculiar. But I don't know what's wrong with it."

"It's that collar over his neck. You people make your horses pull against a strap around the throat. Every time he pulls, the strap cuts into his windpipe and shuts off the poor animal's breath. That collar puts the load on his shoulders. If you were going to pull a load, you wouldn't hitch a rope around your neck to pull it with, would you?"

"Well," said Nevitta dubiously, "maybe you're right. I've been using my kind of harness for a long time, and I don't know that I'd care to change."

Padway shrugged. "Any time you want one of these outfits, you can get it from Metellus the Saddler on the Appian Way. He made this to my specifications. I'm not making them myself; I have too much else to do."

Here Padway leaned against the doorframe and closed his eyes.

"Aren't you feeling well?" asked Nevitta in alarm.

"No. My head weighs as much as the dome of the Pantheon. I think I'm going to bed."

"Oh, my word, I'll help you. Where's that man of mine? *Hermann!*" When Hermann appeared, Nevitta rattled a sentence of Gothic at him wherein Padway caught the name of Leo Vekkos.

Padway protested: "I don't want a physician—"

"Nonsense, my boy, it's no trouble. You were right about keeping the dogs outside. It cured my wheezes. So I'm glad to help you."

Padway feared the ministrations of a sixth-century physician more than he feared the grippe with which he was coming down. He did not know how to refuse gracefully. Nevitta and Fritharik got him to bed with rough efficiency.

Fritharik said: "It looks to me like a clear case of elf-shot."

"What?" croaked Padway.

"Elf-shot. The elves have shot you. I know, because I had it once in Africa. A Vandal physician cured me by drawing out the invisible darts of the elves. When they become visible they are little arrowheads made of chipped flint."

"Look," said Padway, "I know what's wrong with me. If everybody will let me alone, I'll get well in a week or ten days."

"We couldn't think of that!" cried Nevitta and Fritharik together. While they were arguing, Hermann arrived with a sallow, black-bearded, sensitive-looking man.

Leo Vekkos opened his bag. Padway got a glimpse into the bag, and shuddered. It contained a couple of books, an assortment of weeds, and several small bottles holding organs of what had probably been small mammals.

"Now then, excellent Martinus," said Vekkos, "let me see your tongue. Say ah." The physician felt Padway's forehead, poked his chest and stomach, and asked him intelligent-sounding questions about his condition.

"This is a common condition in winter," said Vekkos in a didactic tone. "It is something of a mystery. Some hold it to be an excess of blood in the head, which causes that stuffy feeling whereof you complain. Others assert that it is an excess of black bile. I hold the view that it is caused by the conflict of the natural spirits of the liver with the animal spirits of the nervous system. The defeat of the animal spirits naturally reacts on the respiratory system—"

"It's nothing but a bad cold—" said Padway.

Vekkos ignored him. "—since the lungs and throat are under their control. The best cure for you is to rouse the vital spirits of the heart to put the natural spirits in their place." He began fishing weeds out of the bag.

"How about elf-shot?" asked Fritharik.

"What?"

Fritharik explained the medical doctrine of his people.

Vekkos smiled. "My good man, there is nothing in Galen about elf-shot. Nor in Celsus. Nor in Asclepiades. So I cannot take you seriously—"

"Then you don't know much about doctoring," growled Fritharik.

"Really," snapped Vekkos. "Who is the physician?"

"Stop squabbling, or you'll make me worse," grumbled Padway. "What are you going to do to me?"

Vekkos held up a bunch of weeds. "Have these herbs stewed and drink a cupful every three hours. They include a mild purgative, to draw off the black bile through the bowels in case there should be an excess."

"Which is the purgative?" asked Padway.

Vekkos pulled it out. Padway's thin arm shot out and grabbed the weed. "I just want to keep this separate from the rest, if you don't mind."

Vekkos humored him, told him to keep warm and stay in bed, and departed. Nevitta and Hermann went with him.

"Calls himself a physician," grumbled Fritharik, "and never heard of elf-shot."

"Get Julia," said Padway.

When the girl came, she set up a great to-do: "Oh, generous master, whatever is wrong with you? I'll get Father Narcissus—"

"No, you won't," said Padway. He broke off a small part of the purgative weed and handed it to her. "Boil this in a kettle of water, and bring me a cup of the water." He handed her the rest of the bunch of greenery. "And throw these out. Somewhere where the medicine man won't see them."

A slight laxative should be just the thing, he thought. If they would only leave him alone …

Next morning his head was less thick, but he felt very tired. He slept until eleven, when he was wakened by Julia. With Julia was a dignified man wearing an ordinary civilian cloak over a long white tunic with tight sleeves. Padway guessed that he was Father Narcissus by his tonsure.

"My son," said the priest. "I am sorry to see that the Devil had set his henchmen on you. This virtuous young woman besought my spiritual aid …"

Padway resisted a desire to tell Father Narcissus where to go. His one constant principle was to avoid trouble with the Church.

"I have not seen you at the Church of the Angel Gabriel," continued Father Narcissus. "You are one of us, though, I hope?"

"American rite," mumbled Padway.

The priest was puzzled by this. But he went on. "I know that you have consulted the physician Vekkos. How much better it is to put your trust in God, compared to whose power these bleeders and stewers of herbs are impotent! We shall start with a few prayers. …"

Padway lived through it. Then Julia appeared stirring something.

"Don't be alarmed," said the priest. "This is one cure that never fails. Dust from the tomb of St. Nereus, mixed with water."

There was nothing obviously lethal about the combination, so Padway drank it. Father Narcissus asked conversationally: "You are not, then, from Padua?"

Fritharik put his head in. "That so-called physician is here again."

"Tell him just a moment," said Padway. God, he was tired. "Thanks a lot, Father. It's nice to have seen you."

The priest went out, shaking his head over the blindness of mortals who trusted in *materia medica*.

Vekkos came in with an accusing look. Padway said: "Don't blame me. The girl brought him."

Vekkos sighed. "We physicians spend our lives in hard scientific study, and then we have to compete with these allied miracle-workers. Well, how's my patient today?"

While he was still examining Padway, Thomasus the Syrian appeared. The banker waited around nervously until the Greek left. Then Thomasus said: "I came as soon as I heard you were sick, Martinus. Prayers and medicines are all very well, but we don't want to miss any bets. My colleague, Ebenezer the Jew, knows a man, one of his own sect named Jeconias of Naples, who is pretty good at curative magic. A lot of these magicians are frauds; I don't believe

in them for a minute. But this man has done some remarkable—"

"I don't want him," groaned Padway. "I'll be all right if everybody will stop trying to cure me …"

"I brought him along, Martinus. Now do be reasonable. He won't hurt you. And I couldn't afford to have you die with those notes outstanding—of course that's not the only consideration; I'm fond of you personally …"

Padway felt like one in the grip of a nightmare. The more he protested, the more quacks they sicked on him.

Jeconias of Naples was a little fat man with a bouncing manner, more like a high-pressure salesman than the conventional picture of a magician.

He chanted: "Now, just leave everything to me, excellent Martinus. Here's a little cantrip that'll scare off the weaker spirits." He pulled out a piece of papyrus and read off something in an unknown language. "There, that didn't hurt, did it? Just leave it all to old Jeconias. He knows what he's doing. Now we'll put this charm under the bed, so-o-o! There, don't you feel better already? Now we'll cast your horoscope. If you'll give me the date and hour of your birth …"

How the hell, thought Padway, could he explain to this damned little quack that he was going to be born 1,373 years hence? He threw his reserve to the winds. He heaved himself up in bed and shouted feebly: "Presumptions slave, know you not that I am one of the hereditary custodians of the Seal of Solomon? That I can shuffle your silly planets around the sky with a word, and put out the sun with a sentence? And you talk of casting *my* horoscope?"

The magician's eyes were popping. "I—I'm sorry, sir, I didn't know …"

"Shemkhamphoras!" yelled Padway. "Ashtaroth! Baâl-Marduk! St. Frigidaire! Tippecanoe and Tyler too! Begone, worm! One word from you of my true identity, and I'll strike you down with the foulest form of leprosy! Your eyeballs will rot, your fingers will drop off joint by joint—" But Jeconias was already out the door. Padway could hear him negotiate the first half of the stairway three steps at a time, roll head over heels the rest of the way, and race out of the front door.

Padway chuckled. He told Fritharik, who had been attracted by the noise: "You park yourself at the door with your sword, and say that Vekkos has given orders to let nobody see me. And I mean *nobody*. Even if the Holy Ghost shows up, keep him out."

Fritharik did as ordered. Then he craned his neck around the doorframe. "Excellent boss! I found a Goth who knows the theory of elf-shot. Shall I have him come up and—"

Padway pulled the covers over his head.

✿

It was now April, 536. Sicily had fallen to General Belisarius in December. Padway had heard this weeks after it happened. Except for business errands, he had hardly been outside his house in four months in his desperate anxiety to get his press going. And except for his workers and his business contacts he knew practically nobody in Rome, though he had a speaking acquaintance with the librarians and two of Thomasus' banker friends, Ebenezer the Jew and Vardan the Armenian.

The day the press was finally ready he called his workers together and said: "I suppose you know that this is likely to be an important day for us. Fritharik will give each of you a small bottle of brandy to take home when you leave. And the first man who drops a hammer or anything on those little brass letters gets fired. I hope none of you do, because you've done a good job and I'm proud of you. That's all."

✿

"Well, well," said Thomasus, "that's splendid. I always knew you'd get your machine to run. Said so right from the start. What are you going to print? The *Gothic History?* That would flatter the pretorian prefect, no doubt."

"No. That would take months to run off, especially as my men are new at the job. I'm starting off with a little alphabet book. You know, A is for *asinus* (ass), B is for *braccae* (breeches), and so on."

"That sounds like a good idea. But, Martinus, can't you let your men handle it, and take a rest? You look as if you haven't had a good night's sleep in months."

"I haven't, to tell the truth. But I can't leave; every time something goes wrong I have to be there to fix it. And I've got to find outlets for this first book. Schoolmasters and such people. I have to do everything myself, sooner or later. Also, I have an idea for another kind of publication."

"What? Don't tell me you're going to start another wild scheme—"

"Now, now, don't get excited, Thomasus. This is a weekly booklet of news."

"Listen, Martinus, don't overreach yourself. You'll get the scribes' guild down on you. As it is, I wish you'd tell me more about yourself. You're the town's great mystery, you know. Everybody asks about you."

"You just tell them I'm the most uninteresting bore you ever met in your life."

There were only a little over a hundred free-lance scribes in Rome. Padway disarmed any hostility they might have had for him by the curious expedient of enlisting them as reporters. He made a standing offer of a couple of sesterces per story for acceptable accounts of news items.

When he came to assemble the copy for his first issue, he found that some drastic censorship was necessary. For instance, one story read:

✿

Our depraved and licentious city governor, Count Honorius, was seen early Wednesday morning being pursued down Broad Way by a young woman with a butcher's cleaver. Because this cowardly wretch was not encumbered by a decent minimum of clothing, he outdistanced his pursuer. This is the fourth time in a month that the wicked and corrupt count has created a scandal by his conduct with women. It is rumored that King Thiudahad will be petitioned to remove him by a committee of the outraged fathers of daughters whom he has dishonored. It is to be hoped that the next time the diabolical count is chased with a cleaver, his pursuer will catch him.

✿

Somebody, thought Padway, doesn't *like* our illustrious count. He didn't know Honorius, but whether the story was true or not, there was no free-press clause in the Italian constitutions between Padway and the city's torture chambers.

So the first eight-page issue said nothing about young women with cleavers. It had a lot of relatively innocuous news items, one short poem contributed by a scribe who fancied himself a second Ovid, an editorial by Padway in which he said briefly that he hoped the Romans would find his paper useful, and a short article—also by Padway—on the nature and habits of the elephant.

Padway turned the crackling sheepskin pages of the proof copy, was proud of himself and his men, a pride not much diminished by the immediate discovery of a number of glaring typographical errors. One of these, in a story about a Roman mortally wounded by robbers on High Path a few nights back, had the unfortunate effect of turning a harmless word into an obscene one. Oh, well, with only two hundred and fifty copies he could have somebody go through them and correct the error with pen and ink.

Still, he could not help being a little awed by the importance of Martin Padway in this world. But for pure good luck, it might have been he who had been fatally stabbed on High Path—and behold, no printing press, none of the inventions he might yet introduce, until the slow natural process of technical development prepared the way for them. Not that he deserved too much credit—Gutenberg ought to have some for the press, for instance.

Padway called his paper *Tempora Romae* and offered it at ten sesterces, about the equivalent of fifty cents. He was surprised when not only did the first issue sell out, but Fritharik was busy for three days turning away from his door people who wanted copies that were not to be had.

A few scribes dropped in every day with more news items. One of them, a plump cheerful-looking fellow about Padway's age, handed in a story beginning:

☿

The blood of an innocent man has been sacrificed to the lusts of our vile monster of a city governor, Count Honorius.

Reliable sources have revealed that Q. Aurelius Galba, crucified on a charge of murder last week, was the husband of a wife who had long been adulterously coveted by our villainous count. At Galba's trial there was much comment among the spectators on the flimsiness of the evidence …

☿

"Hey!" said Padway. "Aren't you the man who handed in that other story about Honorius and a cleaver?"

"That's right," said the scribe. "I wondered why you didn't publish it."

"How long do you think I'd be allowed to run my paper without interference if I did?"

"Oh, I never thought of that."

"Well, remember next time. I can't use this story either. But don't let it discourage you. It's well done; a lead sentence and everything. How do you get all this information?"

The man grinned. "I hear things. And what I don't hear, my wife does. She has women friends who get together for games of backgammon, and they talk."

"It's too bad I don't dare run a gossip column," said Padway. "But you would seem to have the makings of a newspaper man. What's your name?"

"George Menandrus."

"That's Greek, isn't it?"

"My parents were Greek; I am Roman."

"All right, George, keep in touch with me. Some day I may want to hire an assistant to help run the thing."

Padway confidently visited the tanner to place another order for vellum.

"When will you want it?" said the tanner. Padway told him in four days.

"That's impossible. I might have fifty sheets for you in that time. They'll cost you five times as much apiece as the first ones."

Padway gasped. "In God's name, why?"

"You practically cleaned out Rome's supply with that first order," said the tanner. "All of our stock, and all the rest that was floating around, which I went out and bought up for you. There aren't enough skins left in the whole city to make a hundred sheets. And making vellum takes time, you know. If you buy up the last fifty sheets, it will be weeks before you can prepare another large batch."

Padway asked: "If you expanded your plant, do you suppose you could eventually get up to a capacity of two thousand a week?"

The tanner shook his head. "I should not want to spend the money to expand in such a risky business. And, if I did, there wouldn't be enough animals in Central Italy to supply such a demand."

Padway recognized when he was licked. Vellum was essentially a by-product of the sheep-and-goat industry. Therefore a sudden increase in demand would skyrocket the price without much increasing the output. Though the Romans knew next to nothing of economics, the law of supply and demand worked here just the same.

It would have to be paper after all. And his second edition was going to be very, very late.

For paper, he got hold of a felter and told him that he wanted him to chop up a few pounds of white cloth and make them into the thinnest felt that anybody had ever heard of. The felter dutifully produced a sheet of what looked like exceptionally thick and fuzzy blotting paper. Padway patiently insisted on finer breaking up of the cloth, on a brief boiling before felting, and on pressing after. As he went out of the shop he saw the felter tap his forehead significantly. But after many trials the man presented him with a paper not much worse for writing than a twentieth-century paper towel.

Then came the heartbreaking part. A drop of ink applied to this paper spread out with the alacrity of a picnic party that has discovered a rattlesnake in their midst. So Padway told the felter to make up ten more sheets, and into the mush from which each was made to introduce one common substance—soap, olive oil, and so forth. At this point the felter threatened to quit, and had to be appeased by a raise in price. Padway was vastly relieved to discover that a little clay mixed with the pulp made all the difference between a fair writing paper and an impossible one.

By the time Padway's second issue had been sold out, he had ceased to worry about the possibility of running out of paper. But another thought moved into the vacated worrying compartment in his mind: What should he do when the Gothic War really got going? In his own history it had raged for twenty years up and down Italy. Nearly every important town had been besieged or captured at least once. Rome itself would be practically depopulated by sieges, famine, and pestilence. If he lived long enough he might see the Lombard invasion and the near-extinction of Italian civilization. All this would interfere dreadfully with his plans.

He tried to shake off the mood. Probably the weather was responsible; it had rained steadily for two days. Everything in the house was dank. The only way to cure that would be to build a fire, and the air was too warm for that already. So Padway sat and looked out at the leaden landscape.

He was surprised when Fritharik brought in Thomasus' colleague, Ebenezer the Jew. Ebenezer was a frail-looking, kindly oldster with a long white beard. Padway found him distressingly pious; when he ate with the other bankers he did not eat at all, to put it Irishly, for fear of transgressing one of the innumerable rules of his sect.

Ebenezer took his cloak off over his head and asked: "Where can I put this where it won't drip, excellent Martinus? Ah. Thank you. I was this way on business, and I thought I'd look your place over, if I may. It must be interesting, from Thomasus' accounts." He wrung the water from his beard.

Padway was glad of something to take his mind off the ominous future. He showed the old man around.

Ebenezer looked at him from under bushy white eyebrows. "Ah. Now I can believe that you are from a far country. From another world, almost. Take that system of arithmetic of yours; it has changed our whole concept of banking—"

"What?" cried Padway. "What do you know about it?"

"Why," said Ebenezer, "Thomasus sold the secret to Vardan and me. I thought you knew that."

"He *did?* How much?"

"A hundred and fifty solidi apiece. Didn't you—"

Padway growled a resounding Latin oath, grabbed his hat and cloak, and started for the door.

"Where are you going, Martinus?" said Ebenezer in alarm.

"I'm going to tell that cutthroat what I think of him!" snapped Padway. "And then I'm going to—"

"Did Thomasus promise you not to reveal the secret? I cannot believe that he violated—"

Padway stopped with his hand on the door handle. Now that he thought, the Syrian had never agreed not to tell anybody about Arabic numerals. Padway had taken it for granted that he would not want to do so. But if Thomasus got pressed for ready cash, there was no legal impediment to his selling or giving the knowledge to whom he pleased.

As Padway got his anger under control, he saw that he had not really lost anything, since his original intention had been to spread Arabic numerals far and wide. What really peeved him was that Thomasus should chisel such a handsome sum out of the science without even offering Padway a cut. It was like Thomasus. He was all right, but as Nevitta had said you had to watch him.

When Padway did appear at Thomasus' house, later that day, he had Fritharik with him. Fritharik was carrying a strong box. The box was nicely heavy with gold.

"Martinus," cried Thomasus, a little appalled, "do you really want to pay off all your loans? Where did you get all this money?"

"You heard me," grinned Padway. "Here's an accounting of principal and interest. I'm tired of paying ten per cent when I can get the same for seven and a half."

"What? Where can you get any such absurd rate?"

"From your esteemed colleague, Ebenezer. Here's a copy of the new note."

"Well, I must say I wouldn't have expected that of Ebenezer. If all this is true, I suppose I could meet his rate."

"You'll have to better it, after what you made from selling my arithmetic."

"Now, Martinus, what I did was strictly legal—"

"Didn't say it wasn't."

"Oh, very well. I suppose God planned it this way. I'll give you seven and four tenths."

Padway laughed scornfully.

"Seven, then. But that's the lowest, absolutely, positively, finally."

When Padway had received his old notes, a receipt for the old loans, and a copy of the new note, Thomasus asked him, "How did you get Ebenezer to offer you such an unheard-of figure?"

Padway smiled. "I told him that he could have had the secret of the new arithmetic from me for the asking."

☼

Padway's next effort was a clock. He was going to begin with the simplest design possible: a weight on the end of a rope, a ratchet, a train of gears, the hand and dial from a battered old clepsydra or water clock he picked up secondhand, a pendulum, and an escapement. One by one he assembled these parts— all but the last.

He had not supposed there was anything so difficult about making an escapement. He could take the back cover off his wrist-watch and see the escapement-wheel there, jerking its merry way around. He did not want to take his watch apart for fear of never getting it together again. Besides, the parts thereof were too small to reproduce accurately.

But he could *see* the damned thing; why couldn't he make a large one? The workmen turned out several wheels, and the little tongs to go with them. Padway filed and scraped and bent. But they would not work. The tongs caught the teeth of the wheels and stuck fast. Or they did not catch at all, so that the shaft on which the rope was wound unwound itself all at once. Padway at last got one of the contraptions adjusted so that if you swung the pendulum with your hand, the tongs would let the escapement-wheel revolve one tooth at a time. Fine. But the clock would not run under its own power. Take your hand off the pendulum, and it made a couple of half-hearted swings and stopped.

Padway said to hell with it. He'd come back to it some day when he had more time and better tools and instruments. He stowed the mess of cog-wheels in a corner of his cellar. Perhaps, he thought, this failure had been a good thing, to keep him from getting an exaggerated idea of his own cleverness.

Nevitta popped in again. "All over your sickness, Martinus? Fine; I knew you had a sound constitution. How about coming out to the Flaminian racetrack with me now and losing a few solidi? Then come on up to the farm overnight."

"I'd like to a lot. But I have to put the *Times* to bed this afternoon."

"Put to bed?" queried Nevitta.

Padway explained.

Nevitta said: "I see. Ha, ha, I thought you had a girl friend named Tempora. Tomorrow for supper, then."

"How shall I get there?"

"You haven't a saddle horse? I'll send Hermann down with one tomorrow afternoon. But mind, I don't want to get him back with wings growing out of his shoulders!"

"It might attract attention," said Padway solemnly. "And you'd have a hell of a time catching him if he didn't want to be bridled."

So the next afternoon Padway, in a new pair of rawhide Byzantine jack boots, set out with Hermann up the Flaminian Way. The Roman Campagna, he noted, was still fairly prosperous farming country. He wondered how long it would take for it to become the desolate, malarial plain of the Middle Ages.

"How were the races?" he asked.

Hermann, it seemed, knew very little Latin, though that little was still better than Padway's Gothic. "Oh, my boss … he terrible angry. He talk … you know … hot sport. But hate lose money. Lose fifty sesterces on horse. Make noise like … you know … lion with gutache."

At the farmhouse Padway met Nevitta's wife, a pleasant, plump woman who spoke no Latin, and his eldest son, Dagalaif, a Gothic *scaio*, or marshal, home on vacation. Supper fully bore out the stories that Padway had heard about Gothic appetites. He was agreeably surprised to drink some fairly good beer, after the bilgewater that went by that name in Rome.

"I've got some wine, if you prefer it," said Nevitta.

"Thanks, but I'm getting a little tired of Italian wine. The Roman writers talk a lot about their different kinds, but it all tastes alike to me."

"That's the way I feel. If you really *want* some, I have some perfumed Greek wine."

Padway shuddered.

Nevitta grinned. "That's the way I feel. Any man who'd put perfume in his liquor probably swishes when he walks. I only keep the stuff for my Greek friends, like Leo Vekkos. Reminds me, I must tell him about your cure for my wheezes by having me put the dogs out. He'll figure out some fancy theory full of long words to explain it."

Dagalaif spoke up: "Say, Martinus, maybe you have inside information on how the war will go."

Padway shrugged. "All I know is what everybody else knows. I haven't a private wire—I mean a private channel of information to heaven. If you want a guess, I'd say that Belisarius would invade Bruttium

this summer and besiege Naples about August. He won't have a large force, but he'll be infernally hard to beat."

Dagalaif said: "Huh! We'll let him up all right. A handful of Greeks won't get very far against the united Gothic nation."

"That's what the Vandals thought," answered Padway dryly.

"*Aiw*," said Dagalaif. "But we won't make the mistakes the Vandals made."

"I don't know, son," said Nevitta. "It seems to me we are making them already—or others just as bad. This king of ours—all he's good for is hornswoggling his neighbors out of land and writing Latin poetry. And digging around in libraries. It would be better if we had an illiterate one, like Theoderik. Of course," he added apologetically, "I admit I can read and write. My old man came from Pannonia with Theoderik, and he was always talking about the sacred duty of the Goths to preserve Roman civilization from savages like the Franks. He was determined that I would have a Latin education if it killed me. I admit I've found my education useful. But in the next few months it'll be more important for our leader to know how to lead a charge than to say *amo-amas-amat*."

CHAPTER V

Padway returned to Rome in the best of humor. Nevitta was the first person, besides Thomasus the Syrian, who had asked him to his house. And Padway, despite his somewhat cool exterior, was a sociable fellow at heart. He was, in fact, so elated that he dismounted and handed the reins of the borrowed horse to Hermann without noticing the three tough-looking parties leaning against the new fence in front of the old house on Long Street.

When he headed for the gate, the largest of the three, a black-bearded man, stepped in front of him. The man was holding a sheet of paper—real paper, no doubt from the felter to whom Padway had taught the art—in front of him and reading out loud to himself:—"medium height, brown hair and eyes, large nose, short beard. Speaks with an accent." He looked up sharply. "Are you Martinus Paduei?"

"*Sic. Quis est?*"

"You're under arrest. Will you come along quietly?"

"*What?* Who—What for—"

"Order of the municipal prefect. Sorcery."

"But … but—*Hey!* You can't—"

"I said *quietly*."

The other two men had moved up on each side of Padway, and each took an arm and started to walk him along the street. When he resisted, a short bludgeon appeared in the hand of one. Padway looked around frantically. Hermann was already out of sight. Fritharik was not to be seen; no doubt he was snoring as usual. Padway filled his lungs to shout; the man on his right tightened his grip and raised the bludgeon threateningly. Padway didn't shout.

They marched him down the Argiletum to the old jail below the Record Office on the Capitoline. He was still in somewhat of a daze as the clerk demanded his name, age, and address. All he could think of was that he had heard somewhere that you were entitled to telephone your lawyer before being locked up. And that information seemed hardly useful in the present circumstances.

A small, snapping Italian who had been lounging on a bench got up. "What's this, a sorcery case involving a foreigner? Sounds like a national case to me,"

"Oh, no, it isn't," said the clerk. "You national officers have authority in Rome only in mixed Roman-Gothic cases. This man isn't a Goth; says he's an American, whatever that is."

"Yes, it is! Read your regulations. The pretorian prefect's office has jurisdiction in all capital cases involving foreigners. If you have a sorcery complaint, you turn it and the prisoner over to us. Come on, now." The little man moved possessively toward Padway. Padway did not like the use of the term "capital cases."

The clerk said: "Don't be a fool. Think you're going to drag him clear up to Ravenna for interrogation? We've got a perfectly good torture chamber here."

"I'm only doing my duty," snapped the state policeman. He grabbed Padway's arm and started to haul him toward the door. "Come along now, sorcer-er. We'll show you some real, up-to-date torture at Ravenna. These Roman cops don't know anything."

"*Christus!* Are you crazy?" yelled the clerk. He jumped up and grabbed Padway's other arm; so did the black-bearded man who had arrested him. The state policemen pulled and so did the other two.

"Hey!" yelled Padway. But the assorted functionaries were too engrossed in their tug-of-war to notice.

The state policeman shouted in a painfully penetrating voice: "Justinius, run and tell the adjutant prefect that these municipal scum are trying to withhold a prisoner from us!" A man ran out the door.

Another door opened, and a fat, sleepy-looking man came in. "What's this?" he squeaked.

The clerk and the municipal policeman straightened up to attention, releasing Padway. The state policeman immediately resumed hauling him toward the door; the local cops abandoned their etiquette and grabbed him again. They all shouted at once at the fat man. Padway gathered that he was the municipal *commentariensius*, or police chief.

At that two more municipal policemen came in with a thin, ragged prisoner. They entered into the dispute with true Italian fervor, which meant using both hands. The ragged prisoner promptly darted out the door; his captors didn't notice his absence for a full minute.

They then began shouting at each other. "What did you let him go for?" "You brass-bound idiot, you're the one who let him go!"

The man called Justinius came back with an elegant person who announced himself as the *corniculatis*, or adjutant prefect. This individual waved a perfumed handkerchief at the struggling group and said: "Let him go, you chaps. Yes, you, too, Sulla." (This was the state policeman.) "There won't be anything left of him to interrogate if you keep that up."

From the way the others in the now-crowded room quieted, Padway guessed that the adjutant prefect was a pretty big shot.

The adjutant prefect asked a few questions, then said: "I'm sorry, my dear old *commentariensius*, but I'm afraid he's our man."

"Not yet he isn't," squeaked the chief. "You fellows can't just walk in here and grab a prisoner any time you feel like it. It would mean my job to let you have him."

The adjutant prefect yawned. "Dear, dear, you're *such* a bore. You forget that I represent the pretorian prefect, who represents the king, and if I order you to hand the prisoner over, you hand him over and that's the end of it. I so order you, now."

"Go ahead and order. You'll have to take him by force, and I've got more force than you have." The chief beamed Billikenlike and twiddled his thumbs. "Clodianus, go fetch our illustrious city governor, if he's not too busy. We'll see whether we have authority over our own jail." The clerk departed. "Of course," the chief continued, "we *might* use Solomon's method."

"You mean cut him in two?" asked the adjutant prefect.

"That's it. Lord Jesus, that would be funny, wouldn't it? Ho, ho, ho, ho, ho!" The chief laughed shrilly until the tears ran down his face. "Would you prefer the head end or the legs end? Ho, ho, ho, ho, ho!" He rocked on his seat.

The other municipal officers dutifully laughed, also; the adjutant prefect permitted himself a wan, bored smile. Padway thought the chief's humor in questionable taste.

Eventually the clerk returned with the city governor. Count Honorius wore a tunic with the two purple stripes of a Roman senator, and walked with such a carefully measured tread that Padway wondered if his footsteps hadn't been laid out ahead of time with chalk marks. He had a square jaw and all the warmth of expression of a snapping turtle.

"What," he asked in a voice like a steel file, "is this all about? Quick, now, I'm a busy man." As he spoke, the little wattle under his jaw wobbled in a way that reminded Padway more than ever of a snapper.

The chief and the adjutant prefect gave their versions. The clerk dragged out a couple of law books; the three executive officers put their heads together and talked in low tones, turning pages rapidly and pointing to passages.

Finally the adjutant prefect gave in. He yawned elaborately. "Oh, well, it would be a dreadful bore to have to drag him up to Ravenna, anyway. Especially as the mosquito season will be starting there shortly. Glad to have seen you, my lord count." He bowed to Honorius, nodded casually to the chief, and departed.

Honorius said: "Now that we have him, what's to be done with him? Let's see that complaint."

The clerk dug out a paper and gave it to the count.

"*Hm-m-m.* '—and furthermore, that the said Martinus Paduei did most wickedly and feloniously consort with the Evil One, who taught him the diabolical arts of magic wherewith he has been jeopardizing the welfare of the citizens of the city of Rome—signed, Hannibal Scipio of Palermo.' Wasn't this Hannibal Scipio a former associate of yours or something?"

"Yes, my lord count," said Padway, and explaining the circumstances of his parting with his foreman. "If it's my printing press that he's referring to, I can easily show that it's a simple mechanical device, no more magical than one of your water clocks."

"*Hm-m-m,*" said Honorius, "that may or may not be true." He looked through narrowed eyes at Padway. "These new enterprises of yours have prospered pretty well, haven't they?" His faint smile reminded Padway of a fox dreaming of unguarded henroosts.

"Yes and no, my lord. I have made a little money, but I've put most of it back in the business. So I haven't more cash than I need for day-to-day expenses."

"Too bad," said Honorius. "It looks as though we'd have to let the case go through."

Padway was getting more and more nervous under that penetrating scrutiny, but he put up a bold front. "Oh, my lord, I don't think you have a case. If I may say so, it would be most unfortunate for your dignity to let the case come to trial."

"So? I'm afraid my good man, that you don't know what expert interrogators we have. You'll have admitted all sorts of things by the time they finish … ah … questioning you."

"Um-m-m. My lord, I said I didn't have much *cash*. But I have an idea that might interest you."

"That's better. Lutetius, may I use your private office?"

Without waiting for an answer, Honorius marched to the office, jerking his head to Padway to follow. The chief looked after them sourly, obviously resenting the loss of his share of the swag.

In the chief's office, Honorius turned to Padway. "You weren't proposing to bribe your governor by chance, were you?" he asked coldly.

"Well … uh … not exactly—"

The count shot his head forward. "How much?" he snapped. "And what's it in—jewels?"

Padway sighed with relief. "Please, my lord, not so fast, It'll take a bit of explaining."

"Your explanation had better be good."

"It's this way, my lord: I'm just a poor stranger in Rome, and naturally I have to depend on my wits for a living. The only really valuable thing I have is those wits. But, with reasonably kind treatment, they can be made to pay a handsome return."

"Get to the point, young man."

"You have a law against limited-liability corporations in other than public enterprises, haven't you?"

Honorius rubbed his chin. "We did have once. I don't know what its status is, now that the senate's authority is limited to the city. I don't think the Goths have made any regulations on that subject. Why?"

"Well if you can get the senate to pass an amendment to the old law—I don't think it would be necessary, but it would look better—I could show you how you and a few other deserving senators could benefit handsomely from the organization and operation of such a company."

Honorius stiffened. "Young man, that's a miserable sort of offer. You ought to know that the dignity of a patrician forbids him to engage in trade."

"You wouldn't engage in it, my lord. You'd be the stockholders."

"We'd be the what?"

Padway explained the operation of a stock corporation.

Honorius rubbed his chin again. "Yes, I see where something might be made of that plan. What sort of company did you have in mind?"

"A company for the transmission of information over long distances much more rapidly than a messenger can travel. In my country they'd call it a semaphore telegraph. The company gets its revenue from tolls on private messages. Of course, it wouldn't hurt if you could get a subsidy from the royal treasury, on the ground that the institution was valuable for national defense."

Honorius thought awhile. Then he said: "I won't commit myself now; I shall have to think about the matter and sound out my friends. In the meantime, you will, of course, remain in Lutetius' custody here."

Padway grinned. "My lord count, your daughter is getting married next week, isn't she?"

"What of it?"

"You want a nice write-up of the wedding in my paper, don't you? A list of distinguished guests, a wood-cut picture of the bride, and so forth."

"Hm-m-m. I shouldn't mind that; no."

"Well, then, you better not hold me, or I shan't be able to get the paper out. It would be a pity if such a gala event missed the news because the publisher was in jail at the time."

Honorius rubbed his chin and smiled thinly. "For a barbarian, you're not as stupid as one would expect. I'll have you released."

"Many thanks, my lord. I might add that I shall be able to write much more glowing paragraphs after that complaint has been dismissed. We creative workers, you know—"

✿

When Padway was out of earshot of the jail, he indulged in a long "*Whew!*" He was sweating, and not with the heat, either. It was a good thing that none of the officials noticed how near he had been to collapse from sheer terror. The prospect of a stand-up fight wouldn't have bothered him more than most young men. But torture …

As soon as he had put his establishment in order, he went into a huddle with Thomasus. He was properly prepared when the procession of five sedan chairs, bearing Honorius and four other senators, crawled up Long Street to his place. The senators seemed not only willing but eager to lay their money on the line, especially after they saw the beautiful stock certificates that Padway had printed. But they didn't seem to have quite Padway's idea of how to run a corporation.

One of them poked him in the ribs and grinned. "My dear Martinus, you're not *really* going to put up those silly signal towers and things?"

"Well," said Padway cautiously, "that was the idea."

The senator winked. "Oh, I understand that you'll have to put up a couple to fool the middle class, so we can sell our stock at a profit. But *we* know it's all a fake, don't we? You couldn't make anything with your signaling scheme in a thousand years."

Padway didn't bother to argue with him. He also didn't bother to explain the true object of having Thomasus the Syrian, Ebenezer the Jew, and Vardan the Armenian each take eighteen per cent of the stock. The senators might have been interested in knowing that these three bankers had agreed ahead of time to hold their stock and vote as Padway instructed, thereby giving him, with fifty-four per cent of the stock, complete control of the corporation.

Padway had every intention of making his telegraph company a success, starting with a line of towers from Naples to Rome to Ravenna, and tying its operation in with that of his paper. He soon ran into an elementary difficulty: If he wanted to keep his expenses down to somewhere within sight of income, he needed telescopes, to make possible a wide spacing of the towers. Telescopes meant lenses. Where in the world was there a lens or a man who could make one? True, there was a story about Nero's emerald lorgnette …

Padway went to see Sextus Dentatus, the froglike goldsmith who had changed his lire to sesterces. Dentatus croaked directions to the establishment of one Florianus the Glazier.

Florianus was a light-haired man with a drooping mustache and a nasal accent. He came to the front of his dark little shop smelling strongly of wine. Yes, he had owned his own glass factory once, at Cologne. But business was bad for the Rhineland glass industry; the uncertainties of life under the Franks, you know, my sir. He had gone broke. Now he made a precarious living mending windows and such.

Padway explained what he wanted, paid a little on account, and left him. When he went back on the promised day, Florianus flapped his hands as if he were trying to take off. "A thousand pardons, my sir! It has been hard to buy up the necessary cullet. But a few days more, I pray you. And if I could have a little more money on account—times are hard—I am poor—"

On Padway's third visit he found Florianus drunk. When Padway shook him, all the man could do was mumble Gallo-romance at him, which Padway did not understand. Padway went to the back of the

shop. There was no sign of tools or materials for making lenses.

Padway left in disgust. The nearest real glass industry was at Puteoli, near Naples. It would take forever to get anything done by correspondence.

Padway called in George Menandrus and hired him as editor of the paper. For several days he talked himself hoarse and Menandrus deaf on How to Be an Editor. Then, with a sinking heart, he left for Naples. He experienced the famous canal-boat ride celebrated by Horace, and found it quite as bad as alleged.

Vesuvius was not smoking. But Puteoli, on the little strip of level ground between the extinct crater of Solfatara and the sea, was. Padway and Fritharik sought out the place recommended by Dentatus. This was one of the largest and smokiest of the glass factories.

Padway asked the doorman for Andronicus, the proprietor. Andronicus was a short, brawny man covered with soot. When Padway told who he was, Andronicus cried: "Ah! Fine! Come, gentlemen, I have just the thing."

They followed him into his private inferno. The vestibule, which was also the office, was lined with shelves. The shelves were covered with glassware. Andronicus picked up a vase. "Ah! Look! Such clearness! You couldn't get whiter glass from Alexandria! Only two solidi!"

Padway said: "I didn't come for a vase, my dear sir. I want—"

"No vase? No vase? Ah! Here is the thing." He picked up another vase. "Look! The shape! Such, purity of line! It reminds you—"

"I said I didn't want to buy a vase. I want—"

"It reminds you of a beautiful woman! Of love!" Andronicus kissed his fingertips.

"I want some small pieces of glass, made specially—"

"Beads? Of course, gentlemen. Look." The glass manufacturer scooped up a handful of beads. "Look at the color! Emerald, turquoise, everything!" He picked up another bunch. "See here, the faces of the twelve apostles, one on each bead—"

"Not beads—"

"A beaker, then! Here is one. Look, it has the Holy Family in high relief—"

"Jesus!" yelled Padway. "Will you listen?"

When Andronicus let Padway explain what he wanted, the Neapolitan said: "Of course! Fine! I've seen ornaments shaped like that. I'll rough them out tonight, and have them ready day after tomorrow—"

"That won't quite do," said Padway. "These have to have an exactly spherical surface. You grind a concave against a convex with—what's your word for *emery?* The stuff you use in rough grinding? Some *naxium* to true them off …"

Padway and Fritharik went on to Naples and put up at the house of Thomasus' cousin, Antiochus the Shipper. Their welcome was less than cordial. It transpired that Antiochus was fanatically Orthodox. He loathed his cousin's Nestorianism. His pointed remarks about heretics made his guests so uncomfortable that they moved out on the third day. They took lodgings at an inn whose lack of sanitation distressed Padway's cleanly soul.

Each morning they rode out to Puteoli to see how the lenses were coming. Andronicus invariably tried to sell them a ton of glass junk.

When they left for Rome, Padway had a dozen lenses, half plano-convex and half plano-concave. He was skeptical about the possibility of making a telescope by holding a pair of lenses in line with his eye and judging the distances. It worked, though.

The most practical combination proved to be a concave lens for the eyepiece with a convex one about thirty inches in front of it. The glass had bubbles, and the image was somewhat distorted. But Padway's telescope, crude as it was, would make a two-to-one difference in the number of signal towers required.

About then, the paper ran its first advertisement. Thomasus had had to turn the screw on one of his debtors to make him buy space. The ad read:

DO YOU WANT A GLAMOROUS FUNERAL?

Go to meet your Maker in style! With one of our funerals to look forward to, you will hardly mind dying!

Don't imperil your chances of salvation with a bungled burial! Our experts have handled some of the noblest corpses in Rome.

Arrangements made with the priesthood of any sect. Special rates for heretics. Appropriately doleful music furnished at slight extra cost.

JOHN THE EGYPTIAN,
GENTEEL UNDERTAKER,
NEAR THE VIMINAL GATE

CHAPTER VI

Junianus, construction manager of the Roman Telegraph Co., panted into Padway's office. He said: "Work"—stopped to get his breath, and started again—"work on the third tower on the Naples line was stopped this morning by a squad of soldiers from the Rome garrison. I asked them what the devil was up, and they said they didn't know; they just had orders to stop construction. What, most excellent boss, are you going to do about it?"

So the Goths objected? That meant seeing their higher-ups. Padway winced at the idea of getting involved any further in politics. He sighed. "I'll see Liuderis, I suppose."

The commander of the Rome garrison was a big, portly Goth with the bushiest white whiskers Padway had ever seen. His Latin was fair. But now and then he cocked a blue eye at the ceiling and moved his lips silently, as if praying; actually he was running through a declension or a conjugation for the right ending.

He said: "My good Martinus, there is a war on. You start erecting these … ah … mysterious towers without asking our permission. Some of your backers are patricians … ah … notorious for their pro-Greek sentiments. What are we to think? You should consider yourself lucky to have escaped arrest."

Padway protested: "I was hoping the army would find them useful for transmitting military information."

Liuderis shrugged. "I am merely a simple soldier doing my duty. I do not understand these … ah … devices. Perhaps they will work as you say. But I could not take the … ah … responsibility for permitting them."

"Then you won't withdraw your order?"

"No. If you want permission, you will have to see the king."

"But, my dear sir, I can't spare the time to go running up to Ravenna—"

Another shrug. "All one to me, my good Martinus. I know my duty."

Padway tried guile. "You certainly do, it seems. If I were the king, I couldn't ask for a more faithful soldier."

"You flatterer!" But Liuderis grinned, pleased. "I regret that I cannot grant your little request."

"What's the latest war news?"

Liuderis frowned. "Not very—But then I should be careful what I say. You are a more dangerous person than you look, I am sure."

"You can trust me. I'm pro-Gothic."

"Yes?" Liuderis was silent while the wheels turned. Then: "What is your religion?"

Padway was expecting that. "Congregationalist. That's the nearest thing to Arianism we have in my country."

"Ah, then perhaps you are as you say. The news is not good, what little there is. There is nobody in Bruttium but a small force under the king's son-in-law, Evermuth. And our good king—" He shrugged again, this time hopelessly.

"Now look here, most excellent Liuderis, won't you withdraw that order? I'll write Thiudahad at once asking his permission."

"No, my good Martinus, I cannot. You get the permission first. And you had better go in person, if you want action."

Thus it came about that Padway found himself, quite against his wishes, trotting an elderly saddle horse across the Apennines toward the Adriatic. Fritharik had been delighted at first to get any kind of a horse between his knees. Before they had gone very far his tone changed.

"Boss," he grumbled, "I'm not an educated man. But I know horseflesh. I always claimed that a good horse was a good investment." He added darkly: "If we are attacked by brigands, we'll have no chance with those poor old wrecks. Not that I fear death, or brigands either. But it would be sad for a Vandal knight to end in a nameless grave in one of these lonely valleys. When I was a noble in Africa—"

"We aren't running a racing stable," snapped Padway. At Fritharik's hurt look he was sorry he had spoken sharply. "Never mind, old man, we'll be able

to afford good horses some day. Only right now I feel as if I had a pantsful of ants."

Brazilian army ants, he added to himself. He had done almost no riding since his arrival in old Rome, and not a great deal in his former life. By the time they reached Spoleto he felt as if he could neither sit nor stand, but would have to spend the rest of his life in a sort of semi-squat, like a rheumatic chimpanzee.

They approached Ravenna at dusk on the fourth day. The City in the Mist sat dimly astride the thirty-mile causeway that divided the Adriatic from the vast marshy lagoons to the west. A faint sunbeam lighted the gilded church domes. The church bells bonged, and the frogs in the lagoons fell silent; then resumed their croaking. Padway thought that anyone who visited this strange city would always be haunted by the bong of the bells, the croak of the frogs, and the thin, merciless song of the mosquitoes.

✿

Padway decided that the chief usher, like Poo-Bah, had been born sneering. "My good man," said this being, "I couldn't possibly give you an audience with our lord king for three weeks at least."

Three weeks! In that time half of Padway's assorted machines would have broken down, and his men would be running in useless circles trying to fix them. Menandrus, who was inclined to be reckless with money, especially other people's, would have run the paper into bankruptcy. This impasse required thought. Padway straightened his aching legs and started to leave.

The Italian immediately lost some of his top-loftiness. "But," he cried in honest amazement, "didn't you bring any *money?*"

Of course, Padway thought, he should have known that the man hadn't meant what he'd said. "What's your schedule of rates?"

The usher, quite seriously, began counting on his fingers. "Well, for twenty solidi I could give you your audience tomorrow. For the day after tomorrow, ten solidi is my usual rate; but that's Sunday, so I'm offering interviews on Monday at seven and a half. For one week in advance, two solidi. For two weeks—"

Padway interrupted to offer a five-solidi bribe for a Monday interview, and finally got it at that price plus a small bottle of brandy. The usher said: "You'll be expected to have a present for the king, too, you know."

"I know," said Padway wearily. He showed the usher a small leather case. "I'll present it personally."

☼

Thiudahad Tharasmund's son, King of the Ostrogoths and Italians; Commander in Chief of the Armies of Italy, Illyria, and Southern Gaul; Premier Prince of the Amal Clan; Count of Tuscany; Illustrious Patrician; *ex-officio* President of the Circus; et cetera, et cetera, was about Padway's height, thin to gauntness, and had a small gray beard. He peered at his caller with watery gray eyes, and said in a reedy voice: "Come in, come in, my good man. What's *your* business? Oh, yes, Martinus Paduei. You're the publisher chap aren't you? Eh?" He spoke upper-class Latin without a trace of accent.

Padway bowed ceremoniously. "I am, my lord king. Before we discuss the business, I have—"

"Great thing, that book-making machine of yours. I've heard of it. Great thing for scholarship. You must see my man Cassiodorus. I'm sure he'd like you to publish his *Gothic History*. Great work. Deserves a wide circulation."

Padway waited patiently. "I have a small gift for you, my lord. A rather unusual—"

"Eh? Gift? By all means. Let's see it."

Padway took out the case and opened it.

Thiudahad piped: "Eh? What the devil is that?"

Padway explained the function of a magnifying glass. He didn't dwell on Thiudahad's notorious nearsightedness.

Thiudahad picked up a book and tried the glass on it. He squealed with delight. "Fine, my good Martinus. Shall I be able to read all I want without getting headaches?"

"I hope so, my lord. At least it should help. Now, about my business here—"

"Oh, yes, you want to see me about publishing Cassiodorus. I'll fetch him for you."

"No, my lord. It's about something else." He went on quickly before Thiudahad could interrupt again, telling him of his difficulty with Liuderis.

"Eh? I never bother my local military commanders. They know their business."

"But, my lord—" and Padway gave the king a little sales talk on the importance of the telegraph company.

"Eh? A money-making scheme, you say? If it's as good as all that, why wasn't I let in on it at the start?"

That rather jarred Padway. He said something vague about there not having been time. King Thiudahad wagged his head. "Still, that wasn't considerate of you, Martinus. It wasn't loyal. And if people aren't loyal to their king, where are we? If you deprive your king of an opportunity to make a little honest profit, I don't see why I should interfere with Liuderis on your account."

"Well, ahem, my lord, I did have an idea—"

"Not considerate at all. What were you saying? Come to the point, my good man, come to the point."

Padway resisted an impulse to strangle this exasperating little man. He beckoned Fritharik, who was standing statuesquely in the background. Fritharik produced a telescope, and Padway explained *its* functions. …

"Yes, Yes? Very interesting, I'm sure. Thank you, Martinus. I will say that you bring your king original presents."

Padway gasped; he hadn't intended giving Thiudahad his best telescope. But it was too late now. He said: "I thought that if my lord king saw fit to … ah … ease matters with your excellent Liuderis, I could insure your undying fame in the world of scholarship."

"Eh? What's that? What do you know about scholarship? Oh, I forgot; you're a publisher. Something about Cassiodorus?"

Padway repressed a sigh. "No, my lord. *Not* Cassiodorus. How would you like the credit for revolutionizing men's idea about the solar system?"

"I don't believe in interfering with my local commanders, Martinus. Liuderis is an excellent man. Eh? What were you saying. Something about the solar system? What's that got to do with Liuderis?"

"Nothing, my lord." Padway repeated what he had said.

"Well, maybe I'd consider it. What is this theory of yours?"

Little by little Padway wormed from Thiudahad a promise of a free hand for the telegraph company, in return for bits of information about the Copernican hypothesis, instructions for the use of the telescope to see the moons of Jupiter, and a promise to publish a treatise on astronomy in Thiudahad's name.

At the end of an hour he grinned and said, "Well, my lord, we seem to be in agreement. There's just one more thing. This telescope would be a valuable instrument of warfare. If you wanted to equip your officers with them—"

"Eh? Warfare? You'll have to see Wittigis about that. He's my head general."

"Where's he?"

"Where? Oh, dear me, I don't know. Somewhere up north, I think. There's been a little invasion by the Allemans or somebody."

"When will he be back?"

"How should I know, my good Martinus? When he's driven out these Allemans or Burgunds or whoever they are."

"But, most excellent lord, if you'll pardon me, the war with the Imperialists is definitely on. I think it's important to get these telescopes into the hands of the army as soon as possible? We'd be prepared to supply them at a reasonable—"

"Now, Martinus," snapped the king peevishly, "don't try to tell me how to run my kingdom. You're as bad as my Royal Council. Always 'Why don't you do this?', 'Why don't you do that?' I trust my commanders; don't bother myself with details. I say you'll have to see Wittigis, and that settles it."

Thiudahad was obviously prepared to be mulish, so Padway said a few polite nothings, bowed, and withdrew.

CHAPTER VII

When Padway got back to Rome, his primary concern was to see how his paper was coming. The first issue that had been put out since his departure was all right. About the second, which had just been printed, Menandrus was mysteriously elated, hinting that he had a splendid surprise for his employer. He had. Padway glanced at a proof sheet, and his heart almost stopped. On the front page was a detailed account of the bribe which the new Pope, Silverius, had paid King Thiudahad to secure his election.

"Hell's bells!" cried Padway. "Haven't you any better sense than to print this, George?"

"Why?" asked Menandrus, crestfallen. "It's true, isn't it?"

"Of course, it's true! But you don't want us all hanged or burned at the stake, do you? The Church is already suspicious of us. Even if you find that a bishop is keeping twenty concubines, you're not to print a word of it."

Menandrus sniffled a little; he wiped away a tear and blew his nose on his tunic. "I'm sorry, excellent boss. I tried to please you; you have no idea how much trouble I went to to get the facts about that bribe. There *is* a bishop, too—not *twenty* concubines, but—"

"But we don't consider that news, for reasons of health. Thank heaven, no copies of this issue have gone out yet."

"Oh, but they have."

"*What?*" Padway's yell made a couple of workmen from the machine shop look in.

"Why, yes, John the Bookseller took the first hundred copies out just a minute ago."

John the Bookseller got the scare of his life when Padway, still dirty from days of travel, galloped down the street after him, dove off his horse, and grabbed his arm. Somebody set up a cry of "Thieves! Robbers! Help! Murder!" Padway found himself trying to explain to forty truculent citizens that everything was all right.

A Gothic soldier pushed through the crowd and asked what was going on here. A citizen pointed at Padway and shouted: "It's the fellow with the boots. I heard him say he'd cut the other man's throat if he didn't hand over his money!" So the Goth arrested Padway.

Padway kept his clutch on John the Bookseller, who was too frightened to speak. He went along quietly with the Goth until they were out of earshot of the crowd. Then he asked the soldier into a wineshop, treated him and John, and explained. The Goth was noncommittal, despite John's corroboration, until Padway tipped him liberally. Padway got his freedom and his precious papers. Then all he had to worry about was the fact that somebody had stolen his horse while he was in the Goth's custody.

Padway trudged back to his house with the papers under his arm. His household was properly sympathetic about the loss of the horse. Fritharik said: "There, illustrious boss, that piece of crow bait wasn't worth much anyhow."

Padway felt much better when he learned that the first leg of the telegraph ought to be completed in a week or ten days. He poured himself a stiff drink before dinner. After his strenuous day it made his head swim a little. He got Fritharik to join him in one of the latter's barbarian war-songs:

> "The black earth shakes
> As the heroes ride,
> And the ravens blood-
> Red sun will hide!
> The lances dip
> In a glittering wave,
> And the coward turns
> His gore to save …"

When Julia was late with the food, Padway gave her a playful spank. He was a little surprised at himself.

After dinner he was sleepy. He said to hell with the accounts and went upstairs to bed, leaving Fritharik already snoring on his mattress in front of the door. Padway would not have laid any long bets on Fritharik's ability to wake up when a burglar entered.

He had just started to undress when a knock startled him. He could not imagine …

"Fritharik?" he called.

"No. It's me."

He frowned and opened the door. The lamplight showed Julia from Apulia. She walked in with a swaying motion.

"What do you want, Julia?" asked Padway.

The stocky, black-haired girl looked at him in some surprise. "Why—uh—my lord wouldn't want me to say right out loud? That wouldn't be nice!"

"Huh?"

She giggled.

"Sorry," said Padway. "Wrong station. Off you go."

She looked baffled. "My—my master doesn't want me?"

"That's right. Not for that anyway."

Her mouth turned down. Two large tears appeared. "You don't like me? You don't think I'm nice?"

"I think you're a fine cook and a nice girl. Now out with you. Good night."

She stood solidly and began to sniffle. Then she sobbed. Her voice rose to a shrill wail: "Just because I'm from the country—you never looked at me—you never asked for me all this time—then tonight you were nice—I thought—I thought—boo-oo-oo …"

"Now, now … for heaven's sake stop crying! Here, sit down. I'll get you a drink."

She smacked her lips over the first swallow of diluted brandy. She wiped off the remaining tears. "Nice," she said. Everything was nice—*bonus, bona,* or *bonum,* as the case might be. "You are nice. Love is nice. Every man should have some love. Love—ah!" She made a serpentine movement remarkable in a person of her build.

Padway gulped. "Give me that drink," he said. "I need some too."

After a while. "Now," she said, "we make love?"

"Well—pretty soon. Yes, I guess we do." Padway hiccuped.

Padway frowned at Julia's large bare feet. "Just—*hic*—just a minute, my bounding hamadryad. Let's see those feet." The soles were black. "That won't do. Oh, it absolutely won't do, my lusty Amazon. The feet present an in-sur-insurmountable psychological obstacle."

"Huh?"

"They interpose a psychic barrier to the—*hic*—appropriately devout worship of Ashtaroth. We must have the pedal extremities—"

"I don't understand."

"Skip it; neither do I. What I mean is that we're going to wash your feet first."

"Is that a religion?"

"You might put it that way. Damn!" He knocked the ewer off its base, miraculously catching it on the way down. "Here we go, my Tritoness from the wine-dark, fish-swarming sea …"

She giggled. "You are the nicest man. You are a real gentleman. No man ever did *that* for me before …"

☼

Padway blinked his eyes open. It all came back to him quickly enough. He tightened his muscles serratus. He felt fine. He prodded his conscience experimentally. It reacted not at all.

He moved carefully, for Julia was taking up two-thirds of his none-too-wide bed. He heaved himself on one elbow and looked at her. The movement uncovered her large breasts. Between them was a bit of iron, tied around her neck. This, she had told him, was a nail from the cross of St Andrew. And she would not put it off.

He smiled. To the list of mechanical inventions he meant to introduce he added a couple of items. But for the present, should he …

A small gray thing with six legs, not much larger than a pinhead, emerged from the hair under her armpit. Pale against her olive-brown skin, it crept with glacial slowness …

Padway shot out of bed. Face writhing with revulsion, he pulled his clothes on without taking time to wash. The room smelled. Rome must have blunted his sense of smell, or he'd have noticed it before.

Julia awoke as he was finishing. He threw a muttered good morning at her and tramped out.

He spent two hours in the public baths that day. The next night Julia's knock brought a harsh order to get away from his room and stay away. She began to wail. Padway snatched the door open. "One more squawk and you're fired!" he snapped, and slammed the door.

She was obedient but sulky. During the next few days he caught venomous glances from her; she was no actress.

The following Sunday he returned from the Ulpian Library to find a small crowd of men in front of his house. They were just standing and looking. Padway looked at the house and could see nothing out of order.

He asked a man: "What's funny about my house, stranger?"

The man looked at him silently. They all looked at him silently. They moved off in twos and threes. They began to walk fast, sometimes glancing back.

Monday morning two of the workmen failed to report. Nerva came to Padway and, after much clearing of the throat, said: "I thought you'd like to know, lordly Martinus. I went to mass at the Church of the Angel Gabriel yesterday as usual."

"Yes?" That Church was on Long Street four blocks from Padway's house.

"Father Narcissus preached a homily against sorcery. He talked about people who hired demons from Satanas and work strange devices. It was a very strong sermon. He sounded as if he might be thinking of you."

Padway worried. It might be coincidence, but he was pretty sure that Julia had gone to confessional and spilled the beans about fornicating with a magician. One sermon had sent the crowd to stare at the wizard's lair. A few more like that …

Padway feared a mob of religious enthusiasts more than anything on earth, no doubt because their mental processes were so utterly alien to his own.

He called Menandrus in and asked for information on Father Narcissus.

The information was discouraging from Padway's point of view. Father Narcissus was one of the most respected priests in Rome. He was upright, charitable, humane, and fearless. He was in deadly earnest twenty-four hours a day. And there was no breath of scandal about him, which fact by itself made him a distinguished cleric.

"George," said Padway, "didn't you once mention a bishop with concubines?"

Menandrus grinned slyly. "It's the Bishop of Bologna, sir. He's one of the Pope's cronies; spends more time at the Vatican than at his see. He has two women—at least, two that we know of. I have their names and everything. Everybody knows that a lot of bishops have one concubine, but two! I thought it would make a good story for the paper."

"It may yet. Write me up a story, George, about the Bishop of Bologna and his loves. Make it sensational, but accurate. Set it up and pull three or four galley proofs; then put the type away in a safe place."

It took Padway a week to gain an audience with the Bishop of Bologna, who was providentially in Rome. The bishop was a gorgeously dressed person with a beautiful, bloodless face. Padway suspected a highly convoluted brain behind that sweet, ascetic smile.

Padway kissed the bishop's hand, and they murmured pleasant nothings. Padway talked of the Church's wonderful work, and how he tried in his humble way to further it at every opportunity.

"For instance," he said, "—do you know of my weekly paper, reverend sir?"

"Yes, I read it with pleasure."

"Well, you know I have to keep a close watch on my boys, who are prone to err in their enthusiasm for news. I have tried to make the paper a clean sheet fit to enter any home, without scandal or libel. Though that sometimes meant I had to write most of an issue myself." He sighed. "Ah, sinful men! Would you believe it, reverend sir, that I have had to suppress stories of foul libel against members of the Holy Church? The most shocking of all came in recently." He took out one of the galley proofs. "I hardly dare show it to you, sir, lest your justified wrath at this filthy product of a disordered imagination should damn me to eternal flames."

The bishop squared his thin shoulders. "Let me see it, my son. A priest sees many dreadful things in his career. It takes a strong spirit to serve the Lord in these times."

Padway handed over the sheet. The bishop read it. A sad expression came over his angelic face. "Ah, poor weak mortals! They know not that they hurt themselves far more than the object of their calumny. It shows that we must have God's help at every turn lest we fall into sin. If you will tell me who wrote this, I will pray for him."

"A man named Marcus," said Padway. "I discharged him immediately, of course. I want nobody who is not prepared to co-operate with the Church to the full."

The bishop cleared his throat delicately. "I appreciate your righteous efforts," he said. "If there is some favor within my power—"

Padway told him about the good Father Narcissus, who was showing such a lamentable misunderstanding of Padway's enterprises …

Padway went to mass next Sunday. He sat well down in front, determined to face the thing out if Father Narcissus proved obdurate. He sang with the rest:

> "Imminet, imminet,
> Recta remuneret.
> Aethera donet,
> Ille supremus!"

He reflected that there was this good in Christianity: By its concepts of the Millennium and Judgment Day it accustomed people to looking forward in a way that the older religions did not, and so prepared their minds for the conceptions of organic evolution and scientific progress.

Father Narcissus began his sermon where he had left off a week before. Sorcery was the most damnable of crimes; they should not suffer a witch to live, etc. Padway stiffened.

But, continued the good priest with a sour glance at Padway, we should not in our holy enthusiasm confuse the practitioner of black arts and the familiar of devils with the honest artisan who by his ingenious devices ameliorates our journey through this vale of tears. After all, Adam invented the plow and Noah the ocean-going ship. And this new art of machine writing would make it possible to spread the word of God among the heathen more effectively.

When Padway got home, he called in Julia and told her he would not need her any more. Julia from Apulia began to weep, softly at first, then more and more violently. "What kind of man are you? I give you love. I give you everything. But no, you think I am just a little country girl you can do anythingyouwantandthenyougettired …" The patois came with such machine-gun rapidity that Padway could no longer follow. When she began to shriek and tear her dress, Padway ungallantly threatened to have Fritharik throw her out bodily forthwith. She quieted.

The day after she left, Padway gave his house a personal going over to see whether anything had been stolen or broken. Under his bed he found a curious object: a bundle of chicken feathers tied with horsehair around what appeared to be a long-defunct mouse; the whole thing stiff with dried blood. Fritharik did not know what it was. But George Menandrus did; he turned a little pale and muttered: "A curse!"

He reluctantly informed Padway that this was a bad-luck charm peddled by one of the local wizards; the discharged housekeeper had undoubtedly left it there to bring Padway to an early and gruesome death. Menandrus himself wasn't too sure he wanted to keep on with his job. "Not that I really believe in curses, excellent sir, but with my family to support I can't take chances …"

A raise in pay disposed of Menandrus' qualms. Menandrus was disappointed that Padway didn't use the occasion to have Julia arrested and hanged for witchcraft. "Just think," he said, "it would put us on the right side of the Church, and it would make a wonderful story for the paper!"

Padway hired another housekeeper. This one was gray-haired, rather frail-looking, and depressingly virginal. That was why Padway took her.

He learned that Julia had gone to work for Ebenezer the Jew. He hoped that Julia would not try any of her specialties on Ebenezer. The old banker did not look as if he could stand much of them.

Padway told Thomasus: "We ought to get the first message from Naples over the telegraph any time now."

Thomasus rubbed his hands together: "You are a wonder, Martinus. Only I'm worried that you'll overreach yourself. The messengers of the Italian civil service are complaining that this invention will destroy their livelihood. Unfair competition, they say."

Padway shrugged. "We'll see. Maybe there'll be some war news."

Thomasus frowned. "That's another thing that's worrying me. Thiudahad hasn't done a thing about the defense of Italy. I'd hate to see the war carried as far north as Rome."

"I'll make you a bet," said Padway. "The king's son-in-law, Evermuth the Vandal, will desert to the Imperialists. One solidus."

"Done!" Almost at that moment Junianus, who had been put in charge of operations, came in with a paper. It was the first message, and it carried the news that Belisarius had landed at Reggio; that Evermuth had gone over to him; that the Imperialists were marching on Naples.

Padway grinned at the banker, whose jaw was sagging. "Sorry, old man, but I need that solidus. I'm saving up for a new horse."

"Do You hear that, God? Martinus, the next time I lay a bet with a magician, you can have me declared incompetent and a guardian appointed."

Two days later a messenger came in and told Padway that the king was in Rome, staying at the Palace of Tiberius, and that Padway's presence was desired.

Padway thought that perhaps Thiudahad had reconsidered the telescope proposal. But no.

"My good Martinus," said Thiudahad, "I must ask you to discontinue the operation of your telegraph. At once."

"What? Why, my lord king?"

"You know what happened? Eh? That thing of yours spread the news of my son-in-law's good fort—his treachery all over Rome a few hours after it happened. Bad for morale. Encourages the pro-Greek element, and brings criticism on me. *Me*. So you'll please not operate it any more, at least during the war."

"But, my lord, I thought that your army would find it useful for—"

"Not another word about it, Martinus. I forbid it. Now, let me see. Dear me, there was something else I wanted to see you about. Oh, yes, my man Cassiodorus would like to meet you. You'll stay for lunch, won't you? Great scholar, Cassiodorus."

So Padway presently found himself bowing to the pretorian prefect, an elderly, rather saintly Italian. They were immediately deep in a discussion of historiography, literature, and the hazards of the publishing business. Padway to his annoyance found that he was enjoying himself. He knew that he was abetting these spineless old dodderers in their criminal disregard of their country's defense. But—upsetting thought—he had enough of the unworldly intellectual in his own nature so that he couldn't help sympathizing with them. And he hadn't gone on an intellectual debauch of this kind since he'd arrived in old Rome.

"Illustrious Cassiodorus," he said, "perhaps you've noticed that in my paper I've been trying to teach the typesetter to distinguish between U and V, and also between I and J. That's a reform that's long been needed, don't you think?"

"Yes, yes, my excellent Martinus. The Emperor Claudius tried something of the sort. But which letter do you use for which sound in each case?"

Padway explained. He also told Cassiodorus of his plans for printing the paper, or at least part of it, in Vulgar Latin. At that Cassiodorus held up his hands in mild horror.

"Excellent Martinus! These wretched dialects that pass for Latin nowadays? What would Ovid say if he heard them? What would Virgil say? What would any of the ancient masters say?"

"As they were a bit before our time," grinned Padway, "I'm afraid we shall never know. But I will assert that even in their day the final s's and m's had been dropped from ordinary pronunciation. And in any event, the pronunciation and grammar have changed too far from the classical models ever to be changed back again. So if we want our new instrument for the dissemination of literature to be useful, we shall have to adopt a spelling that more or less agrees with the spoken language. Otherwise people won't bother to learn it. To begin with, we shall have to add a half dozen new letters to the alphabet. For instance—"

When Padway left, hours later, he had at least made an effort to bring the conversation around to measures for prosecuting the war. It had been useless, but his conscience was salved.

Padway was surprised, though he shouldn't have been, at the effect of the news of his acquaintance with the king and the prefect. Well-born Romans called on him, and he was even asked to a couple of very dull dinners that began at four P.M. and lasted most of the night.

As he listened to the windy conversation and the windier speeches, he thought that a twentieth-century after-dinner speaker could have taken lessons in high-flown, meaningless rhetoric from these people. From the slightly nervous way that his hosts introduced him around, he gathered that they still regarded him as something of a monster, but a well-behaved monster whom it might be useful to know.

Even Cornelius Anicius looked him up and issued the long-coveted invitation to his house. He did not apologize for the slight snub in the library, but his deferential manner suggested that he remembered it.

Padway swallowed his pride and accepted. He thought it foolish to judge Anicius by his own standards. And he wanted another look at the pretty brunette.

When the time came, he got up from his desk, washed his hands, and told Fritharik to come along.

Fritharik said, scandalized: "You are going to *walk* to this Roman gentleman's house?"

"Sure. It's only a couple of miles. Do us good."

"Oh, most respectable boss, you can't! It isn't done! I know; I worked for such a patrician once. You should have a sedan chair, or at least a horse."

"Nonsense. Anyway, we've got only one saddle-horse. You don't want to walk while I ride, do you?"

"N-no-not that I mind walking; but it would look funny for a gentleman's free retainer like me to go afoot like a slave on a formal occasion."

Damn this etiquette, thought Padway.

Fritharik said hopefully: "Of course there's the workhorse. He's a good-looking animal; one might almost mistake him for a heavy cavalry horse."

"But I don't want the boys in the shop to lose a couple of hours' production just because of some damned piece of face-saving—"

Padway rode the work-horse. Fritharik rode the remaining bony saddle-horse.

Padway was shown into a big room whose ornamentation reminded him of the late Victorian gewgaw culture. Through a closed door he could hear Anicius' voice coming through in rolling pentameters:

"Rome, the warrior-goddess, her seat had taken,
With breast uncovered, a mural crown on her head.
Behind, from under her spacious helmet escaping,
The hair of her plumed head flowed over her back.
Modest her mien, but sternness her beauty makes
*   awesome.*
Of purple hue is her robe, with fang-like clasp;
Under her bosom a jewel her mantle gathers.
A vast and glowing shield her side supports,
Whereon, in stout metal cast, the cave of Rhea—"

The servant had sneaked through the door and whispered. Anicius broke off his declamation and popped out with a book under his arm. He cried: "My dear Martinus! I crave your pardon; I was rehearsing a speech I am to give tomorrow." He tapped the book under his arm and smiled guiltily. "It will not be a strictly original speech; but you won't betray me, will you?"

"Of course not. I heard some of it through the door."

"You did? What did you think of it?"

"I thought your delivery was excellent." Padway resisted a temptation to add: "But what does it *mean*?" Such a question about a piece of post-Roman rhetoric would, he realized, be both futile and tactless.

"You did?" cried Anicius. "Splendid! I am greatly gratified! I shall be as nervous tomorrow as Cadmus when the dragon's teeth began to sprout, but the approval of one competent critic in advance will fortify me. And now I'll leave you to Dorothea's mercy while I finish this. You will not take offense, I hope? Splendid! Oh, daughter!"

Dorothea appeared and exchanged courtesies. She took Padway out in the garden while Anicius went back to his plagiarism of Sidonius.

Dorothea said: "You should hear father some time. He takes you back to the time when Rome really was the mistress of the world. If restoring the power of Rome could be done by fine talk, father and his friends would have restored it long ago."

It was hot in the garden, with the heat of an Italian June. Bees buzzed.

Padway said: "What kind of flower do you call that?"

She told him. He was hot. And he was tired of strain and responsibility and ruthless effort. He wanted to be young and foolish for a change.

He asked her more questions about flowers—trivial questions about unimportant matters.

She answered prettily, bending over the flowers to remove a bug now and then. She was hot too. There were little beads of sweat on her upper lip. Her thin dress stuck to her in places. Padway admired the places. She was standing close to him, talking with grave good humor about flowers and about the bugs and blights that beset them. To kiss her, all he had to do was reach and lean forward a bit. He could hear his blood in his ears. The way she smiled up at him might almost be considered an invitation.

But Padway made no move. While he hesitated his mind clicked off reasons: (a) He didn't know how she'd take it, and shouldn't presume on the strength of a mere friendly smile; (b) if she resented it, as she very likely would, there might be repercussions of incalculable scope; (c) if he made love to her, what would she think he was after? He didn't want a mistress—not that Dorothea Anicius would be willing to become such—and he was not, as far

as he knew, in need of a wife; (d) he was in a sense already married …

So, he thought, you wanted to be young and foolish a few minutes ago, eh, Martin, my boy? You can't; it's too late; you'll always stop to figure things out rationally, as you've been doing just now. Might as well resign yourself to being a calculating adult, especially as you can't do anything about it.

But it made him a little sad that he would never be one of those impetuous fellows—usually described as tall and handsome—who take one look at a girl, know her to be their destined mate, and sweep her into their arms. He let Dorothea do most of the talking as they wandered back into the house to dinner with Cornelius Anicius and Anicius' oratory. Padway, watching Dorothea as she preceded him, felt slightly disgusted with himself for having let Julia invade his bed.

They sat down—or rather stretched themselves out on the couches, as Anicius insisted on eating in the good old Roman style, to Padway's acute discomfort. Anicius had a look in his eye that Padway found vaguely familiar.

Padway learned that the look was that of a man who is writing or is about to write a book. Anicius explained: "Ah, the degenerate times we live in, excellent Martinus! The lyre of Orpheus sounds but faintly; Calliope veils her face; blithe Thalia is mute; the hymns of our Holy Church have drowned Euterpe's sweet strains. Yet a few of us strive to hold high the torch of poetry while swimming the Hellespont of barbarism and hoeing the garden of culture."

"Quite a feat," said Padway, squirming in a vain effort to find a comfortable position.

"Yes, we persist despite Herculean discouragements. For instance, you will not consider me forward in submitting to your publisher's eagle-bright scrutiny a little book of verses." He produced a sheaf of papyrus. "Some of them are not really bad, though I their unworthy author say so."

"I should be very much interested," said Padway, smiling with effort. "As for publication, however, I should warn you that I'm contracted for three books by your excellent colleagues already. And between the paper and my schoolbook, it will be some weeks before I can print them."

"Oh," said Anicius with a drooping inflection.

"The Illustrious Trajanus Herodius, the Distinguished John Leontius, and the Respectable Felix Avitus. All epic poems. Because of market conditions these gentlemen have undertaken the financial responsibility of publication."

"Meaning—ah?"

"Meaning that they pay cash in advance, and get the whole price of their books when sold, subject to bookseller's discounts. Of course, distinguished sir, if the book is really good, the author doesn't have to worry about getting back his cost of publication."

"Yes, yes, excellent Martinus, I see. What chances do you think my little creation would have?"

"I'd have to see it first."

"So you would. I'll read some of it now, to give you the idea." Anicius sat up. He held the papyrus in one hand and made noble gestures with the other:

☼

"Mars with his thunderous trumpet his lord acclaims,
  The youthful Jupiter, new to his throne ascended,
  Above the stars by all-wise Nature placed.
  The lesser deities their sire worship,
  To ancient sovereignty with pomp succeeding—"

☼

"Father," interrupted Dorothea, "your food's getting cold."

"What? Oh, so it is, child."

"And," continued Dorothea, "I think you ought to write some good Christian sentiment sometime, instead of all that pagan superstition."

Anicius signed. "If you ever have a daughter, Martinus, marry her off early, before she develops the critical faculty."

☼

In August Naples fell to General Belisarius. Thiudahad had done nothing to help the town except seize the families of the small Gothic garrison to insure their fidelity. The only vigorous defense of the city was made by the Neapolitan Jews. These, having heard of Justinian's religious complexes, knew what treatment to expect under Imperial rule.

Padway heard the news with a sick feeling. There was so much that he could do for them if they'd only let him alone. And it would take such a little accident to snuff him out—one of the normal accidents of warfare, like that which happened to Archimedes. In this age civilians who got in the way of belligerent armies would be given the good old rough and ruthless treatment to which the military of his own twentieth century, after a brief hundred and fifty years of relatively humane forbearance, had seemed to be returning.

Fritharik announced that a party of Goths wanted to look Padway's place over. He added in his sepulchral voice: "Thiudegiskel's with them. You know, the king's son. Watch out for him, excellent boss. He makes trouble."

There were six of them, all young, and they tramped into the house wearing swords, which was not good manners by the standards of the times. Thiudegiskel was a handsome, blond young man who had inherited his father's high-pitched voice.

He stared at Padway, like something in a zoo, and said: "I've wanted to see your place ever since I heard you and the old man were mumbling over manuscripts together. I'm a curious chap, you know, active-minded. What the devil are all these silly machines for?"

Padway did some explaining, while the prince's companions made remarks about his personal appearance in Gothic, under the mistaken impression that he couldn't understand them.

"Ah, yes," said Thiudegiskel, interrupting one of the explanations. "I think that's all I'm interested in here. Now, let's see that bookmaking machine."

Padway showed him the presses.

"Oh, yes, I understand. Really a simple thing, isn't it? I could have invented it myself. All very well for those who like it. Though I can read and write and all that. Better than most people, in fact. But I never cared for it. Dull business, not suited to a healthy man like me."

"No doubt, no doubt, my lord," said Padway. He hoped that the red rage he was feeling didn't show in his face.

"Say, Willimer," said Thiudegiskel, "you remember that tradesman we had fun with last winter? He looked something like this Martinus person. Same big nose."

Willimer roared with laughter. "Do I remember it! *Guths in himinam!* I'll never forget the way he looked when we told him we were going to baptize him in the Tiber, with rocks tied to him so the angels couldn't carry him off! But the funniest thing was when some soldiers from the garrison arrested us for assault!"

Thiudegiskel said to Padway, between guffaws: "You ought to have been there, Martinus. You should have seen old Liuderis' face when he found out who we were! We made him grovel, I can tell you. I've always regretted that I missed the flogging of those soldiers who pinched us. That's one thing about me; I can appreciate the humor of things like that."

"Would you like to see anything more, my lord?" asked Padway, his face wooden.

"Oh, I don't know—Say, what are all those packing cases for?"

"Some stuff just arrived for our machines, my lord, and we haven't gotten around to burning the cases," Padway lied.

Thiudegiskel grinned good-naturedly. "Trying to fool me, huh? I know what you're up to. You're going to sneak your stuff out of Rome before Belisarius gets here, aren't you? That's one thing about me; I can see through little tricks like that. Well, can't say I blame you. Though it sounds as though you had inside information on how the war will go." He examined a new brass telescope on a workbench. "This is an interesting little device. I'll take it along, if you don't mind."

That was too much even for Padway's monumental prudence. "No, my lord, I'm sorry, but I need that in my business."

Thiudegiskel's eyes were round with astonishment. "Huh? You mean I can't have it?"

"That, my lord, is it."

"Well … uh … uh … if you're going to take that attitude, I'll pay for it."

"It isn't for sale."

Thiudegiskel's neck turned slowly pink with embarrassment and anger. His five friends moved up behind him, their left hands resting on their sword hilts.

The one called Willimer said in a low tone: "I *think*, gentlemen, that our king's son has been insulted."

Thiudegiskel had laid the telescope on the bench. He reached out for it; Padway snatched it up and smacked the end of the tube meaningfully against his left palm. He knew that, even if he got out of this situation in one piece, he'd curse himself for a double-dyed knight-erranting idiot. But at the moment he was too furious to care.

The uncomfortable silence was broken by the shuffle of feet behind Padway; he saw the Goths' eyes shift from him. He glanced around. In the doorway was Fritharik, with his sword belt hitched around so the scabbard was in front, and Nerva, holding a three-foot length of bronze bar-stock. Behind them came the other workmen with an assortment of blunt instruments.

"It seems," said Thiudegiskel, "that these people have no manners whatever. We should give them a lesson. But I promised my old man to lay off fighting. That's one thing about me; I always keep my promises. Come along boys." They went.

"*Whew!*" said Padway. "You boys certainly saved my bacon. Thanks."

"Oh, it was nothing," said George Menandrus airily. "I'm rather sorry they didn't stay to fight it out. I'd have enjoyed smacking their thick skulls."

"You? *Honh!*" snorted Fritharik. "Boss, the first thing I saw when I started to round the men up was this fellow sneaking out the back door. You know how I changed his mind? I said I'd hang him with a rope made of his own guts if he didn't stick! And the others, I threatened to cut their heads off and stick them on the fence palings in front of the house." He contemplated infinite calamities for a few seconds, then added: "But it won't do any good, excellent Martinus. Those fellows will have it in for us, and they're pretty influential, naturally. They can get away with anything. We'll all end in nameless graves yet."

Padway struggled mightily to get the movable parts of his equipment packed for shipment to Florence. As far as he could remember his Procopius, Florence had not been besieged or sacked in Justinian's Gothic War, at least in the early part.

But the job was not half done when eight soldiers from the garrison descended on him and told him he was under arrest. He was getting rather used to arrest by now, so he calmly gave his foremen and editor orders about getting the equipment moved and set up, and about seeing Thomasus and trying to get in touch with him. Then he went along.

On the way he offered to stand the Goths drinks. They accepted quickly. In the wineshop he got the commander aside to suggest a little bribe to let him go. The Goth seemed to accept, and pocketed a solidus. Then when Padway, his mind full of plans for shaving his beard, getting a horse, and galloping off to Florence, broached the subject of his release, the Goth looked at him with an air of pained surprise.

"Why, most distinguished Martinus, I couldn't think of letting you go! Our commander-in-chief, the noble Liuderis, is a man of stern and rigid principles. If my men talked, he'd hear about it, and he'd break me sure. Of course I appreciate your little *gift*, and I'll try to put in a good word for you."

Padway said nothing, but he made a resolve that it would be a long day before he put in a good word for this officer.

(to be continued in Issue 9)

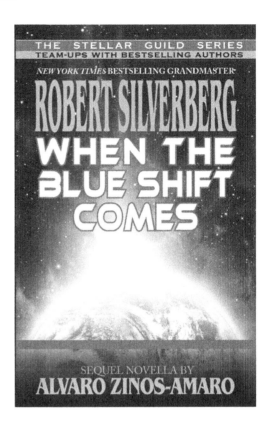

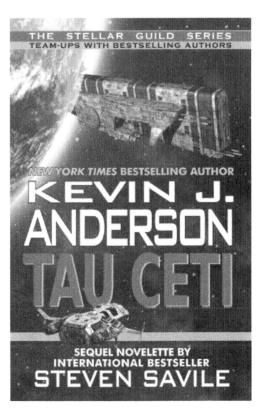

CPSIA information can be obtained at www.ICGtesting.com
Printed in the USA
BVOW10s2321180514

353734BV00003B/9/P

9 781612 422022